A Low Carbohydrate, Ketogenic Diet Manual

"No Sugar, No Starch" Diet

Dr. Eric C. Westman, MD MHS

1

Medical Disclaimer

The material in this book is for informational purposes only and is not intended as a substitute for the advice and care of your physician. Any new lifestyle program as outlined in this book should be followed only after first consulting with your physician to make sure it is appropriate for your individual circumstance.

The author and its publisher disclaim responsibility for any adverse effects that may result from the use or application of the information contained in this manual.

Introduction

This way of eating is a diet low in sugary and starchy foods. Because starches are easily digested to sugar, starchy foods are similar to sugar, and must be avoided as well. This way of eating focuses on eating "real' food and includes meat, fish, cheese, eggs, salads, and vegetables. This eating plan will provide your body with the nutrition that it needs, and will change the fuel that your body uses from mainly sugars and starches to mainly fat.

Sugars and starches are also known as carbohydrates and can be measured in 'grams.' Your carbohydrate intake will be 20 grams or less per day. This means that you will need to avoid sugar, bread, fruit, flour, pasta, or any other sugary/starchy food that has a lot of carbohydrates. When you limit the carbohydrate intake, your hunger will go away, and if you have extra weight on your body, you will eat less and lose weight. A list of the foods initially allowed is provided to assist you in changing your eating patterns.

Medical supervision is recommended for any weight loss program, especially if you are currently taking any medications. As your weight decreases and your medical conditions improve, medications will probably have to be adjusted. Blood work should be checked periodically to make sure that your values are within the normal range. Many people report that their regularly-scheduled appointments help to ensure that they follow the diet.

"No Sugar, No Starch" Diet

List of Permitted Foods

This diet is focused on providing your body with the nutrition it needs (protein and fat), while minimizing foods that your body does not need (carbohydrates). To be most effective, you will need to keep the dietary carbohydrate to **less than 20 grams per day**. Your diet is to be made up exclusively of foods and beverages from this handout. It doesn't matter how the food is cooked. Food can be cooked in a microwave oven, baked, boiled, stir-fried, sautéed, roasted, fried (with no flour, breading, or corn meal), or grilled.

When hungry, EAT AS MUCH AS YOU WANT OF THE FOLLOWING FOODS. (These foods have no carbs.)
Meat: Beef (hamburger, steak, etc.), pork, ham, bacon, lamb, veal, sausage, pepperoni, hot dogs, or other meats.
Poultry: Chicken, turkey, duck, or other fowl.
Fish & Shellfish: Any fish including tuna, salmon, catfish, bass, trout, shrimp, scallops, crab, and lobster.
Eggs: Whole eggs are permitted without restrictions.
Don't avoid the fat. Oils and butter have no carbs.
You do not have to deliberately limit quantities, but you should stop eating when you feel full.

Salad greens and nonstarchy vegetables MUST BE EATEN EVERY DAY, but the amount is limited:
Salad greens: _2_ cups a day. Includes: arugula, bok choy, cabbage (all varieties), chard, chives, endive, greens (all varieties including beet, collards, mustard, and turnip), kale, lettuce (all varieties), parsley, spinach, radicchio, radishes, scallions, and watercress. (If it is a leaf—you can eat it.)

Nonstarchy vegetables: 1 cup (measured uncooked) a day. Includes: artichokes, asparagus, broccoli, Brussels sprouts, cauliflower, celery, cucumber, eggplant, green beans (string beans), jicama, leeks, mushrooms, okra, onions, peppers, pumpkin, shallots, snow peas, sprouts (bean & alfalfa) sugar-snap peas, summer squash, tomatoes, rhubarb, wax beans, zucchini.

If you do not have high blood pressure (hypertension) or heart failure, then use bouillon AS NEEDED during the first few weeks of the diet to minimize headache or fatigue.
Bouillon: up to 2 times daily—as needed for sodium replenishment. Clear broth (consommé) is strongly recommended. Unless we tell you that you need to restrict your salt intake, DO NOT USE LOW SODIUM BOUILLON.

FOODS THAT ARE ALLOWED IN LIMITED QUANTITIES:
(Check the labels to be sure there is not added carbohydrates.)
Cheese: up to 4 ounces a day. Includes: hard, aged cheeses such as Swiss, cheddar, brie, camembert, bleu, mozzarella, Gruyere, cream cheese, goat cheeses. Check the carbohydrate count.
Cream: up to 2 tablespoonfuls a day. Includes whipping, heavy, light, or sour cream.
Mayonnaise: up to 2 tablespoons a day.
Olives (black or green): up to 6 a day.
Avocado: up to 1/2 of a fruit a day.
Lemon/lime juice: up to 2 teaspoonfuls a day.
Soy sauces: up to 2 tablespoons a day.
Pickles, dill or sugar-free: *up to 2 serving a day.*

Zero Carb Snacks: Sugar-free jello, pork rinds; pepperoni slices; ham, beef, turkey, beef jerky, deviled eggs

Possible Side Effects

The "no sugar, no starch" diet does have some possible side effects, as does any effective weight loss program. Although they will not seriously impact your health and will disappear quickly, they can be bothersome. These side effects include sugar cravings, and flu-like symptoms, constipation, and bad breath. The following recommendations can help you avoid or minimize these side effects.

Drink Lots of Liquids: It is important to drink an **adequate** amount of fluid per day – preferably water or another non-caffeinated beverage.

Constipation: If you are experiencing constipation (hard stools or hard-to-pass stools), there are a number of ways that you may address the issue.

- use 1 teaspoon of milk of magnesia at bedtime daily
- add ½ cup of fiber-rich vegetables to your diet per day
- have 1 to 2 servings per day of sugar-free gum or sugar-free candy that contains sorbitol or another sugar alcohol
- use sugar-free Metamucil twice a day

When we have determined which approach will be best for you, you may use that method until symptoms resolve. If the issue persists and you need additional assistance, consult your health care provider.

Breath: Some people experience bad breath in the initial stages of a "no sugar, no starch" diet. This can usually be avoided by drinking plenty of water and performing good oral hygiene. This includes seeing a dentist, brushing your teeth twice a day (including your tongue), and flossing your teeth daily. If the problem persists, try sugar-free gum or mints.

Sugar cravings: As your body adjusts to your new way of eating, you may initially experience cravings for the sugary/starch foods that are not on this diet, but the cravings will pass. Like stopping anything that you are accustomed to, or addicted to, the fewer carbohydrates you have in your diet, the sooner the cravings will subside. Sugar cravings can be temporarily treated with a sugar-free beverage, such as diet soda or a sugar-free flavoring, or sugar-free jello with whipped cream.

Bouillon: Occasionally, people can experience fatigue, headaches, body aches, difficulty concentrating, or other flu-like symptoms when they stop eating carbohydrates. These symptoms are usually fairly mild and pass quickly; they are a sign that your body is going through a transition period from burning carbohydrates to burning fat for fuel. To help prevent these symptoms, we recommend drinking beef or chicken broth one to three times a day. Do not use bouillon if you have high blood pressure or heart failure. To make the broth, drop a cube of bouillon into a cup of hot water and drink it. Although your energy levels will soon return to normal, many patients have reported they enjoy the broth and continue drinking it beyond the first week.

Ketosis
Ketosis is okay—it just means that your body is burning fat. (Ketosis is commonly confused with 'ketoacidosis'- a serious condition that can occur in individuals with diabetes.) You can measure your urine or blood ketones at home if you wish with urinary or blood ketone test strips. Not everyone has measurable ketones in the urine even when they are successfully fat-burning and losing weight. So if there are no ketones in the urine, it does not necessarily mean that you are not burning fat.

7

What happens if I "slip"?
Once you begin this way of eating, you must follow it strictly. If you eat carbohydrates, even a little bit, you may stop the weight loss process for up to three days. This means you will come out of ketosis (fat-burning), and you may even gain back several pounds of water weight. The most important thing to do if you do eat carbohydrates is to get right back on track with the next meal. You may be surprised that it is not difficult to be strict because your hunger will be decreased or gone entirely.

Vitamins and Supplements
Although the "no sugar, no starch" diet is very nutritious, we recommend that you take an iron-free multivitamin to be sure that you are getting all of the vitamins and minerals that you need, unless you are told to take iron by your doctor.

Cholesterol
Many people ask how the "no sugar, no starch" diet will affect cholesterol levels since it isn't a low-fat diet. The predictions about how this way of eating would adversely affect the blood cholesterol didn't come true when the studies were finally done. This way of eating reduces the cardiac risk factors by lowering blood triglycerides and increasing the good cholesterol (HDL). To ensure happens for you, have your health care provider measure your fasting lipid profile periodically.

Your weight is not the only thing that will improve.
If you adhere to your new way of eating, you can expect to lose pounds and inches. You may experience improved energy levels, better appetite control, and, in general, a reduction in the frequency and severity of the symptoms of a number of health problems you may have experienced before.

If you have diabetes, you can expect better blood sugar control and a reduction in your diabetes medications may have to be made on the day you stop eating carbohydrates. Some people are able to stop taking their diabetes medications completely. However, if you are taking diabetes medications, including insulin, do not change the dosage or stop taking without consulting with your health care provider.

Increasing Activity and Reducing Stress

In addition to changing your eating habits, you may wish to change some other aspects of your lifestyle in order to improve your overall health. Stress and inactivity can negatively impact your health and even make it more difficult for you to lose weight. Stress management techniques may improve your ability to handle dietary temptations, sugar cravings, and emotional eating patterns. Increasing your activity level may help reduce stress, decrease appetite, build muscle, and improve bone density.

The Main Restriction: Carbohydrates

On this diet, no sugars (simple carbohydrates) and no starches (complex carbohydrates) are eaten. The only carbohydrates we encourage are the nutritionally-dense, fiber rich vegetables listed on page 4 and 5.

Sugars are simple carbohydrates. **Avoid these kinds of foods**: white sugar, brown sugar, honey, maple syrup, molasses, corn syrup, beer (contains barley malt), milk (contains lactose), flavored yogurts, fruit juice, and fruit.

Starches are complex carbohydrates. **Avoid these kinds of foods**: grains (even "whole" grains), rice, cereals, flour, cornstarch, breads, pastas, muffins, bagels, crackers, and "starchy" vegetables such as slow-cooked beans (pinto, lima, black beans, etc.), carrots, parsnips, corn, peas, potatoes, French fries, potato chips, etc.

Fats and Oils

All fats and oils, even butter, are allowed. Olive oil and peanut oil are especially healthy oils and are encouraged in cooking. Avoid margarine and other hydrogenated oils.

For salad dressings, use oil and vinegar, bleu cheese, ranch, Caesar, Italian. Avoid "lite" dressings, as these commonly have more carbohydrate. Chopped eggs, bacon, and/or grated cheese may also be included in salads.

Fats, in general, are important to include because they taste good and make you feel full. You, therefore, can eat the fat or skin that is served with the meat or poultry that you eat, as long as there is no breading on the skin. **Do not attempt to follow a low-fat diet!**

Sweeteners and Desserts

If you feel the need to eat or drink something sweet, you should select the most sensible sweetener(s) available—just not sugar. Some available alternative sweeteners are: Splenda (sucralose), Nutrasweet (aspartame), Truvia (stevia/erythritol blend), Sweet & Low (saccharin), sugar alcohols (sorbitol, maltitol). Sugar alcohols can occasionally cause stomach upset.

Beverages

Drink as much as you would like of the allowed beverages, but do not force fluids beyond your capacity. The best beverage is water. Essence-flavored seltzers (zero carbs) and bottled spring and mineral waters are also good choices.

Caffeinated beverages: Some patients find that their caffeine intake interferes with their weight loss and blood sugar control. With this in mind, you may have **up to _3 servings** of coffee (black, or with artificial sweetener and/or cream), tea (unsweetened or artificially sweetened), or caffeinated diet soda per day.

Alcohol

At first, we ask that you avoid alcohol consumption on this diet. As weight loss and dietary patterns become well-established, alcohol in moderate quantities may be added back into the diet at a later point in time. We can help you make the best choices for low-carbohydrate alcoholic beverages if needed.

Quantities

Eat when you are hungry; stop when you are full. The diet works best on a "demand feeding" basis; i.e., eat when you are hungry. If you are not hungry, you don't have to eat. Learn to listen to your body. A low-carbohydrate diet has a natural appetite reduction effect to ease you into the consumption of smaller and smaller quantities comfortably. You do not have to eat everything on your plate "just because it's there." You are not counting calories. Enjoy losing weight comfortably, without hunger or cravings.

Important Reminders

The following items are NOT on the diet: sugar, bread, cereal, flour-containing items, fruits, juices, honey, whole or skimmed milk, yogurt, canned soups, dairy substitutes, catsup, sweet condiments and relishes.

Avoid these common mistakes: Beware of "fat-free" or "lite" diet products and foods containing "hidden" sugars and starches (such as coleslaw or sugar-free cookies and cakes). Check the labels of liquid medications, cough syrups, cough drops, and other over-the-counter medications that may contain sugar. Avoid products that are labeled "Great for Low-Carb Diets!"

Books and Websites

You may find the following books and websites informative:
The New Atkins for a New You (especially as you transition to a low-carbohydrate lifestyle.)
Dr. Atkins Diabetes Revolution, Dr. Atkins' New Diet Revolution, Atkins for Life, and *Dr. Atkins' New Diet Cookbook, Protein Power,* 1001 *Low-Carb Recipes* by Dana Carpender; *The Low-Carb Cookbook* and *Living Low-Carb,* both by Fran McCullough.

Linda's Low-Carb Menus & Recipes:
> http://genaw.com/lowcarb/ This has a terrific collection of kitchen-tested recipes.

Active Low-Carbers Forum: http://www.lowcarb.ca
Dana Carpender's website: http://www.holdthetoast.com
Jackie Eberstein's website: http://www.controlcarb.com
Jimmy Moore's website:
http://www.livinlavidalocarb.blogspot.com
Lauren Benning's Healthy Low-Carb Treats:
http://www.healthyindulgences.blogspot.com

Although the information in these books and websites may be helpful to you, if there is conflicting information, use the information from this book--not diet instruction from another book or website.

Low-Carb Menu Planning

What does a low-carb menu look like? You can plan your daily menu by using the following as a guide:

Breakfast
Meat or other protein source (usually eggs)
Fat source -- *This may already be in your protein, for example, bacon & eggs have fat in them. But if your protein source is "lean", add some fat in the form of butter, cream (in coffee), or cheese.*
Low-carb vegetable (if desired) – *This can be in an omelet or breakfast quiche.*

Lunch
Meat or other protein source
Fat source -- *If your protein is "lean"—add some fat with butter, salad dressing, cheese, cream, avocado, etc.*
1 to 1 ½ cups of salad greens or cooked greens
½ to 1 cup of vegetables

Snack
Low-carb snack that has protein and/or fat

Dinner
Meat or other protein source
Fat source -- *If your protein is "lean"—add some fat with butter, salad dressing, cheese, cream, avocado, etc.*
1 to 1 ½ cups of salad greens or cooked greens
½ to 1 cup of vegetables

They Made Me Laugh

(Illustration by Judy Price)

They Made Me Laugh

A Novel

BJ McCall

Red Raven Publishing Port Orchard, Wash.
A division of Red Raven Enterprises

This is a work of fiction. Names, characters, places and incidents are the product of the author's imagination or are used fictitiously, and any resemblance to any persons living or dead, business or government establishments, events, or locales is entirely coincidental.

They Made Me Laugh
Copyright © 2015 by BJ McCall
All rights reserved.

First Printing: 2015
Printed in the United States of America
First Edition
ISBN: 0991416104
ISBN 9780991416103

Dedicated to my parents Adolf and Lillian Maas and my grandmother "Aunt Mary".

Acknowledgements

A novel that's memoir based does not have space for all of those who made it possible, but some must be mentioned: my four children, Raelissa, Calvin, Cabot and Risa, without whom there would have been only half as much to write; my sons-in-law Kim and Don and daughter-in-law Angela who made possible my four grandchildren, Brandon, Sean, Skyler and Lillian who continue to make any problems I may have had raising their parents worth every minute; my parents Lillian and Adolf Maas and my grandmother (Aunt Mary) who demonstrated what love, integrity and determination can accomplish; my twenty-five year collection of wonderful and wonderfully varied students, the other half of my novel; and the six supportive members of my writing group; Bruce Lawson, our lone (but not lonely male), Darlene Dubay, Judy Price, Mary Ann Schradi, Melba Burke and Morna Frazier and in memoriam Harold (Doc) Warsinski.

Two quotations come to mind:

- "Everybody gives us something; some, perhaps, only to set an example of what not to be." ~ my Mom
- "As a factual memoir, this novel is pretty good fiction." ~ my daughter Risa

Thank you.

.

Chapter One

I looked forward to this day, shivering with pleasure when the August breeze lifted my hair, tickling my neck. Maybe I was just one more anonymous link in the endless chain of freeway commuters slowly creeping south, but I smiled out my open windows at drivers in lanes on either side of me. A few smiled back. Here we all were, trapped in traffic, breathing toxic fumes, and smiling at strangers. In the distance, clouds obscured the base of Mt. Rainier, but not its snow covered peak glittering in the morning sun. It seemed to be the beginning of another pleasant day.

Half an hour later, humming, I turned onto the familiar curving drive leading to the single story school just beyond the parking lot. To its right lay the grass covered playground, its green mottled with brown dusty patches. I stopped moving and caught my breath. Before me brilliant white-gold shafts of light from the rising sun pierced the branches of the bordering maple trees, throwing dramatic black shadows over the ground. Slowly they receded as the sun continued its ascent above the trees and I coasted forward, scoping out the area.

I smiled, elated as I snagged my favorite spot. On the opening day of each new school year, arriving early established parking space squatter's rights. Unless I wanted to spend the well known western Washington winter weather mimicking a soggy mop, I needed a parking spot close to the building's entrance, because my hair, left on its own, drooped like cocker spaniel ears. It took

1

time to bend it to my will and I didn't appreciate the wind and rain tearing it apart in seconds.

Before closing my window, I assessed the other early arrivals, and felt fairly certain that neither the ostentatious long black Lincoln Continental parked in the space marked *principal*, nor custodian Mark Smythe's white Ford pick-up truck parked in the far corner would be contenders for my parking spot. The verdict was out on the older brown Chevy next to Mark's pick-up. It looked familiar, but after three months away, who remembers old brown Chevies? It was into this drab assortment of black, brown and white vehicles that I added my ruby red, thrice waxed Rambler Rebel that, like most Ramblers, began its life an insipid pale green. But that was before I bought it the make-over that fire trucks envied.

Opening the car door, I breathed in the pungent mixture of warming macadam and recently cut grass and stretched across the seat to haul out my supplies. Swinging my feet to the ground, I slung the strap of my purse, red to match my car, over my left shoulder and wedged the thermos under my armpit, while with my other hand I hugged two packages of Oreos and a bag of multicolored hard candies to my chest along with my brown bag lunch, and hip bumped the door shut.

Workshop days, of necessity, called for casual dress, and I strode, not walked, in patriotic splendor in my faded blue jeans, new white Keds and a not very sexy red cotton blouse, its sleeves rolled up to my elbows. Unexpectedly, my purse strap snapped and my purse fell on my foot, nearly tripping me, turning my confident stride into an awkward lurch. Desperately clutching the cookies, candies and lunch bag, I flung my left arm out to avoid falling and the steel thermos slithered from under my arm and clanged to the pavement. I stood for a moment gazing down on it, before resignedly muttering, "Oh, heck. What are a few more dents? It already tilts like a Chianti-sodden Tower of Pisa."

Rescue was at hand. There, almost my mirror image in blue jeans, red shirt and white sneakers, was one of my favorite colleagues, John Cipriano. He was pulling open one of the school's heavy double doors with one hand and waving the other about attempting to hurry the tell-tale smoke drifting away. "Hey, John," I yelled before he could escape, "wait up!"

He bent to pick up the cigarette butt he'd stepped on, and flashed me a smile as bright as his trade-mark red plaid shirt, before he hurried to scoop up my thermos and purse. Even dangling my purse, he looked masculine and at 60, better than lots of younger men. The summer sun had deepened his olive complexion, accentuating his black hair and dark eyes. "Hey, hey, hey, ole buddy BJ, good to see you again," he said.

I noticed he wasn't meeting my eyes, but looking somewhere below my chin. "OK, John," I said, "Stop ogling my. . ."

"Ogling? I'm not ogling your. . ." he flushed, searching for an acceptable euphemism.

"My Oreos," I said, finishing my sentence and laughing at his discomfiture.

He grinned, lifted his eyes from the Oreos and scrambling for a safe way to change the subject, his words came out in a jumbled rush. "I like your choice of colors, but aren't you worried people will think we're twins? Those Oreos for me? How was your summer?" He ran out of breath.

I copied his breathless delivery, responding in reverse order, "My summer? You asking about all of it, or just the highlights? And no, the Oreos aren't for you, but I'll give you a couple. The bag of candy is for the lounge, and I'll get a seeing-eye dog for anyone who thinks we're twins. And even though you didn't ask, I'm fine and it's good to see you again, too."

He laughed and held the door for me. "I'm open for any amount of the Oreos, but please, feel free to edit your summer doings extensively, even the highlights." Inside, we glanced toward the principal's office, but the privacy curtain was closed and the outer office was dark, so we bypassed it and went to the lounge. John flipped on the lights and I laid the Oreos on the counter before I walked across the room to dump the candy on the table before bending to stuff my lunch into the small old fashioned fridge.

When I looked up, John held the opened Oreo container toward me, now minus two cookies. "I love cookies, especially Oreos. My wife worries about my weight, but she said cookies are OK, just no candy." He shot me a wicked grin as he twisted one of the cookies apart and scraped off its filling with his teeth. He finished both Oreos and said, "Well, I guess it's time to hit the old classroom." Picking up my thermos he asked hopefully, "Anything else you want me to carry?"

"No," I answered, "and get your eyes off my Oreos."

At my classroom door, I retrieved my thermos and asked, "Have you seen this year's roster yet? We forgot to stop by the office to pick one up."

A shadow crossed his face and his smile faded as he shook his head. "No, but I do know who our new principal is."

I waited. "So?" I prodded after a long pause, "Who is it? What's he like? I assume it's a he?"

"Yes. His name's Rick Roark. Mean anything to you?" he answered in an uncharacteristic monotone.

"No, not that I remember. So, tell me. You seem to know who he is."

"I worked with him for awhile at Roosevelt Elementary." John walked to his classroom door where he turned with a smile more like a grimace, said, "See ya," and went in.

"Now what the heck was that all about?" I wondered as I put the packages of Oreos in the top drawer of my file cabinet, carefully balanced my wobbly thermos on my desk, and reattached the strap on my purse before stashing it in the bottom drawer of my desk. "Oh, nuts, I'd better go get whatever's in my mailbox," I thought. I retrieved my purse and hurried back to the office.

I passed the still dark and curtained principal's office, but now the outer-office lights were on. I swept through to the adjoining workroom after passing Marla LaPierre, the school secretary, who was intent on a stack of papers on her desk. She glanced up, returned my, "Good morning," greeting and continued sorting. My mailbox held nothing particularly interesting, just a couple of fliers, a packet of ballpoint pens, another of number 2 pencils and the staff bulletin. "Hi, again, Marla," I said on my way out.

She smiled. "Yeah, same to you."

For the next four and a half hours, I focused all my energy and thoughts on turning my nondescript box of a classroom into an inviting place of learning. The spotless carpet of uninspiring beige and gleaming windows testified to Mark's efforts. With optimistic fervor, I dragged desks and chairs into place, hauled books from the storeroom, selected poster paints, construction paper, crayons and scissors and sharpened half a dozen pencils, while visions of brilliantly executed bulletin boards danced in my head. That these visions were unrealistic, considering my non-existent artistic talent, was irrelevant. It was a long time since I believed in the 9 to 3 workday or that teachers had nothing to do when the kids weren't present.

Hoping for some cross ventilation, I opened the three windows, the door to the outside and the hallway door. Judging by my sweat soaked hair and clinging wet shirt, it was an unrealized hope. Instead, hot desultory breezes carried in dust as well as fumes from the power mower, whose relentless roar made my eardrums vibrate. Along with the dust and the roar and the fumes, huge, ugly, black flies, swarmed in, buzzing in circles and diving at me and even contaminating my coffee cup. I flapped my arms and swatted at them to no avail. "You'd better be glad I don't have a fly swatter," I snarled, "or you'd be on your way to fly heaven by now." They ignored me.

❧❧

"Lunch?"

Intent on maintaining my balance on the student chair I used as a step ladder, I jumped at the unexpected sound and the alphabet letters I was stapling above the white board scattered. I flailed wildly for something to catch hold of. What I grabbed just happened to be the head of my friend and colleague, Ethel.

"Hey, cut out all the theatrical huggy stuff," she said, maintaining a tight grip on my arm until she was sure I was OK. "I just came by to see if you wanted to have lunch with me. It is noon, you know—the time lots of people eat lunch." She waved a brown bag I assumed was her lunch toward the clock for emphasis. "Oh, by the way," she said, trying to sound casual without success, "notice anything?" She pirouetted, holding one arm in what would have been a graceful arch above her head, except for the dangling brown bag.

Of course, the response she hoped for was obvious, but I couldn't resist teasing, "Oh, yes, I noticed it immediately. Your white streak is wider—you have more gray hair!" Ethel took great pride in her beautiful dark hair, through which a single streak of enhanced white (never gray) hair swooped back from her left temple. Her withering glance confirmed this was not the right answer.

"I know, I know," I said with mock excitement, "You have a new grubbie dress! I love that shade of purple on you. Is that the shade called puce?" Nearly everyone else wore slacks or jeans to set up their rooms. Ethel never wore jeans. An astute woman, she recognized that at 5 foot 3, and just under 200 pounds, slacks did not emphasize her best assets, just her most prominent ones.

"It's not purple and it certainly isn't puce, it's mauve, but you're getting closer, at least."

"You must have done lots of chasing your grandchildren this summer. You've lost weight."

"Brilliant observation. Over 20 pounds. Now let's go eat."

I replaced the tipsy thermos on my desk after I filled my cup, slung my purse with its reattached strap over my shoulder and we left to extract my brown bag lunch from the faculty fridge before heading out of doors. We ate, we talked, we laughed and talked some more, enjoying the feel of the sun-warmed concrete bench along the wall. Ethel munched her carrot sticks and apple with slow deliberation like all the diet gurus advocated, while I chewed energetically on my cold, rubbery leftover pizza, thinking it had been more satisfying last night. Maybe I should have given it a ten second zap in the lounge.

Involved, as good friends are who haven't seen each other for three months, we were oblivious to the world around us as we relived, shared and embellished the events of our summer vacation. We looked up when a shadow fell across us. "Hey, you two look like you need a masculine point of view," John said, as we made room for him on the bench. "So, what's the topic of conversation?"

"I just told Ethel I'm taking my kids to the ocean on our next three day weekend. Do we get Columbus Day off?"

Instead of answering my question, he asked, "Why not take them to a dude ranch? Kids love riding horses."

"No way," I said, "I rode a horse once. Every time it went up, I came down. Hard. I can think of a lot better reasons to spread my legs than slamming myself down on a leather saddle."

John bolted.

Ethel looked shocked, but couldn't help laughing. "Do you always say what you're thinking?" she asked. "It could get you in trouble."

"I have no idea where that comment came from. It just kind of tumbled out. But it is how I feel about horseback riding, I've just never said it out loud before." A stab of contrition made me add, "I know John never makes off color remarks in front of women, so I guess I'd better apologize next time I see him."

A short while later I asked, "Ethel, do you know anything about our new principal?" She didn't bolt, but her smile vanished.

"Yes, I've worked with him before. His name's Rick Roark. Since you don't know who he is, I'll let you meet him and draw your own conclusions."

Chapter Two

"Ye gods," John growled from the door, "don't they ever ventilate the teachers' lounge? It's so hot in here I'm already sweating and it stinks!" Of course the room stank; a reminder it used to be the faculty smoking room, John's favorite hangout. I laughed at the irony, even as I agreed with his opinion. After a quick scrutiny of the room, he walked to the sofa where I sat between Annie Edwards and Wanda Chan.

"Oops, be careful," I yelped. My coffee sloshed as I scooted to my right, almost ramming into Annie to avoid being sat on by John. Fortunately, my bulky red leather purse was the major recipient of my coffee, so I wasn't burned, but now rivulets of brown liquid drizzled onto my lap and down my leg. I looked and felt yucky.

"You don't expect me to help hold the wall up, do you?" John asked after his unceremonious plopping between Wanda and me. Wanda was tiny, so that's probably why the ancient faux leather sofa, built to hold three, merely sagged without collapsing under the four of us.

"That's your idea of an apology?" I muttered, using the last of my tissues to dab coffee off my purse, but I didn't have enough tissues for my jeans. My purse still glistened wetly, but I leaned forward to relocate it on the floor between my feet anyway, ignoring John's, "Why do you drag that ubiquitous bag of junk everywhere?" Regaining my previous upright position on the over-crowded sofa proved impossible, so I settled for looking more like Quasimodo than Rodin's *Thinker* and planted my elbows on my knees. At least that allowed me to drain the remaining dregs of my coffee as well as look toward John without our rubbing noses. "Does anyone have any idea why we were told to attend this command performance?" I asked, hoping someone in the room had an answer.

"I would guess to meet our new principal, Rick Roark," Vic's unmistakable voice boomed from behind me.

"Well, where is he then? I need this workshop day to get my room ready for the kids, and sitting around waiting isn't accomplishing much." In a lower voice, I said to John, "When the intercom order, 'All personnel are required to meet in the lounge at 1330 hours' I thought maybe Hal on *2001 A Space Odyssey* had taken over." He pretended not to hear me. I knew I sounded bitchy, so I shut up and without thinking, leaned back, but jerked forward when my head collided with John's chin.

Figuring he'd just poke me in the ribs, I kept my blisteringly brilliant bon mot to myself, merely thinking, "For Pete's sake, just because this lounge looks like a cast-off army barracks doesn't mean this is a military base—it's a school and I'm a teacher." I looked at the tasteless Formica topped table, surrounded by its eight equally tasteless steel framed chairs, crowded between the four of us on the sofa and the wall. Any cushioning under the black plastic seats was long gone, and I knew from experience their occupants, while less crowded, were even less comfortable than we were. I guessed I should feel lucky to be one of the twelve who weren't standing. Most were leaning against the walls or the imitation wood counter on which a brown microwave oven and time-worn coffee urn were positioned between the no longer white sink and fridge. It was my contention that a colorblind misanthrope created this masterwork of beige, brown or black. Everything, rugs, walls, furniture and cabinets, even the witches' brew, euphemistically referred to as coffee, that many actually drank, fit the criteria. My Oreos didn't— they had bright white centers. But they were in my classroom.

I couldn't help comparing our cramped lounge with its too many bodies in too little space, sans ventilation, charm or comfort, to the swarm of portable classrooms that, like horny rabbits, multiplied on the playfield every year. Lacking insulation they were stifling on hot days and frigid on cold days, noisy, and never as sanitary as real buildings. The powers-that-be excused this by calling them a *temporary quick fix*, an insult to the overflow students they contained. But no one thought it necessary to find even a quick fix for the over-crowded restrooms, staff lounge, gym and music rooms, while playground aides contended with increased arguments and fights as the space decreased.

"You know, John," I sniped, "considering the new air conditioning and carpets in the admin offices, I wonder if it would bankrupt the district to spring for some fresh paint and acoustical tile in here." I didn't mind that John gave my question the silent treatment; it was rhetorical anyway. But I did flash him an exasperated look and turned for comfort to my cup and a sip of coffee, forgetting I was wearing most of it. After double checking that only the aroma remained, I glanced toward the communal urn, and suppressed a shudder. No way was whatever was simmering there contaminating my cup.

Facing me from across the table, Ethel realized my cup was empty and flashed me an impish grin, wiggled the fingers of one hand while with the other raised her cup to her lips. She brought her coffee from home, too. With a ferocious scowl, I mouthed, "I'll get you for that." She raised her cup again.

"BJ..." John started to say, so close his breath tickled my ear, but stopped as everyone fell silent and looked toward the door. A man I'd never seen before, and therefore assumed was the new principal, stood rigidly erect for several seconds in the entry, before saying, "Good afternoon, Staff. I am Rick Roark, your new principal."

Of course it was. Although sounding slightly less robotic than it had over the intercom, that clipped, impersonal voice was unmistakable. An irreverent urge to laugh made me turn to John to say, "Oh, no! I was right. They've reactivated Hal!" but John's narrowed eyes locked on Roark, and the thin tight line of his lips, stopped me.

"Thank you for coming," Roark said, his voice as neutral as his body language.

"Not too many options," I thought, suppressing a grin. I scanned my colleagues. In unsmiling silence, some were looking toward Roark, but most were looking down toward the floor or staring off in space. Ethel was studying her hands.

Apparently Roark expected no response, for without pausing he continued, "I have been transferred here for two reasons. The first one is, Matt Preston, your previous principal, has retired. Secondly, the administration feels this school has suffered from weak and inefficient management."

"Wow, Mr. Sensitivity!" I thought as I felt John stiffen. As far as I knew, everyone admired Matt, but John was his personal friend as well.

Oblivious to any reaction to his words, Roark went on, "I have been sent here to correct this problem. I am well aware that behind my back, some of the staff in my previous school referred to me as a hatchet man. I am proud to say, that is probably a very good assessment."

"Yep. It's Hal. At least the hatchet wielding tin woodman wanted a heart," I thought. Roark stopped talking long enough to give several of us an appraising once over. I returned the favor, thinking as I took in his ramrod spine and clipped brown hair that he'd have fit beautifully in the military. Perhaps a bit too old—at least forty, and hoping he didn't intend to run the school like an academy.

Completing his once-over, Roark said, "I see some familiar faces," although he'd shown no signs of recognition, "but I need to know the names of those who are new to me." With his back to those of us on the sofa and the rest of the room, he faced the ones seated at the table or standing against the wall behind them, and stared silently at Mark.

"Uh, I'm Mark," he said, twisting around and raising his head in order to face Roark, "Mark Smythe. School custodian. Been here nearly twenty years." The usually garrulous Mark was almost stuttering. Relief washed over his face when Roark shifted his gaze to Mary who sat next to him.

Like Mark, she had to turn and raise her head in order to look up at Roark. She smiled and said, "I am Mary Johnson. Third grade." Ignoring her smile, Roark moved on without acknowledgement.

"I was right!" I thought. "It really is Hal."

Finished with those at the table and along the wall, he turned to stand directly in front of Wanda, who, in order to make eye contact was compelled to look up at him like a supplicant.

"You're not pulling that intimidation crap on me," I thought indignantly as his belt buckle moved into my line of vision. I briefly considered addressing myself to his fly, but chose instead to tilt my head, resting it coquettishly on John's shoulder. I slanted a look up at Roark from the corner of my eye and in my teacher voice announced, "BJ. Fifth grade." Go ahead, make something of that, I thought. He stood, looking down at me through narrowed eyes a moment longer and a prickly chill darted down my spine although the room was still sticky hot.

His last victim, Patricia Soames, who was squatting against the back wall, broke the pattern. She rose smoothly, moving away from the wall to her full five foot ten, forcing Roark to take a step back. Almost nose to nose she stated, "I am Patricia Soames. I teach sixth grade. I have done so in this school for six years and ten years elsewhere." When he made no response she relaxed back against the wall, and slid back down to a squat. Patricia and I had never particularly enjoyed each other's company, but at that moment I really, really, really admired her.

Staff introductions over, it was Roark's turn. "It is important that you not only know who I am, but what my philosophy is: I believe subordinates do not question their superiors. When my superiors say 'Jump', I jump and I expect the same discipline from my subordinates."

When my jaw dropped, I accomplished the impossible, I kept my mouth shut. But I couldn't stop my eyes from blinking. Superiors? Subordinates? I sucked in a sudden breath. John noticed, and he jabbed my ribs, and for a second I quit breathing. When I quit blinking and gave no indication of talking, John pulled his elbow back. "Is some college giving out degrees in dictatorship?" I wanted to ask. Instead I forced myself to look attentive as Roark reeled out the same laundry list of expectations and rules I'd heard at the beginning of every school year. But for the first time it was completely unrelieved by a smile or touch of humor.

My breathing was almost back to normal when Roark reiterated his superiors, subordinates inanity. I pinched my lips together and glowered at John, daring him to elbow me again. Superiors? Subordinates? The words created knots in my guts. Well, of course, I'm a teacher. Maybe administrators see it that way. But if they do, most of them are smart enough to keep it quiet. I figured I'd do well to follow suit, just keep quiet—not every stupid remark had to be responded to. I recalled one of my college instructors saying, "If you are a person who rocks the boat or raises your head above the average, do not become a teacher. You'll never succeed in the system."

I had no desire to rock the boat, so I gave myself a figurative shake and tried to find something safe to concentrate on until these dumb-ass superior/subordinates references ended. I moved my head off John's shoulder and slumped forward, giving me an excellent view of most of the floor and a lot of shoes.

It was no surprise that Roark in his spit-polished black loafers was the only one not wearing white canvas shoes. Whoops, my mistake. Patricia Soames was decked out in white Oxfords so wide I figured they may have come with oars. I tried to suppress the giggle triggered by this idea, but it erupted as a snort, whereupon the room became a vacuum devoid of sound or movement. Any further impulse to giggle died when I looked up and found myself impaled on Roark's glacial glare.

"BJ, isn't it?"

I flushed, hoping I only imagined the warning in his voice. In mute embarrassment, I faced him and saw his eyes almost matched his icy blue tie.

"Well, BJ, don't you believe you should defer to your superiors?"

Shaken and frustrated at having no safe response I grew hotter and sweatier by the second. My armpits itched. My vision blurred. Sweat scalded my eyelids and dripped to my chin. Knowing he'd interpret my tears as a sign of weakness made it worse. Of course I didn't agree with this arrogant martinet. Years ago I'd challenged my college instructor, telling him I believed the boat-rockers and above average teachers were precisely what children deserved. But this man was my new boss and I needed my job.

Well?" he demanded.

Struggling to keep my face from registering the contempt I felt, I bit my tongue and remained silent, holding back the answer I didn't dare utter.

"Well?" he said again in a tone that demanded a response.

"Uh, well, maybe?" I babbled, knowing I sounded stupid, but at least it wasn't dishonest or insubordinate.

"Maybe?" he mimicked, his voice heavy with sarcasm. "My question was, 'Don't you believe you should defer to your superiors?' and you answer, 'Maybe'. What does that mean?"

I wasn't an idiot, but I'd always been a lousy liar, and, unfortunately, an even worse diplomat. I took a deep breath. "Maybe means that maybe I would if I found someone I thought was superior to me. And it's never happened yet." I knew I should stop, but stopping in free-fall isn't an option and I finished my suicidal plunge. "What's more, I haven't heard the words superior and subordinate used so much since the Nuremberg Trials."

I'd never heard so much silence. Wasn't anybody breathing? John's elbow was gouging clear through to my other side. "Too late," I wanted to tell him. But I think he knew. As my grandpa used to say, I was too late smart.

Roark froze. Only his eyes, now narrow slits, moved as he focused somewhere over my head, before enunciating with cold precision the remainder of his agenda: the programs planned, supplies ordered, opening day procedures, and all the other housekeeping details for the new year. Finally it was over. Hot, sweaty and an emotional wreck, I heaved a sigh of relief. I heaved it too soon. Roark had a parting shot.

"One last thing before you go," he said. "I want you all to know that I adhere to an open door policy. My office door is always open to everyone: teachers, staff, parents, students. In fact, I want to encourage every one of you to feel free to come to me any time you disagree with any of my policies or regulations so I can show you where you're wrong."

"If he had a sense of humor," I thought, "I could believe he was kidding. I guess I'll just have to hope my ribs hold out. And be grateful a year is only nine months long."

.

Chapter Three

When my contract day ended, I beat everyone else out the door. Once on the freeway I kept the odometer at one mile under the speed limit, and looked forward to stretching out on my lawn chair on the deck, being lulled by the sun's warmth and the occasional tickle of a late summer breeze. Our home perched on the edge of a ravine that muffled the sounds of civilization, and I reveled in the near silence. About an hour later, still in daydream mode, I coasted down my driveway into the carport and felt a leap of joy as my welcoming committee of four dashed to greet me. I opened the car door, but before I could get out, they clamored, "Can we go to the beach? Huh? Huh? Can we? Huh? It's so hot and we're all sweaty."

"School doesn't start till tomorrow, so I don't have any homework, yet," Lissa said.

"Me, either," the other three chimed in.

"You promised we could have MacDonald's hamburgers and fries so you wouldn't have to think about dinner on your first day of work, so we have lots of time," Cal added.

"We even have our swimsuits on under our clothes already," Cabot said, lifting his tee shirt to prove it.

They trailed me into the house. Dreams die hard, but it was time to concede defeat. "OK. OK. Just let me put my stuff away and change my clothes and get a cup of coffee first."

"I knew you'd say that," Lissa said, holding a steaming cup toward me, while Cal hauled my satchel to my room and Risa set my thermos on the counter..

Laughing, I took the coffee to my bedroom and dropped into my chair by the nightstand. It wasn't exactly the same as a deck chair in the sun, but I relaxed a moment, holding the warm cup in both hands and taking a few sips before setting it on the dresser and going into the closet to switch into shorts and sandals. There wasn't a sound in the house, so I figured the kids were already in the car. I fished my keys out of my purse, made a run through the house, checking that all windows were closed, before opening the front door.

"Hey, look, Mom," Cabot yelled the moment he saw me. "We're taking the raft we made in the woods so we can sail on it."

My purse fell from my numb fingers as, with horror I saw, tied to the top of my shiny red car, the most ungainly conglomeration of 2 x 4s and badly weathered sheets of plywood sandwiching an oversized, overinflated truck inner tube. Poking skyward from its center was another eight foot 2 x 4 with one of the boys' cowboys and Indians bed sheets wrapped around it and secured with what appeared to be a narrow rope. From beneath the raft, like signal pennants on a ship, dangled the corners of four beach towels: Cabot's red one, Cal's orange one, Lissa's blue one and Risa's purple one.

"But don't worry, Mom," Cal assured me, "we'll put your clothesline back up when we get home. Except for some twine, it was the only rope we could find." He smiled with pride. "And did you see what we did? We put a whole bunch of towels under the raft so it wouldn't scratch your car. Cool, huh?"

While I struggled to regain my voice, there was an eerie wolf-like howl from the trunk. "It's just Laddie," Cal explained. "He wants to go to the beach with us, and I knew you wouldn't let him ride in the car, so we used some of the rope to tie the lid down, but we used the spare tire to hold it part way open so Laddie wouldn't suffocate."

My mouth was open, but no words were coming out. Being able to breathe is necessary if one wants to talk.

"Just don't blame me," Lissa said. "I was making cookies."

"I was putting the milk and paper cups in the picnic basket, so I didn't do it, either," Risa hastened to add.

"Hey!" Lissa's unexpected shout made my ears ring. "Is that MY bath towel under your yucky old raft?" Dropping the basket and thermos, she made a lunge for Cal, who dove headfirst through the window into the back seat. He'd wisely left the window open after he looped the rope securing the raft, through both back windows. She leaned in, shaking her fist, but he'd scooted to the far side, out of her reach. Unable to attack Cal, she turned toward Cabot, who, by now, was scrambling in the opposite window after his brother. Cal slid away from imminent collision and before Lissa could return, swiftly wound the window up.

"I'll climb over the front seat and get you!" she threatened, seeing Cabot raising his window, too.

I sighed, picked up the thermos and picnic basket and returned them to Lissa, checked that Risa had the beach blanket, retrieved my purse and after locking the front door, motioned both girls into the front seat. Hoping to head off further warfare, I said, "Lissa, how about if I let you use my towel?" as I started the car.

She smiled triumphantly over her shoulder at Cal. My towel was larger and more luxurious than the others, one of my last gifts from my parents, and until this moment, off-limits to anyone but me.

Cognizant of the monstrosity riding above us, I backed with greater care than usual up the driveway. The beach we liked best was less than five miles away and I drove slowly, fearing speed or an abrupt stop would launch the raft from the roof of the car onto the hood. Hearing no sound from the trunk, I assumed Laddie was resigned to his ignominious mode of transportation.

I kept my eyes on the road, ignoring the startled looks of people on the sidewalk or in approaching cars. In the rear view mirror I noted that no vehicle drove within ten car lengths of me. Well, that's one way to discourage tailgaters. Lissa slouched as far out of sight as her seatbelt allowed, but the boys kept up excited chatter about who got to use the raft first, who was captain and who was crew and how envious others on the beach would be when they saw the wind catching the sail as they glided down the beach.

"I have my life preserver, so I get to ride with you," Risa announced, wiggling in anticipation.

"Not me," Lissa said, "I plan to lie on Mom's towel and get a suntan."

In the nearly empty parking lot, I was spared any further astonished or puzzled stares from strangers. The boys worked as a team, removing my clothesline and coiling it before tossing it into the back seat, then undid some twine I recognized as from my gardening supplies. Without damage to the car, they slid the raft off the roof, leaving the towels, and with one boy on each side, carried it toward the water. I slung the towels over my shoulder and scooped up the discarded twine which I tossed into the back seat on top of the rope, before handing Lissa the blanket to carry to the beach. Risa skipped alongside her, toting the thermos and the food. I locked the car and paroled Laddie, who leaped from the trunk and raced to the boys who were already bobbing just off-shore.

"Laddie!" they shouted happily. "Here, boy. Come here, boy." Laddie was a water dog, and he woofed and dogpaddled through the few feet of water separating him from the would-be Huck Finns. Each time either boy moved, their half submerged raft tilted and wobbled, but its ability to float became more precarious still when they hauled Laddie on board. Standing in knee deep water, Risa eyed it and her brothers, who sat on opposite sides with Laddie between them, and changed her mind about joining them. When a sudden gust of wind caught the bed sheet sail, the boys whooped with pleasure, but Laddie plunged overboard, and the raft capsized, catapulting both boys into the water. Their heroic efforts to right it forced it farther from land until, with heavy hearts, the boys waved farewell, watching as it drifted out of their reach.

That night after dinner, at McDonald's as promised, I stood on the deck watching the moon-glow filter through the leaves of the tall maple tree below me, the one we called the boys' tree. Hundreds of trees grew on the sides of the ravine, but nine year old Cal and Cabot, a year younger, built their private tree house, actually no more than a platform, high in this particular maple, hidden by its dense foliage that created a natural security curtain. A breeze of evergreen fragrance, rustled its way up the ravine, its coolness reminding me it was almost autumn. I needed a sweater, so I slid the glass door open and came back inside.

From the kitchen came the raised voices of Cal and thirteen year old Lissa, bickering over something. I had no idea over what, and with no desire to find out, I slipped quietly toward my room. Passing the living room, I stopped, confronted by a remnant of my youthful bad taste sitting stolidly in front of the fireplace. Even if guests had to sit on the floor, the time had come for that chair to go. "Lissa, Cal," I called, "Come here. I need your help."

"Yeah? What?" Cal demanded as Lissa scowled, happy to let her brother do the talking.

I ignored their lack of enthusiasm and pointed at the heavy monstrosity. "I want you to haul that ugly pink chair out of the living room and put it in the rec room."

"Why us?" Cal demanded.

"It's too heavy," Lissa said.

"You two because I said so. And it isn't too heavy if you work together."

"What if she drops it and it falls on me and I get hurt?" Always one to play the odds, Cal figured nothing was ever lost by arguing, and there was a chance he might win.

"She won't drop it because I'll be standing right there at the top of the stairs and. . ." inspiration struck, "if she does, then she has to do all your work for a week."

"Even make my bed and clean the toilet?" Cal asked.

"Of course," I answered.

"Well, what if he drops it on me?" Lissa asked.

"Same deal, in reverse. Now get going."

Grunts and complaints, warnings and threats echoed up the stairwell, punctuated with thumps on every stair, but soon the chair was sitting in all its glowing pink ugliness in the basement rec room. No injuries were sustained, so both kids were stuck doing their own chores.

Cabot, who had come out to observe remained silent until it was over, then commented, "I bet Laddie will like lying in it." From behind him the shaggy sheep dog, hearing his name, woofed agreement.

"Well," I responded wryly, "I guess that qualifies it as a win-win. Laddie has furniture he can climb on and I won't have to look at it again."

I was almost right.

Chapter Four

"Hi-ho, hi-ho, it's off to work I go, da, da, da, da. . ." What I lacked in musical talent I compensated for with volume, so it seemed only fair I spare my fellow commuters by keeping the window closed and the air vent open. Mile after bumper-to-bumper mile I sang my way south on I-405 toward my first day with my new class. Sometimes I wondered how anyone, meaning me, who barely tolerated school, could love teaching so much. Just another of life's mysteries.

On this perfectly wonderful day, the rising sun's rays ricocheted off the freshly waxed hood of my car sending flashes of red lightning back into space. Every turn and curve in the road alternately hid or exposed glimpses of Mt. Rainier, like a game of hide-and-seek. I stopped singing long enough to take a sip of coffee, and seeing a Coca Cola truck attempting to merge, I slowed. Because I'd found Coca Cola drivers to be unfailingly courteous, I always made a space for them. Besides, one of the perks of arriving at work an hour or so early, meant time was not an issue. The strident horn blast from the car behind me indicated one commuter disagreed.

Half an hour later, another perk awaited me—my chosen parking spot was open. However, another perk faded and died when I saw Hatchet Man's car, meaning he'd arrived ahead of me and I'd have to go past him to use the copy machine. I pocketed my keys, took a deep breath, and reached back to hoist the over-loaded satchel from the back seat. "Thank goodness I can leave some of this stuff in my classroom from now on," I grunted. Before clutching it in my right hand, I slid the battered thermos under my arm and cinched the strap of my hefty purse on my left shoulder and lumbered from the car. Too weighed down to stride purposefully, I waddled toward the entrance.

The closer I got, the more nervous I got. My salary, unlike that of some of my female colleagues, was not added income, it was my only income, and I tried to keep people like Roark from finding out. Inside, somewhere, I knew he was waiting, and after yesterday's fiasco I worried, wondering if he was just inside the door, poised to attack; to demand an explanation, or worse, a retraction? "If he does, how do I respond? Lie and say I'm sorry and didn't mean what I said?" But lying has never been my strong suit, and I kind of wanted to keep it that way. Maybe I could make just an appearance of denying everything, but I had no idea how. "Guess I'll just play it by ear. *Que sera, sera.*" I reached out and reluctantly pulled the heavy door open and scoped out the hallway, relieved he was nowhere in sight and his office door was closed.

Tip-toeing to keep my heels from clicking on the tile floor was difficult under all the weight I was carrying, and hurrying was impossible, so when I reached the relative safety of my classroom, I sighed with relief, dropped the satchel on the floor next to my desk, fell into my chair and shoved my purse into the bottom drawer, pulled my thermos from under my arm and treated myself to a half cup of coffee. "There is no fragrance on earth like good, freshly brewed coffee," I thought, inhaling deeply as I sipped. "It's the little luxuries that make life wonderful."

Golden shafts of sunlight blazed through the tall windows as I pulled aside the ugly dark drapes, puzzling yet again at some bureaucrat's execrable taste. With a shrug, I turned away, scanning the room to check everything was ready for my new students. I was pleased with how well the double row of alphabet letters I'd stapled above the white board turned out. During the summer my kids and I had outlined each letter with glitter, and now it sparkled in the sunlight. I hoped my students would enjoy them as much as I did.

Below the letters, I wrote my name and the date with a bright red felt pen, the erasable kind. The smell of whatever chemical was in them made my nose twitch, but twitching was better than sneezing from chalk dust. I retrieved my lesson plan book from the satchel, laid it open on my desk and rechecked my plans for the day, making just a few changes. I felt that what I'd finished the day before looked good. So I refilled my cup, slung my purse strap over my shoulder and set off to find John and Ethel and whoever else was around.

It was early and except for Edna, the first grade teacher sitting at the table, the lounge was deserted. She was leaning forward, holding her head in her hands, and didn't appear to be aware of me, so I turned to continue my search for Ethel. When Edna called out so softly I almost didn't hear her, "Hi, BJ. You're here early, too," I turned back.

"Hi, Edna," I said, and after a moment walked over to sit across the table facing her. I seldom saw into Edna, and when our paths did cross, she was so quiet that little more than a courteous nod passed between us. Three years ago, when we first met, I'd been struck by her badly pock-marked face, but over time it was her gentle voice and warm personality I noticed. Judging by the comments of my students who'd been in her class, this was what they remembered, too. "Yes, I like getting here early," I answered before asking, "Are you OK?"

Her slumped shoulders and depressed expression indicated otherwise. "Well, I guess I'll be fine," she murmured so softly I barely heard her. "I just have to redo my bulletin boards."

"Bummer," I said. Bulletin boards are the bane of my teaching life. I couldn't imagine redoing mine unless they caught fire. Maybe not even then. "What happened to yours?" I asked.

She was silent for a couple of seconds. Without looking up, she answered, "Mr. Roark says they don't portray the message he wants for the school. They're too immature."

I started to laugh, but something warned me not to. "Too immature?" I parroted. "Unless you're not telling me something, you teach first graders, who, the last time I checked, were kind of immature." I thought a moment. "OK, I give up. What the heck did he mean by *the message for the school*? I didn't know we had one." She didn't answer, so I asked, "What did he say to put up instead?"

"He didn't say." She sounded close to tears. "He said that I'm a professional and it's my job to figure it out."

"That's stupid," I burst out. "Just tell him that if what you've done doesn't suit him, then he needs to explain exactly what's wrong and what he wants done. That's his job." Even in my indignation, I knew this was quite a stretch. I couldn't imagine quiet Edna confronting Roark. As far as I knew, she was the only one who called him Mr. Roark instead of Roark, or Rick, so I shut up and reached across the table to lay my hand on her wrist, just as three primary teachers came into the lounge holding empty cups and heading for the coffee urn.

Annie Edwards carried a tray laden with cookies and made my day by placing it on the table between Edna and me. "Ohhh," I moaned in pleasure as I caught their cinnamon and butter aroma, "homemade snickerdoodles. Thank you Annie," I said, taking one as Edna stood and left the room. I watched her go, wondering if I should do something. Nothing came to mind, so I reached for another cookie, letting its cinnamony sweetness melt on my tongue. Annie sat down in the chair vacated by Edna, and I said, "Annie, your cookies are delicious." I debated telling her about Roark's treatment of Edna, but wasn't sure I should.

Slowly both the noise level and humidity had risen as more of the staff came into the lounge. Ethel wasn't among them, so I smiled, reached for a couple more cookies, and left to find her. She likes cookies, too.

Finding her was easy. She was in her classroom, busy as usual. Her sky blue dress accessorized with a yellow scarf flipped jauntily over her right shoulder, was new to me. "Hey, Foxy Lady with gray hair," I said, putting one of the cookies on her desk, "I brought you something." She kept her back to me and continued placing construction paper folders of every color on the students' desks and then, without the slightest hesitation, waggled her rear end at me—I thought she was mooning me, but I wasn't sure. "Hey," I repeated, "be nice or I'll eat your cookie." Deliberately not looking at me, she side-stepped to her desk and snatched the cookie.

Electricity snaps and crackles. So does color. Ethel's room fairly vibrated with color, predominantly those of autumn: scarlet, orange, brown, and gold. Maple leaves and grinning paper pumpkins vied for dominance over green and red apples, all zigzagging around the room, above doors, windows and bulletin boards. A three dimensional life-size scarecrow, its arms dangling to the floor, with a broom of straw lying across its knees, slouched in a vintage folding chair, guarding the door. Alphabet letters marched above her white board, lacking flashy glitter, but with no paint, crayon or felt pen left unused.

"Think you have enough color in here?" I asked.

"Unless you just plan on being a nuisance," she said in her no nonsense voice, "start over there by the window and put a name tag on top of each of these folders. They're in alphabetical order." Holding her cookie between her index finger and thumb, she waved imperiously in the direction of a stack of name tags lying on a nearby desk. Along with everyone else, I learned long ago that the price for entering her classroom was being put to work. No exceptions— she was an equal opportunity task master of parents, teachers, students, anyone capable of following orders, and that included our previous principal, but I had my doubts about our new one. For her, it was a matter of survival. With thirty-two morning students and another thirty-one afternoon students, twice as many to evaluate, prepare materials for and address the strengths and weaknesses of, as any other teacher, she shanghaied any help she could. No one who has ever dealt with children would assume that 63 kids are the same as 32 or 31 just because they aren't all there at the same time. But administrators don't deal with living students, just numbers and bottom lines. I was willing to bet that if they were responsible for no more than that nightmare called *Report Card Time,* things would change in a hurry.

Trailing her around the room dropping off name tags, I said, "I just saw Edna. She was in tears. She said Roark made her redo her bulletin boards."

Ethel actually stopped what she was doing and asked, "Why?"

"He said they were too immature. She said she wasn't sure what he meant, so I told her to insist he explain exactly what it was he wanted. And to do it before she took them down."

"She won't." She sighed, and with a look of resignation, said, "Edna belongs to some religious group that prohibits women from challenging men, raising their voices, wearing make-up, dressing provocatively and a bunch of other things."

"Oh, then her complexion isn't a reaction to make-up? I always assumed it was."

"All I know," Ethel said, "is that girl has been to more dermatologists than I knew existed. We talked about it sometimes last year. She's tried everything they've prescribed or suggested, but nothing seems to help."

I was quiet, thinking this over.

Ethel flashed me a wicked grin, "But, hey, we're running out of time." She shoved some papers at me, "So while you're passing these out, tell me what's new that we didn't get to yesterday. Any wild adventures? What's going on with your kids? How's your love life?"

I ducked the latter question. The less said, the better, and responded with, "Oh, Ethel, you know better than to ask about my kids. I've got three months' worth of their clever sayings, incredible exploits and loveable characteristics to regale you with. And I have to tell you about their raft. How much time do we have?"

She threw up her hands in mock surrender. She'd met each of my four offspring, and always expressed the opinion that each of them was brilliant, creative, beautiful and perfect. I wished their teachers and our neighbors were as smart as Ethel.

"I think I'd better hurry home after work today to find out how their first day back in school went and see which of their new bottomless pit friends are helping them clean out the refrigerator." More soberly I added, "Not to mention discovering what vital supplies their teachers say I have to run out and buy before tomorrow. Last year I barely made it to the hardware store for Lissa's science class before closing time. Hope those kids leave something for tomorrow's lunches." I glanced at the clock. "Whoops. Gotta run. Classes start in 20 minutes and I want to re-review my roster. Almost every name on it is new to me, and I'm awful with names. Hope you have a wonderful day." I ran out of breath, finished leaving papers on desks and handed her the leftovers.

"See you at lunch," she said, hugging me with the arm that wasn't full of old magazines and papers. Ethel's kindergarteners demolish stacks of magazines every year, converting them into interesting collages and piles of recyclable trash.

At the door, I raised my eyebrows almost into my hairline, looked askance at her bulletin boards, and in my best Roark imitation, asked, "But are you sure these are not too immature?" I fled, hastily shoving the door closed, so her eraser hit it and not me.

On my way back, I ducked into the lounge hoping to renew my energy with another snickerdoodle. This was my lucky day. Not only were there a few cookies remaining, there was a different group of adults, which meant I wouldn't appear greedy when I took one more. Appearance is everything. Figuring it would be my last one, I savored it fully on my return to my classroom while I scanned my roster for the umpteenth time, trying to familiarize myself with each name and where I'd written it on the seating chart. Leaning back sipping coffee, I wished I had another cookie, and stared into space, recalling as many names as I could. Irritated, I scowled, when the intercom intruded on my concentration.

"Good morning, Staff. At this time I wish to inform all teachers they are to report to their classrooms no later than five minutes before the bell. This applies not only in the morning, but after each break. It is now seven minutes before the bell." There was a click.

A desire to yank the thing off the wall and stick it where I thought it would be appropriate wasn't an option, so I settled for sticking my tongue out at it. I would have added giving it a raspberry, but didn't want to spray coffee all over my desk.

From behind me, a chorus of hoots and uninhibited laughter made me spin around. Pressed up against and smearing the length of my windows, was a wavy line of moist noses and grinning mouths.

Busted!

Chapter Five

With a burst of laughter, a little louder than might be considered ladylike, I hurried to open the door and join them. "Good morning," I said, struggling to look and sound more teacher-like.

When, as if on cue, all the faces turned from the window and responded in unison, "Good morning, Ms. McCall," I cracked up. Their puzzled looks followed by polite laughter set me off yet again.

When I was able to speak normally, I said, "Oh, so you know who I am," in mock surprise.

At this, the wavy line evolved into a semi-circle of high spirited individuals, effectively pinning me to the wall. Answers filled the air, running over and into each other, creating a tangled skein of sound. "My sister had you last year." "I saw you on the playground lots of times." "My Mom told me." "That's what they said in the office."

"OK, OK, OK!" I said, raising my hands in surrender. I searched unsuccessfully for a familiar face in this dazzling array of fluorescent orange and green tee shirts scattered among the various shades of red, blue and yellow ones, most anchored to blue jeans and white tennis shoes. Like all children, they moved constantly, creating a liquid collage of color as varied as that of oil sheen on water. "Well," I said in a break in the sound, "it looks like you know me, but I don't know you. How many of you will be in my class this year?"

Hands shot into the air, along with a deafening chorus of "Me," "I am," "I will." I could see I'd have to be careful how I phrased future questions.

"There sure are lots of you," I acknowledged. "How about if I call out a name and if it's yours, you raise your hand." Nods and smiles met this suggestion, so I guessed they liked it. Some seemed so eager to be called on, they never took their eyes off me. Recalling some of the names on my roster, I called out, "Chris." Three hands flew up. Three? I remembered seeing only two. "Which Chris are you?" I asked the blond boy hopping up and down on one foot in his eagerness to respond.

"I'm Chris Amundsen, really Christopher, but everybody just says Chris," he said, continuing to hop. "Sometimes when she's mad, my mom calls me Christopher, but usually she calls me Chris. And..."

"Thank you, Chris Amundsen."

Before I could ask, a slim girl with a shiny cap of curly red hair Orphan Annie would have loved, worked her way close to me and, as if afraid of not being called on, took hold of my arm and said seriously, "I'm Chris James and I'm glad I'm going to be in your class."

I replied solemnly, "Thank you, Chris James. I'm happy to have you." It took a moment before she smiled and melted back among her peers.

I looked at the third child who raised his hand. "I don't remember three Chrisses. Which one are you?" I asked.

"I'm Chris Bronson, but I'm not in your class." He flashed me an impish look and added, "You asked ALL the Chrisses to raise their hands and my name is Chris, so I did." He looked around at his audience, and grinned delightedly at its burst of laughter. I fully expected him to take a bow.

"Gotta watch those vague questions," I warned myself, "kids are literal." I joined the laughter, regretting this little clown wasn't going to be one of my students.

"I'm Billy," a freckle-faced redhead announced. "My name is Billy McGuire and I'm glad I'm going to be in your class."

"I'm glad, too," I told him.

"My last year's teacher didn't say that," he said matter-of-factly.

The bell rang, saving me from having to find a response to this bit of information. In a flurry of noise and motion, those not in my class scattered, those who remained scrambled into line quickly as they'd been taught since kindergarten. It didn't seem possible, but the noise level actually rose as they jockeyed for position. I raised my hand, signaling for quiet. Three or four quit talking. Briefly. With my finger to my lips, I walked the length of the line. Talking stopped only when I so instructed each child individually. It was awhile before I opened the door for my silent class, and with my finger to my lips, motioned them in.

As each one filed past, I pointed to the coat rack with a shelf for lunches above it, then to the board where I'd written, "Please sit at the desk with your name tag on it." To my whispered, "What is your name?" they each responded, in a whisper. Often whispering is often an effective means for bringing classes to order. Humoring me, the children filed in, placed any wraps or lunches where I'd indicated, and sat in their assigned seats, all in utter silence. Pleased at the success of my strategy, I turned to close the door and the room erupted in sound. Every child was talking, some in groups of two or three, others wandering about, looking at their new surroundings. A few waited in a line for a drink from the fountain at the back of the room. Talking. This time the finger on the lips didn't work and the whispering was ineffective.

Exasperated, I resorted to my teacher voice, which rose above the din. "I would like each of you to sit down. Now! Quietly." They shrugged and returned to their seats, except for Billy. Casting a "Whatever you say, Teacher," look at me, he complied. Literally. He dropped to the floor, nearly on my foot. Very quietly, of course.

"But you said. . ." he began, looked at the expression on my face, and jumped to his feet and scampered to his seat.

"Well, Billy," I thought, resisting the impulse to laugh, "you have reminded me once again that I need to be precise in my instructions." With everyone seated, I surveyed the room and saw that one desk had no occupant. Forgetting the advice I'd just given myself, I asked, "Whose name is on that desk?" and was deafened as answers were shouted from every direction, "Martin Muller."

"It's Martin Muller's desk." "Martin Muller is absent." "He wasn't on the bus either."

I scribbled Martin Muller on an attendance slip, read the name tag on the desk nearest me and said, "Allison Barker, will you please take this to the attendance office?" Allison stood and reached for the slip, gave her short brown pony tail a flip and looked at me with innocent brown eyes that crinkled as she shot an impish glance at her classmates. Before she reached the door, I remembered Billy and Chris. "And come right back," I ordered. I was learning.

Every year I faced a new group of students, each one unique, but this one promised some new challenges. Between admonitions to stop talking, to sit down and to stop asking how long until lunch, I managed to squeeze in the list of my class expectations, the school's rules and an overview of daily and weekly agendas. It was nearly noon before, per district requirement, I was able to read to them the official process of disciplinary actions. I hurried through it as quickly as possible. Although corporal punishment was still on the list, I had never used nor approved of it, so I added, "But I promise you, I will never hit you or ask anyone else to do so." They were silent, absorbing this, then Billy, with his trademark wicked grin lighting up his freckled face asked, "Not even if we're bad?"

Returning his grin with an equally wicked one of my own, I replied using my scariest voice, "There is something you should know, Billy, I'm the mother of the baddest kid you've ever seen, so believe me, I know lots of ways to deal with bad behavior. Trust me, what I know how to do makes hitting you seem nice." With what I hoped was an ominous look, I asked, "Care to test me?"

Billy studied me a moment, threw up his arms in an act of surrender, and said, "Naw, I think maybe I'll just be good."

I swallowed the laugh that bubbled up, and nodded my approval. "Good choice, Billie. There's the bell for lunch. Let's eat."

Above the ensuing pandemonium, I watched some of the boys high-fiving Billy and saying, "I think I'd rather be good, too. I don't think she's kidding." My own kids had explained the meaning of two people raising their right hands and smacking them, so I wasn't worried it was some kind of secret society rite.

How they could talk so much and eat so fast amazed me, for in less than ten minutes, all evidence of lunch, except its smells of peanut butter, tuna fish and pizza disappeared, and the last student left the room. Noisy and exuberant as they were, they left the room clean. A few chairs may have been out of place, but there weren't any wrappers, napkins, crumbs or spills on the desks or floor. Unbelievable.

I rebalanced my thermos after filling my cup and although it was hot, I almost finished the coffee before retrieving my purse and striding quickly to the lounge. One advantage was that my nearly empty cup posed no threat of spilling when I leaned down to pull my bag lunch from the fridge. Taking one last gulp, I set both the now empty cup alongside my lunch on the table, dropped my purse under my chair, and plopped down next to John, and nodded at Mary and Patricia sitting across from us, and announced, "That is absolutely the busiest, the noisiest, the most non-stop class I've ever had!"

"Well, gee, BJ, I'm fine, thank you for asking," John said, raising one sardonic eyebrow. "And how are you today?"

"That's one for you, John," I said laughing and started over, "Hi, John. How are you doing today? Good class? You look well. That shirt looks good on you. Plaid, isn't it? Is that a salami sandwich you're eating?" I could see the little bits of pink slices sticking out of the crusty bread. But my nose gave me the real info.

Before he could respond, Mary leaned across the table. "Believe me, BJ, I know which class you have. Every primary teacher remembers that class. Working with them is like trying to lasso corn popping in an open pan." Her blue eyes danced with remembrance. "While you're riding herd on one, six others are skittering about."

"Looks like you have your hands full this year, BJ," John said, followed by a Woody Woodpecker laugh.

"They may be a handful," Mary said, laughing at John's dreadful imitation, "but on the plus side, they're one of the kindest group of kids you'll ever have, not a mean or rude one among them." She paused a moment, before adding, "Well, maybe one. But for the rest, if you get mad or snap at them, they look absolutely chagrined and apologize and promise to do better. And they do. For awhile."

Not wanting to be found insensitive twice in one day, I smiled and said, "I appreciate the insight, Mary. I welcome any help I get." She gave me a wide grin, as I added with real sincerity, albeit faux French, "I like your new hair style—eeet eees so tres chic." I knew the lovely pale blond shade that complemented her complexion, wasn't all natural, but then, neither was mine. Everybody knew my color was out of a bottle. Probably from the time I turned it Kelly green for St. Pat's Day, or maybe when I turned it candy cotton pink for Easter. I figured that's why god gave women more hair than she gave men.

Mary took a breath as if to speak, but before she could, John enlightened us all, with, "I'm doing OK. Great class, no problems. Do you really like my new shirt? And yes, it's salami. Want a bite?"

It took a moment before the three of us realized what John, who delighted in creating confusion with non-sequiturs, was doing.

"I love your new shirt. Red plaid is really your color. And no," I shuddered, "I think I'll pass on the salami and just eat my own lunch." I gave him my steely stare and added, "And John, before you get too smug, just remember, the class I have today, is your class next year."

Patricia put down her sandwich and said seriously, "You do know John won't get them all. Half will be mine."

"Right," I said, thinking what a good sixth grade team they made: John—so off-the-wall and Patricia so literal and down to earth. And both so dedicated to kids.

It was time I started eating. The clock was ticking, and five minutes before the bell was almost here. Or did he say seven?

Chapter Six

In the predawn dark, I broke free of the tangled bedding, silenced the shrieking alarm and, without turning on a light, staggered to the bathroom. Tired as I was when I fell into bed the night before, the dread I might not survive the school year with Rick Roark as my boss, and haunted by a need to establish classroom control, sleep eluded me and I thrashed most of the night. My burning eyes and aching head notwithstanding, I turned on the bathroom light and prayed the mirror above the wash basin lied. Nothing still living should look that haggard. Of course I knew I was still living, because any funeral director who left a corpse looking this bad would be out of business. Sloshing my face with cold water helped a little. Applying some make-up did, too, but a lot less than I hoped for. Only a cock-eyed optimist doesn't recognize a lost cause when it's staring back at her in the mirror, so I faced reality and gave up. Moments later in my unlit closet I pulled on whatever I touched first, not really caring if anything matched, before returning to the bathroom to brush my hair.

"Mom!" My almost 13 year old daughter Lissa's yell reverberated off the bathroom walls, assaulted my nerves, and made my ears ring. Before I could answer, she yelled again, "Mom!" Her tone implied my not responding fast enough was a form of child abuse. About to enter her teens, everything was right now, except homework and getting up in the morning.

45

Spritzing some needed highlights on my hair's newest color, autumn russet, I yelled back, "Yes? If you want me, I'm in the bathroom."

"I know. I'm right here. I can't make the sandwiches. Cal ate all the peanut butter." At least from the doorway she'd lowered her voice. But not by much.

Big surprise. At nine, Cal thought peanut butter was the only food worthy of consumption, and he ate it straight out of the jar when he thought no one was looking. How he stayed so skinny, considering the quantities of peanut butter he consumed, made me envious. Besides peanut butter, he loved the family's big sheep dog, Laddie, almost as much as Cabot did, and took delight in tormenting his siblings.

"Mom!" Lissa's frustrated tone matched her rigid body language as she stomped into the bathroom. She was the only person I knew who could stomp stiff-legged and barefooted. She wedged herself between me and the mirror. With an impatient toss of her head, she flicked back her naturally blond hair, and glared at me. "Mom, it's my week to make lunches and Cal ate all the peanut butter. What am I supposed to use?"

"No I didn't," Cal yelled from somewhere in the house, probably the kitchen. "Besides, there wasn't hardly any left."

I knew which half of his answer I believed.

"Mom, make him stop! First he eats all the peanut butter, then he says he doesn't, then I see his yucky finger marks in it, and even if there's some left, no one wants to eat it." Lissa was on a roll, and I had to leave for work. It was hard enough getting four kids up, dressed, fed and ready for school by 6:30, on the few days they didn't stall, bicker with each other, or argue with me. It looked like today I was in for all three.

"The stupid bus doesn't come until 8:30, so how come we have to get up so early. Why can't we sleep in?" Cal yelled, trying to take the pressure off the peanut butter accusation.

"Because, for the hundredth time, when I let you, you overslept, didn't eat, forgot books and lunches and Risa went to kindergarten looking like the rag-picker's kid." I sure didn't need this ploy or the peanut butter controversy. "Cal," I yelled, as if there hadn't been enough yelling already this morning, "get in here." He swaggered in, the glint in his eye announcing louder than words that he was loving this. He thrived on tormenting Lissa.

"Yes, Mom?" he said, oozing innocence like melting Jello. He cocked his head and lounged against the door frame, his version of macho insouciance.

"Cal, we've been over this a million times. What do I have to do to make you stop eating out of the peanut butter jar? And while we're at it, stop drinking out of the milk container. It's gross. And it's unfair."

He smiled, trying to look rueful and failing miserably. "I don't know. Maybe I'm a psycho. I just can't seem to help myself. It's a compulsion." He'd been reading my child psychology books again. If he'd write a book report on it for his teacher, his grades would improve.

"Yeah, that's some compulsion," I agreed, sardonically, "and maybe you just like hogging all the peanut butter for yourself."

"But, Mom, it's the only thing I like. I don't eat the stuff they like."

"As far as I can tell, the only things you don't eat are green veggies. You seem to do OK with macaroni and cheese and roast beef."

"Well, I don't complain if they hog all the green veggies, do I?"

Struggling to hold back a hoot of laughter left me momentarily speechless, but inspiration struck Lissa.

"Mom," she said, casting an evil look at her brother, "I know how to make it fair. There was a lot of broccoli left over last night. I certainly don't want to be a hog. Why don't we share ours with Cal? I'll even make him a sandwich out of it, since we're out of peanut butter." She faced him with a triumphant smirk.

"Yeah, yeah, do it, Mom. We don't want to be hogs, either," Cabot and Risa implored. It was easy to see why so much broccoli was left over.

I shook my head No, and laughed at the sheer outrageousness. A broccoli sandwich sounded nasty, even to me.

But, if desperation is the mother of invention, I was about to give birth, again. Bending my knees just enough to be at his eye level, I said, "I'll make you a deal, Cal. You stop eating out of the family's containers and I'll buy an extra jar of peanut butter, and an extra gallon of milk that will be all yours." A calculating look crossed his face as he weighed the possibilities in this. Was it my imagination or did the green flecks in his hazel eyes actually flash? "I'll even put your name on yours, and no one else will touch them. You can stick your fingers in the jar or drink straight from the container all you want." I knew I had his undivided attention, so I closed in for the kill: "BUT, you have to promise never to touch any of ours."

"Cool, Mom," he grinned, "I can live with that."

I figured he could. But, I knew this kid. For this to work, there had to be a downside, or once his was gone, he'd find a way to eat whatever was available. For him, there was no such thing as enough peanut butter.

"Mom," Lissa wailed, "that's not fair. He gets a whole jar just for being gross." Risa and Cabot nodded, too smart to get between Lissa and Cal verbally.

I knew Lissa was right. To be fair, there had to be something in it for the other three as well. "What," I wondered, "do they want that would effectively keep Cal's fingers out of their peanut butter?" A slow, calculating smile inched across my face, as my eyes narrowed into the hooded look he'd dubbed my snake eyes. "There'ss jusst one ssmall thing, Cal," I said, drawing out the sibilants.

"Yeah?" he said warily, calculating that what was coming probably wasn't something he wanted to hear.

"None of the other peanut butter is yours. If you touch it," I stopped for emphasis, "even touch it, you owe the others a payment. Something they want as much as you want peanut butter." Except for Laddie's snuffling, the room was silent. I had the absolute attention of all four of them. "So, instead of cleaning the bathroom only on your week, you will have to clean it for each of their weeks.

That's four weeks—a whole month. But, that's only if you touch their peanut butter. Or drink from their milk container."

"What?" he howled.

"Why is that a problem? You weren't planning on eating their peanut butter as well as your own, were you?" Pasting my snaky smile back on, I said sweetly, "I'm sure you'd never do that. But, it's not negotiable. Either you get your own jar of peanut butter and container of milk with this deal, or you don't get them, but you still have to clean the bathroom if we ever catch you eating out of the family's supply again. Your choice."

I could almost hear the wheels of their minds spinning plots. But when I saw the gold flecks in Lissa's blue eyes flash, I knew my imagination had to be working over-time. I figured she was already planning ways to tempt him into eating from the family jar. The possibility of getting out of the hated bathroom clean-up by outsmarting Cal was her idea of heaven on earth. A brief pang of sympathy for Cal swept over me.

Eight year old Cabot, so like Cal with his wide forehead and hazel eyes, and so unlike him in temperament, was high-fiving Risa. Younger and often ignored, they were allies, and the prospect of non-germed peanut butter was a major victory. They didn't experience many victories, so they were savoring the moment. Like me, they figured Cal was already searching for the loophole he was sure existed, confident that before his jar of peanut butter was gone, he'd find it. They were all so different, my four, unique and creative and never, never dull.

"OK, Mom. So how soon till I get my own peanut butter and milk?" Cal demanded, adding defiantly, "And nobody better even touch MY milk and peanut butter!"

"Well, I do hope tonight after work will be soon enough to suit you," I said. Not waiting for his answer, I grabbed my stuff and ran for the door. I was later than usual, but took time to I hug each one, grateful they were mine. Not even Paul Newman, the man of my dreams, could lure me away from them.

A thick gray fog hid the mountain and caused the heavy traffic to move erratically through its slowly dissipating patches. I drove with intense concentration, gripping the steering wheel, and keeping an eye on the taillights ahead of me. Abruptly, the driver behind me flashed his high beams, and I shook my head in disbelief when he darted past and cut in front of me. I dropped back, leaving lots of space between us. He looked like an accident on its way to happen, and I didn't want any part of it. I guessed other drivers felt the same, because even in bumper to bumper traffic, no one filled that space.

Cresting a low hill that rose above the fog, I forgot the traffic and the obnoxious driver, as Mt. Rainier appeared, towering in the distance. For the remainder of my drive, I thought of my class and my kids and peanut butter. Peanut butter as bait? Or, in Cal's case, would bribery be more accurate? No, it had a hook, so bait was the right word. Was there a comparable bait I could use with my students? I surely hoped so or there wouldn't be much learning done this year. I entered the building with my mind still on peanut butter, so intent, I forgot to look in on Ethel or check for cookies in the lounge, and almost missed the calculating look from Roark as we passed in the hall.

Almost.

Fortunately, the ritual of opening curtains, writing assignments on the board, laying out materials, and pouring coffee in a cup can be done mechanically. Finished, I gazed out the window, above the trees into the sky, but my thoughts stayed on peanut butter. A school bus's squealing brakes broke the silence, followed by the sounds of children running and calling out. A stream of students waved to me as they raced to the play areas, making me smile as I waved back. No brilliant flash of insight had struck by the time the bell rang, so I relegated my search for the peanut butter solution to the back of my mind and focused on the here and now.

Watching my students tearing out the door when the recess bell rang, eager to begin running, playing and being with their friends, sowed the seeds of my epiphany. With a light heart, a half cup of hot coffee, and my purse swinging jauntily from my shoulder, like the kids, I was eager to be with my friends.

I had my peanut butter.

Chapter Seven

Back in my room five minutes before the bell, I watched from the window as the little scamps raced about, unaware their days of unrestrained confusion in the classroom were about to end. After four years and three weeks of considering the school their own delightful social club, their teacher, who proclaimed herself to be the mother of the baddest kid of all, was about to put the lid on their metaphorical peanut butter. The bell rang and with a smile I opened the door.

How angelic they looked as they waited for me to admit them into the building, returning my smile as I passed along their silent line. Too bad they had no psychic powers to warn them I was not fooled. That I knew this was the calm before the storm, and that like a cyclone they'd whirl and roar as soon as the door closed behind them. Standing in the doorway I said, "Boys and girls, today we are going to do something new. It's really important that each of you can hear me, so instead of going to your seats, I want you to sit on the floor at the front of the room facing me. Then I'll tell you my big surprise." I stepped aside and they surged past me.

Rampant speculation reigned. "What does she mean?" "What kind of surprise?" "Maybe no school today." With his arms waving like windmill paddles, and paying no attention to where he was going as he talked to Kevin, Billy was blind-sided. Intent on being one of the first through the door, Roger plowed into Billy, sending him sprawling across the entry way and nearly taking Kevin with him. Without losing a decibel, the line came to an instant stop. When tiny Chris James, following just behind Billy, leaned down, extending her hand to help him up Billy's face glowed. Every downside has an upside.

Roger, however, looking beyond the line of children in front of him to where he planned to sit, didn't see Chris's outstretched hand as he stepped over Billy, and sent her sprawling as well. At that, several solicitous hands reached to help the two embarrassed students to their feet. Muttering a perfunctory, "Sorry," Roger hugged the wall, squeezing past the fallen pair, and clomped heavy footed to where Walter and Geoff sat in the center of the front row. Realizing his intent, they scooted apart before he dropped heavily between them. Self preservation out-ranked right of possession.

Roger watched me as I shut the door and, without a word, shot him a knowing look, but addressing his improper behavior could wait. In the unprecedented quiet, I chose not to risk losing the class' undivided attention. I had a more important issue and timing is everything. Solemnly I sat down and leaned forward, looking at each student individually. I smiled at Chris on my left, then at Billy on my right, each surrounded by a small circle of friends. Billy, whose eyes were on Chris, was oblivious to me. Chris was oblivious to Billy, and returned my smile. Behind the others, Derek sat alone, looking down at his hands folded in his lap, uninvolved.

Only the humming of a dying fluorescent light overhead broke the stillness of the room. I knew a good thing when I didn't hear it and said, "I want to tell each of you, that I think you are an exceptionally nice class." They smiled and nodded in agreement. "You are kind to each other." More nods and smiles. Chris's Orphan Annie curls bobbed, Billie high-fived his circle of friends, and without turning his head, Roger slanted a look at Skye. "Besides that," I continued, "you play well on the playground, the work you hand in is done carefully and on time and I really enjoy being your teacher, so I would like to give you a reward." I stopped.

They waited for the punch line. Shaking my head, I gazed at them with a look of bewilderment. "But I don't know what I can give you." Instantaneous cacophony erupted in a deluge of suggestions. I let them brainstorm for a couple of minutes, before I signaled for their attention, somewhat surprised when I got it.

"If I had magical powers or tons of money or even control of the school board, I'd give you whatever you choose. But, as you may have guessed, I don't have any of these and that creates a few restrictions. You know, like it has to be something your parents and the principal would allow." When this elicited a few groans, I laughed. "Yeah, that's a bummer," I agreed, "and it also has to be something everyone receives equally. And don't forget, I don't have much money. I'm a teacher, and hardly any of us are millionaires." They laughed politely. "Now, who has an idea?" I asked and waited, but not for long.

"Candy." "A's on our report cards." "No homework." "Longer vacations."

"Whoa," I interrupted, "slow down. I'm going to put all your ideas on the board, but I think I'd better list those restrictions first."

- OK with parents, principal and school board;
- Everyone receive equally;
- Cheap

Turning to face them, I said, "Now, let's get **your** ideas on the board." Ideas flowed faster than I could write in my usual careful penmanship, but capturing all their hopes took precedence. Soon the board was covered in words scribbled in red. After awhile, the waves of ideas ebbed, followed by silence.

"What a lot of interesting suggestions," I said, shaking the writer's cramp from my right hand. "Our next job is to narrow them down. Since this is to be your reward, I think you should make the final decision. Why don't you gather in groups of four or five and see which ones we probably won't be able to use because of the three restrictions. Those that remain we'll talk about."

In full voice they coalesced into small groups throughout the room. No one could accuse them of being unable to walk and talk at the same time. That was one multitask they had down to a science.

As I strolled among them, I discovered they were as adept at elimination as they were at developing. In short order, they identified which items would be parent vetoed, which the school administrators wouldn't permit, and which ones I couldn't afford.

Leaving them in their various groups, I stood waiting in the front of the room, facing them. Sooner than I expected, I had their attention, and said, "As I walked around, I saw you eliminating many of your good ideas when you found they didn't meet the criteria. So, let's talk about the ones you think we could use." There was no response. I scanned the room. Seeing no raised hands, I chose a student at random. "Allison, which one did your group like best?"

"None of our ideas work," she answered, so dejected even her flippy pony tail appeared to droop.

"None?" I asked.

"No. It was those darn restrictions." She frowned. "Without them, we liked lots of the ideas." Murmurs of agreement met her assessment.

"Are you telling me there isn't any reward I can give you?" I asked. "Didn't any of you come up with even one usable idea?"

A depressed silence pervaded my class. Hesitantly, Skye Zimmerman, possibly my most reticent student, raised her hand. "I think my group has kind of an idea?" she said, her voice rising, making it sound like a question.

"Tell us what it is, Skye, we could really use an idea."

"Could you give us an extra recess? Nobody said that before." She focused her gray-blue eyes on my face, watching for my reaction.

"Hmmm," I mused. "A recess" . . . I let my voice trail off. "Let me think about that."

I couldn't believe she found within minutes, the idea it took me two days to come up with. I furrowed my brow, as if in deep internal debate. What began as a low buzz, escalated to their normal sound level, as possibilities and enthusiasm replaced dejection.

"Skye," I said, unable to suppress a huge smile, "I think you may have found the answer." When the class turned to look admiringly at Skye, her pleasure was evident. Roger appeared mesmerized.

"While I'm pretty sure the administration would never let me take a whole fifteen minutes out of your class time, and your parents probably wouldn't be too happy, either, it definitely meets the third criterion—it's cheap."

This got the laugh I hoped for.

"You know, there might be some way I could arrange to give you three or four minutes once in a while," I shrugged deprecatingly, "but how much good are three or four minutes? Besides, when would you want them?"

Deflated, they nodded, acknowledging that three or four minutes were hardly worth considering. But depression was alien to this group, and shortly their imaginations kicked in, as well as pandemonium. Possibilities abounded, some, like "middle of spelling," "end of the day," "before going to music class," and "during a test," elicited hoots of laughter before being discarded. During a lull, ever logical Sarah said, "I know when I'd like them. If you can only give us three or four minutes, I'd like them just before recess."

"Oh? Why would you choose then?" I asked.

"Well, if we can leave for recess three or four or even two minutes early, we won't have to wait to use the ball fields or slides or equipment or other stuff like we do when all the other classes get there ahead of us. Our room is the farthest away and we're almost always last."

"Yeah," Joey, my smallest student, jumped to his feet and called out, "and we would get to choose teams instead of waiting to get picked. Maybe even be captain." His face glowed with anticipation. His enthusiasm was infectious. All semblance of order was gone. High fiving was everywhere. I gave them a moment before, still laughing, I held up my hand for quiet, and was again surprised when I got it. Twice, or was it three times in one day? It might be a record. I hoped it was the beginning of a trend.

"I think you have a great idea here. No one can object to our using just a very few minutes of class time, and all of you seem to be in favor. Does anyone not like this idea?" I waited. A happy silence reigned. Then I broke it with the dreaded "H" word.

"However, once again, there are a couple of restrictions." I waited for the groaning to stop. "Come on, did you forget this is a school? Restrictions are what school is all about." They laughed. "You're right. School's about a lot more than restrictions, but, restriction number one is this: the time can't be used before lunch recess. You already eat faster than anyone, kids, adults, or cartoon dinosaurs, I've ever seen, and I'm not eager to deal with upset stomachs or parents calling me because their kids aren't finishing their lunches."

Accepting this as reasonable, if not desirable, they nodded.

"Now, the next thing is, the school board says we have to have a certain number of minutes of instruction every day. We don't want them wrecking everything telling us we can't take even two minutes away. However," I paused. This time when I used the H word, any looks of disappointment became hopeful. I waited until I had their complete attention. "However," I repeated, "I do have a way to get you these minutes, but it will take cooperation on your part. Do you want to hear it?" It took awhile for each of them, one by one, to assure me they did.

"OK, here it is. I asked the other teachers how long it takes for their classes to come in each morning, hang up coats, sign up for lunch and begin studying. The shortest time any of them said was ten minutes." This was a bright group, but I got lucky—no one asked why I had asked for this information. "So now, as I see it, if we are allowed ten minutes before instruction has to start, what if we could do all that in less than ten minutes. Then, whatever time we didn't use, would legally be ours and we could use it any way we wanted. Right?"

The light was dawning.

"For instance, if you were in your seats quietly working on your assignments in seven minutes, to be fair, the school would owe you three minutes. At least, that's how I see it. Is that how you see it?"

They agreed with their trademark cacophony that took me a few minutes to subdue.

"But you know, to be completely fair, I think we owe the school more study time than we've been giving it." They looked puzzled. "What I mean is, your parents pay lots of tax money for you to learn. Then the school board pays the teachers and principal and custodian and others a lot of money for you to learn. And everybody makes sure you get time to eat lunch and have a recess." It was clear they had no idea where this was going, and waited for me to explain.

"I've been keeping track, and discovered that, on some days, we get lots less learning time than they are paying for. Did you know that?"

With wide-eyed innocent looks Cal could learn from, they shook their heads.

"Well, it's true. I watched the clock, and sometimes we lose five and ten and sometimes as much as fifteen minutes until the room is quiet. I think that's not very honest." I mirror their wide-eyed innocent looks. "And you are not dishonest, are you?"

"No way." "I don't cheat." "Me neither," echoed around the room.

"I agree," I said. "I believe you just forget and use time that it isn't fair for you to use. It's kind of an accident. I know that if you remembered, you'd stop taking this time and use it the right way." I nodded at them. "If you think I'm right, raise your hand." Most hands flew into the air.

Only Derek sat without moving. Odd. I'd noticed he seldom left his seat or talked with others during class time, seeming to prefer reading a book to socializing. I made a mental note to look into this.

"OK," I said. "Here's how I can help you. See this clangy old cow bell I brought with me today?" they nodded. "Here's what it sounds like." I gave it a hefty shake and at the resulting racket many of the kids covered their ears and Billy took his eyes off Chris, but only for a moment. I scowled at the bell, "Awful, isn't it?" Their agreement was unanimous. And loud.

When I could be heard, I said, "I really hate its noise. But what if, whenever I think you are taking time unfairly, I ring this bell, so when you hear it, you remember to stop talking and start being fair again?" This was accepted with considerably less enthusiasm.

"And then, if you hear the bell twice during the day, you trade back all the minutes you earned in the morning." This was met with blank stares but no disagreement. "But," I dropped my voice and added a note of sadness, "if you hear it a third time, then we probably need a discussion about being honest, and we can do that instead of going to recess." This did not elicit any high fives.

Billie raised his hand. "Ms. McCall, what if we just skip the bell part?"

Resisting the urge to laugh, I used my most serious tone to answer, "I understand, Billie, but it's a package deal, unless you want to skip winning the extra minutes in the morning. We could skip just that part. But the rest of it stands."

He stared at me. "I get it," he said, as if thinking out loud. "That's what you meant when you said you have the baddest kid ever."

"And not all peanut butter comes in a jar," I added silently.

Chapter Eight

An early morning mist spread across my windshield, nature's notice that summer was gone and fall was here. Morning light arrived later each day, and today the freeway still glowed in the beams of car headlights. To the west, the dark was broken by runway lights of Boeing Field, and ahead, only the peak of Mt. Rainier caught the rays of the rising sun.

Soon parked in the slot I'd laid claim to, at least in my own mind, I leaned on the steering wheel for a moment, looking beyond the protective chain link fence to the line of leafless maple trees. Outlined against the black night sky slowly shifting to gray, they looked liked a line of skinny chorus girls with their scraggy arms entwined.

I left the car and a chilly breeze filled my nose with the acrid smoke of burning leaves. I sneezed. I hurried toward the door, almost ahead of a stronger breeze that tangled its way through my previously well coiffed hair. I gazed with some irritation at my reflection in Ethel's window, and I got an idea that made me grin. Almost running down the hall to Ethel's room, I stopped long enough to lose the grin before I flung the door open and called out, "Hi, Ethel." Her back was to me as she leaned over a student desk. But with a wariness born of experience, I remained in the doorway. I wanted to know what job she might assign me to before I entered.

"Hi, BJ," she said, not looking up from whatever it was she was doing. I scanned the room, and just like always, saw that every bit of space on walls and counter tops as well as most windowpanes, were filled with children's work: collages, drawings, laboriously printed lower case letters "b", while 11 inch by 14 inch papers covered with drying poster paint nearly covered the floor. Exactly how a kindergarten should look.

I waited, hoping she'd come to the door. She didn't. She didn't even look around, so I took the risk and strode over to her, if you can call weaving and detouring around desks and chairs and paintings striding. "Ethel, it's important. I need your unbiased opinion," I said, pulling her arm in feigned urgency. "Come over here by the window for a minute." The window ledge held small open jars of poster paint, and I could only imagine the tie-dyed look her spotless gray dress would have by the end of the day. Ethel started every day spotless, but seldom left that way.

She heaved an exasperated sigh, dumped the papers she was holding onto the nearest desk and muttered, "Oh, all right. What is it?"

"Look. Now that the sun is up, I want you to look at the leaves on the ground under those maple trees." I checked to see if she was looking where I was pointing. She was. "I really want to know if my beautician got those colors right—I told her I wanted my hair exactly the same colors as those maple leaves. I even took a bag of leaves with me." I stepped closer, facing Ethel, and tilted my head slightly so she'd have a better view of my hair. "So, did she? Get the colors right?"

For a long moment she simply stared at me. Her mouth dropped open, but no words came out. Then, "You took a bunch of leaves to your beautician? And expected her to match your hair color to them? And now you want my opinion? I have an opinion, all right, but it's not about your hair!" Her voice had risen as her stare changed from disbelief to indignation. Then, remembering who she was talking to, she started laughing.

I clenched my teeth and held my breath, struggling to keep a straight face and lost. Talking while you're laughing is almost impossible, but I choked out, "Darn! I almost gottcha, didn't I?"

She shook her head. "BJ, for a couple of minutes, I actually fell for it. Dumping a bunch of leaves on your beautician. You know, I'll never get an ulcer as long as you're around. You have the weirdest sense of humor!"

"Weird? You called me weird! Just for that, I'm going to flounce out of here." But with all that stuff lying on the floor and hanging off desks between me and the door, flouncing was impossible, but I did manage several dismissive sniffs and more than one haughty toss of my head. I regretted having such short hair; long hair would have added so much to my head tosses. All the way down the hall, even through the closed door, I could hear her laughing. I love starting my day with Ethel.

Next stop, the lounge, now occupied by only four people. Standing near the window were Mary Johnson and Marla, the school secretary, talking with a woman who was probably a parent volunteer, but I didn't recognize her as one of mine. Unwilling to interrupt, I smiled and gave them a half wave, which they returned. Marla's dark chignon and wine red sheath dress alongside Mary's short blond curls and well designed blue pants suit created a picture of sophisticated glamour, and I felt just a slight tinge of envy. Fortunately, I looked good in green.

I walked to the table, where Edna was sitting alone. Her unadorned beige dress and dark brown hair nearly matched the brown surface of the table on which her elbows rested. As if for warmth, both her hands encircled a mug, which I assumed held herbal tea, since her religion prohibited tea and coffee and lot of other stuff. Her shoulders were slumped and she looked exhausted. She nodded, but didn't look up when I said, "Hi, Edna." I waited to see if she'd look up or indicate a desire to talk, but she continued to look away. In the middle of the table was a plate of cookies. Sugar cookies. Homemade. I love sugar cookies. I took two, wishing I dared take three. They're great for dunking, but always make such a mess on my desk. Thinking of my desk reminded me of the student papers stacked on it, that weren't going to correct themselves. With another look toward Edna, I called goodbye from the door and waved with the hand not holding the cookies. She did not respond.

Amply fortified with sugar cookies and coffee, I picked up a red marker and began writing the day's assignments on the white board. Only the squeaking of the marker broke the stillness of my empty room, and I jumped when the door banged open and John strode in saying, "Good grief! Are trying to cover your entire board in red ink? It looks like blood spatter from a crime scene."

Sticking my nose in the air so I could look down it, I asked in my most hoity-toity voice, "It most assuredly does not. And who asked you? I happen to like red." John didn't laugh, he guffawed, forcing me to retaliate. "And it would appear you like red, too, or hadn't you noticed your shirt contains humungous blobs of flaming red? But enough of the social pleasantries, do enlighten me—why are you really here? An irresistible attraction to my magnetic personality or did you want to borrow my red marker?"

He cringed. "No way do I want your creepy red marker and we can discuss your dubious irresistible charms later." Concern replaced his banter as his smile faded. "I need to talk to you about one of your kids, a boy named Roger. Roger Lumley." He paused a long time, searching my face, as if looking for a clue how to continue.

I knew what was coming wasn't good. Big, lumbering Roger. Roger who was sent to the principal's office at least once a week by the playground aides, or the music teacher, or the PE teacher. I'd come to expect the constant flow of disciplinary notices. But this was a first from easy going, kid-friendly John. "What's he done, John?" I asked, dreading the answer.

Hesitantly, John said, "You know my noon recess baseball games?"

I nodded. Everyone knew John's games. He spent every one of his noon lunch breaks organizing and supervising the older kids, reducing a lot of the problems faced by the playground aides. Everyone, aides, kids, and parents, liked and appreciated John. This had to be serious.

Clearly uncomfortable, he held his hands out, palms up, saying, "I don't know how it happens, but whenever he shows up, arguments and even fights break out—and I can never trace their source. He's always in it somewhere, but I can never be sure it's his fault. But by the time things are calmed down, recess is over and the game's ruined. If I could just say it's his fault and send him out of the game, I would. But I can't. I feel guilty and angry no matter what I do or don't do. Help me out. Do you have any ideas?"

My coffee and sugar cookies began an uneasy churning. Roger was my responsibility and John was my friend and I hadn't a clue what to do. Swallowing hard to force the cookies and coffee down out of my throat, my voice was almost a croak when I said, "John, I'm so sorry. I have no idea what I can do. Everyone is on his case, and I've tried to get him to cooperate. So far with no luck, but I'll keep looking for an answer."

"That's OK. Maybe there aren't any answers." He got as far as the door before he turned, and a trace of his usual smile flitted across his face. "Don't take this wrong, but you bloody well should try a blue or black marker." The door clicked shut. He'd gotten in the last word and I could hear him laughing all the way to his classroom. I laughed, wondering when he'd started using British slang.

I set the uncorrected papers aside and leaned back, mentally reviewing everything I knew about Roger. Almost from the first day in September he'd been in trouble. Almost every recess the playground aides sent him to the principal's office or made him stay in an area away from the other kids. His class assignments were messy, incomplete or not handed in. I knew the other kids avoided him, and I had to insist they include him in group projects. Skye actually refused to be in any group with him and told me, "He's mean and I'm afraid of him and my mom told me to stay away from him."

I thought about all the times I'd talked to him. I knew the aides talked to him. More than once the principal talked to him. We wrote notes home to his parents and they said they talked to him. But nothing changed. Following one staff meeting, I'd had a conversation with three of his previous teachers, giving them a brief run-down of my problem. "You've all had Roger in your classes," I said. "Did any of you have problems with him?" I asked, knowing my question was rhetorical.

Joan, who used to teach first grade but now taught second said, "Back when he was in my first grade class he was bigger than average, and he was a bully. The other kids were afraid of him and lots of them refused to play with him." Her dark eyes closed for a moment as if remembering, then said, "You know, I don't remember ever seeing him smile."

Nodding, Mary agreed, "I saw that, too, in second grade. Besides that, he spent most of the day staring out the window, so his work was hardly ever done and his tests scores were always below average."

Joan shrugged. "I guess about all you can do is keep him away from the other kids, ignore him as much as you can, notify his parents when you have to, and wait for June when you can send him on to another teacher. It's what I finally did."

I could see myself doing this about the same time Satan's sinners started throwing snowballs. But I thanked them for their input.

The morning bell returned me to the present. Seeing the papers I should have been correcting gave me a guilt trip, so I covered them with my plan book. "Good morning, class," I said, smiling and holding the door.

"Good morning, Ms. McCall," they replied, quietly following our new morning routine.

Minutes later, I watched Sarah, who was this week's class secretary write "3" on the board, then announce, "Today we took seven minutes, so we get three extra minutes," creating lots of smiles. Roger and Derek appeared indifferent.

Not for the first time, I watched Roger, hoping for some kind of insight. "I sure wish a genie would just appear and offer me three wishes, because right now I'd skip the world peace and unlimited wealth ones, and go straight to mind reading." No genie appeared, so I began the day's lessons.

It was a rewarding morning. I was pleased as my students segued smoothly from math to language arts, where they kept me laughing with their opinions and analyses of *The Cremation of Sam McGee* that I read as an introduction to our poetry unit. Some of their comments took the form of charades as they exhibited horror and freezing and blast furnace heat. Roger remained impassive. While they began writing their evaluations of the poem, I collected their math papers and fanned them out on top of my plan book, noting that Roger's was both messy and incomplete.

A sudden silence made me look up. My class sat like statues, their hands folded on cleared desks, staring intently at the clock— three minutes before the hour. Standing against the door I hastily opened, I saw that lambent rays of the autumn sun had dissipated the morning mist, creating a perfect recess day. At my nod, my sagacious scholars swept past me in record time, to claim the minutes they'd earned. As he passed me, I laid my hand lightly on Roger's arm saying, "Please don't leave yet," quickly adding when he tensed, "You're not in any kind of trouble, I just want to talk to you."

He stepped out of line to stand beside me, staring at the floor, wary and defiant and it was obvious he didn't believe me. I had no plan of action and no idea where to begin. He'd already heard everything every authority figure had to say. How I wished Roark was a principal I could have discussed this with, but I knew he'd attribute any request as weakness and use it to downgrade my evaluation.

I sighed, something I seemed to be doing a lot of today. "Maybe," I thought hopefully, "I should just excuse Roger and think about it awhile." But realizing this would be just a lame postponement, I walked back and sat at my desk, motioning him to pull up a chair and sit facing me. "Roger," I said, "we've got a problem."

"His cynical look let me know he thought my comment was as dumb as I thought it was.

"I think you know what I'm talking about. I've talked to you about fighting and so has just about every adult in the school. You haven't paid much attention to any of what we've said."

He sat, silent, staring now at the floor.

I waited, studying him as though I'd discover the secret to success through his physical appearance. No use. All I saw was what I always saw, a stocky boy, big for a ten year old, in blue jeans and white tee shirt like many of his classmates, with his brown hair falling over his eyes. He sat slouched in his chair, scowling. For a ten year old, he looked almost intimidating. I could see why his classmates avoided him. "Roger," I said. He raised his head and, with a look more guarded than hostile, stared directly at me. I saw his eyes were hazel. Why hadn't I seen that before? Both my sons inherited my hazel eyes, so it's something I usually noticed. I pulled my thoughts back on track, and in a neutral tone said, "I really mean it, Roger. We need to talk."

He dropped his head again. "Yeah, right—*we* need to talk. Like you're going to let *me* talk." Snapping upright, he glared at me, his eyes narrow angry slits. "Everybody in this school talks, but nobody in this school ever listens. At least not to me." His voice wasn't loud, but the anger was unmistakable. And the words were rude, as truth often is.

The hostility told me that at this moment, I embodied the ev*erybody*. Choosing each word carefully, I said, "Roger, you've been in my class over a month. I've always tried to be honest. Do you think I try to tell the truth?" When he didn't respond, a sick feeling swept through me.

He dropped his head again. With an almost imperceptible nod, in a voice barely above a whisper he said, "Yeah, you tell the truth. But you don't listen to me, either. Nobody does."

"You're right, Roger," I said, and stopped, waiting for him to raise his head and look at me. He didn't. I said, "Thank you, Roger. Will you, believe when I tell you that from now on when we talk, we, not just I, will talk? And I will really listen to you?"

It was a promise I had to keep. He trusted me and I couldn't risk losing that.

He made no sign he'd heard me. Recess was almost over. Desperate to hold on to our tenuous thread of communication, I said softly, "Roger, I'm sorry I used up your whole recess. Would you come back on another recess? Or at least think about it?"

"Yeah, why not?" he said, still not looking at me. "Besides, I hate recess."

Chapter Nine

It was one of those days. Risa upchucked her breakfast, Cal lost a shoe and Laddie wanted to play catch me if you can with Cabot. One delay followed another, before I was on my way and discovered to my delight, that leaving home later had an up-side. Instead of being hidden behind a gray predawn mist, my mountain's crest was a dazzling splash of pink and white that late October morning, and when another driver slowed in response to my signal to change lanes, I waved a surprised, but pleased, thank you.

Roger had been in my mind intermittently since our meeting and I recognized he had shown me a possible way to reach him, a small opening in the wall he'd erected as a defense against the criticism and rejection he'd encountered. I wanted to go through, but how? I looked up from the freeway and the cars and the mundane world toward my mountain, hoping for inspiration, and I remembered his words, "Everybody talks to me, but nobody ever listens to me." Maybe it was time for me to just shut up and listen and see what happens..

In my preoccupation with Roger, I lost track of time and found myself coasting into my favorite parking slot. The lot was full, but I guess I'd been accorded squatter's rights. I stepped from my car into a world of warmth and sunlight, fall's bonfire fragrances, and an orchestra of bird trills above the bass notes of distant traffic. A moment later I pulled the heavy school door open, headed toward the world of 'what if'.

Laughter and voices drew me to the lounge, along with the hope of finding cookies and Ethel. The small room was jammed and everyone brandished a cup of freshly brewed coffee. I knew from its fragrance it was fresh-brewed, but I also knew, from experience, its flavor did not match its aroma. I eyeballed the crowd. No Ethel. Worse, no cookies. I could catch Ethel later, so I shrugged, resigned to go to my classroom, undernourished as I was. Before I could leave, John called out, "Hey, hey, hey, BJ, not leaving without saying good morning are you?"

I looked in the direction of his voice, but saw Vic Koslowsky, not John. With a wink, Vic raised his arm into the football Statue of Liberty position, and John poked his head out from behind him grinning. Vic extended his arm and John ducked under it. Their Mutt and Jeff act cracked me up, along with everyone else in the room, to John and Vic's great delight. Vic's massive six foot four reminded me of a Mack truck that could block from view anything smaller than a VW and compared to him, John was much smaller than a VW—more like a go-cart.

Laughing, I made a bee-line for them. Vic threw his arms up in mock terror as I lurched to a stop within and inch or less of smacking into him. "Whoops. Sorry," I said, "almost ran into you. Didn't see you standing there."

"Yeah," Vic boomed, "that happens a lot to us little guys. Even when we wear bright red sweat shirts." Bright didn't begin to describe the one he wore today. It was so bright, it bordered on fluorescent.

"Oh, I thought you wanted to be twinsy with John," I said, dramatically shading my eyes.

"Quit slandering my shirts," John growled. "Besides, everyone knows that one of your drippy red markers smeared itself all over Vic's sweatshirt—it used to be white."

"Oh, oh," Vic said looking at his watch, "gotta run. Promised a couple of kids on my team, I'd come in early and try to show them how to toss a basketball so it lands somewhere near the hoop. Oh, yeah, John, here's the end of the blond story." He turned away and lowered his voice so I couldn't hear, but from their wicked laughs

I knew better than to ask what was funny. Vic smacked John on the back, started to pat me on the head, thought better of it, patted me on the shoulder, and strode to the door, cradling his nearly overflowing coffee cup.

As people moved aside to let him pass, I saw Edna, huddled on the sofa, her dark hair shrouding her face, her hands lying limp in her lap. Joan Westerman sat next to her, and Patricia Soames, one arm resting across Edna's shoulder, sat on her other side. My throat constricted. I looked questioningly at John.

"It's Roark," he whispered. "He's definitely chosen her as his victim of the year."

"His what?" I asked.

"Remember, I told you I worked with him before? I recognize his *modus operandi*."

"Huh?" was my brilliant response.

Darting a glance around, he took my elbow saying, "It's kind of public in here, let's go into the nurse's office. It's probably empty right now." As we walked down the hall, John kept his voice low, "Every year he picks one staff member to harass, usually someone he figures won't or can't fight back." Shoving the door to the nurse's room open, he turned the light on. I followed him in, wrinkling my nose at the acrid antiseptic smell. We were now far enough away, that there was little chance of being overheard, but, ever wary of gossip, we left the door wide open.

"I agree, John, Edna is the least likely person I know to fight back, but she's a really good primary teacher. The kids and their parents always like her. Harassing her makes no sense."

"Making sense has nothing to do with it. Roark knows Edna's religion won't let her challenge him. Coupled with that, he thinks Edna is ugly, and he hates anyone he considers ugly, fat or handicapped. It's like he sees them as a personal affront to his sense of esthetics. His next victim will probably be someone fat, or someone old that he thinks should retire." He paused, "Like me." I started to laugh but one look at his face warned me he was dead serious.

I flared. "Everything you've told me is absolutely reprehensible! Educators are supposed to be intelligent and to use common sense. The welfare of the students is supposed to be their primary concern. In my opinion, Roark needs to go, not Edna, and certainly not you!"

"Hey, take it easy. I agree, but I'm not gone yet. Unlike Edna, I may fight back," John said with an effort at a grin.

Still angry, I asked, "What did he do to Edna this time? She looks absolutely beaten."

"I'll tell you, if you keep your voice down. The door's open and the lounge isn't in the next county."

I rolled my eyes, but nodded in agreement.

"Do you remember at the beginning of the year, when he made her redo her bulletin boards?"

"Yeah," I replied, not bothering to curtail the sarcasm, "he said they looked too immature. Good grief, first grade is immature. If you can't be immature in first grade, when can you?" I thought back a moment. "I think I told her to insist that he describe exactly what he wanted, preferably in writing, and if he wouldn't, to just ignore him."

Sadness mingled with frustration as John shook his head. "She tried, but he dumped it back on her, adding a guilt trip. He's good at that, and Edna's not good at standing up for herself, especially to authority figures. Anyway, when I came in this morning, I heard Edna telling Patricia and Joan about a bulletin board she saw in a teaching magazine that she thought met his demands. So she bought the materials for it, using her own money, and then spent over a week assembling it, and yesterday she put it up."

"Don't tell me! The ass rejected it." I stormed, shaking with anger. "No way would I do all that!" John's warning look indicated my voice may have risen a tad above the advisable level. Again.

"You've got to be more careful, BJ, Roark has his toadies and you may recall you are not his favorite person." I looked toward the door expecting to see a dark shadow looming there.

"Gee, thanks for that reminder, John. But you're right. I'll keep my voice down and since you didn't respond, can I assume that this effort didn't meet with Hatchet Man's approval either?"

John shook his head. "No, when she showed it to him, he said it was not what he told her to do. When she asked him to tell her what he did want, he just repeated that she was a professional and should not expect him to do her thinking for her."

"That's exactly what he said to her the other time," I said.

"I know," John said, "but that's not all. This time, he really went for the jugular." Capturing perfectly Roark's cold, clipped voice, John said, "Don't waste any more time on your bulletin boards. You are obviously incapable of doing them correctly. Just get busy on your lesson plans. They are woefully inadequate."

The mimicry was so perfect it made me shudder. "Woefully inadequate? Woefully inadequate?" I squeaked, "What does that mean? I thought she was a really good teacher. Last year she was nominated our teacher of the year. And Matt Preston thought she was great."

"We all did. In fact, except for Roark, we all still do. But since he replaced Matt, being a good teacher isn't important. Roark needs a victim. And Roark only likes pretty."

I'd already figured out the victim part, but the need for pretty was new to me. "So what did Hatchet Man say was wrong with her plans?" I asked.

"Get real. He didn't explain, and Edna was too demoralized to ask. You saw her. Joan and Patricia have been trying to get her to stop crying all morning. But unless she stands up to him, he's going to drive her out. He's done it before and he's good at it." John shook his head as if shaking off a bug, lifted his hand in an abrupt wave and walked out the door.

After turning off the light and shutting the door, I followed him. From the hall I saw that only Edna, Patricia and Joan, remained in the lounge. I went over to them, wishing I had more to offer than the words, "I'm so sorry." Joan and Edna looked up with wan smiles. Patricia ignored me.

·

Chapter Ten

My footsteps dragged on my return to the classroom, where I stashed my purse in the bottom desk drawer and emptied books and papers from my tote bag. Impatient and angry, I ignored the steam rising from the coffee I poured, and jumped when I burned my mouth. Of course it slopped, so now I had a mess on my desk, a wet brown blotch on my blue slacks, and a scalded leg. "This," I griped, "is not turning out to be my best day yet," as I sopped up what I could of the mess with a handful of paper towels. "I sure wish genies came with this job, so I could wish for a thousand angry bees to get trapped in Roark's shorts." The picture this conjured up made me giggle, so I added, "Ah, to bee or not to bee."

A tapping on my window interrupted this gratifying vision of vengeance. Grinning and waving good morning were about a dozen students, three of whom were mine. My heart lifted and I smiled. When I returned their waves, they grinned again and ran back to their play.

With less than twenty minutes left, I reviewed my lesson plans, checking I had everything under control, at least academically, and was startled when the hall door opened. Of the three who entered, I didn't recognize the man striding toward me, but I knew the girl ahead of Roark was one of Nick Archer's students, Jody Kerr. I was happy she was one of his students and not one of mine. According to Nick, Jody was allergic to discipline, cooperative behavior and completing assignments. When she became too argumentative, Nick sent her to the office for a time-out, but these, as well as her resultant low grades, always brought Daddy Kerr in on the war path. I assumed the unknown man was Daddy Kerr, but what brought this unholy trio into my classroom was a mystery I wasn't sure I wanted to solve. Being left ignorant was not to be an option.

"Ms. McCall, Mr. Roark and I agree that Jody should be transferred to your classroom," the man I was now sure was Mr. Kerr, stated without preamble. Behind him Roark made no attempt to hide a smile. It was then I noticed Jody was carrying her books and other belongings.

Playing for time, I rose and extended my hand. "Good morning. I assume you are Jody's father?" He looked surprised, so I smiled, nodded at Roark, and turning to look at her said, "Good morning, Jody." She smiled back. To her father I said, "May I ask why you've made this decision, Mr. Kerr?"

"It is our desire that she be placed with a female teacher. I am fed up with her being sent to the office. I am fed up with the notes criticizing her that are sent to her mother and me. And I am especially fed up with Mr. Archer's unwillingness to cooperate with us. A good teacher must be cognizant of students' needs and have the ability to work with them. My daughter is an independent thinker, and I expect you to take this into account, since you have many more years' teaching experience than Mr. Archer. I hope you don't find this too difficult." I detected a hint of sarcasm in this final remark, but I let it pass. I was still ticked off by his swipe at my age.

He turned, nodded at Roark and ignoring Jody strode toward the door, with just the slightest touch of a goose-step in the click of his heels across the floor. Before the door closed behind him, I caught a glimpse of a thirty-something, nondescript woman waiting in the hall. He took her arm, so I assumed it was his wife, and wondered why he'd left her in the hall.

Jody stood frozen where he left her. Forcing a smile, I said, "Well, welcome to your new classroom, Jody. You can put your things on that empty desk by the wall and go out with the other kids until the bell rings."

After tossing her stuff toward the desk I indicated, she fled.

I looked at Roark who held out a stack of papers and files. "Here are all the data you'll need. I assume you have no questions." It was a statement, not a question and he was gone.

"Thank you for your concern," I snarled at the closing door. Then sighed, "Move over, Edna, it looks like you aren't Roark's only victim this lovely day."

Things got better as the day progressed. It always did when Roark left the building and today there was an administrative meeting. By the end of the school day, things were pleasantly back to normal.

At home that evening, while waiting for the potatoes to boil, I scooped up a load of dirty clothes and ran down the stairs and through the rec room to the utility/store room. I stuffed the laundry into the washer, started it going and, concerned the potatoes might burn, dashed to the foot of the stairs, where I turned to look back, thinking, "There's something different in here." On a closer look it was obvious; the pink chair was missing. "Hey", I yelled up the stairs, "Cal, Cabot, Lissa, Risa, I need you to come down here."

"Yeah?" they yelled back, clomping their way down. "What do you want?"

"Where is the pink chair?" I asked.

"I don't know," Risa said.

"It's missing," Lissa said after looking around.

"What pink chair?" the boys asked in unison.

"You know exactly what pink chair. The huge, ugly one you brought down here last month."

"I don't know what pink chair you're talking about," Cal said, assuming his innocent look. Cabot struggled for an equally innocent look, but less successfully.

I gave up. The potatoes were about to burn and I was hungry. "OK, let's go eat dinner," I said. Lucky for them I hated that chair.

After dinner, I carried the table cloth to the deck to shake out the crumbs, and stood for a moment, mesmerized by the flickering light from the setting sun filtering through the few remaining leaves of the tall maple tree. And there, in all its garish color, perched high in the tree on the platform the boys called their tree house, was the pink chair.

"Cal, Cabot, I've found the lost pink chair," I called.

"I don't see any pink chair," Cal said, skidding to a stop beside me.

"Me, neither," Cabot said, ever loyal to his brother.

Right. I saw no point in making an issue of it. Who knew? Maybe they needed glasses. Besides, I hated that chair.

Chapter Eleven

It's a new day. My classroom held only me. Roark was gone. Mr. Kerr was gone. I had a new student. I did not have a plan for Roger. The bell rang. Warm sunlight enveloped me when I opened the door. Self preservation dictated I press myself against the building and tuck in my toes. Like flying missiles, from every section of the playground, my students converged on the open door, calling out enthusiastic choruses of, "Good morning, Ms. McCall". Not in any flight of fancy could I imagine a better way to begin a day. Following the plan, they trooped in quietly, dropped completed assignments on my desk, began the assignment on the board and earned two extra recess minutes. Any lingering thoughts of Roark evaporated.

I introduced Jody and was pleased when Allison's hand flew into the air. "Can I be the one who tells her all our rules and stuff?" she asked.

"That's a good idea, Allison, I said. Jody gave me a small smile, but I didn't know her well enough yet to interpret it. "You can start by telling her how you earn minutes. And oh, yes, tell her how you use them." Allison dragged her chair to Jody's desk and began an animated explanation.

Roger was absent and I couldn't decide whether I was relieved or disappointed. With everyone intent on the board assignments, I took a moment to organize the student papers now scattered over my desk. I riffed through them, hoping to see Derek's name on at least one, but no such luck. With a sigh I looked across the room and called softly, "Derek." He looked up, and I motioned him to come to my desk.

With great deliberation, he placed a marker in his book, closed and laid it to one side, slid his chair back, and rose.

I studied him as he approached, wishing his physical being would somehow unravel the mystery of his missing assignments. He was taller than most of his classmates, nearly as tall as my 5'8". Without his summer tan, the tiny freckles below his light blue eyes were visible and the golden sun streaks were gone, leaving his hair a darker, sandy brown. He moved with the youthful awkwardness of growth outstripping coordination. Upon reaching my desk, he stood looking at me in silence.

I kept my voice low, "Derek, I've just gone through the papers due today. I didn't see one from you. Did you forget to turn yours in?" I asked, although sure this was not the case.

"No." he answered.

I waited to see if he'd offer an explanation. When he didn't, I said, "I think we need to talk about this, but now isn't a good time. I'd like you come see me during afternoon recess."

With no change of expression, he nodded and returned to his seat and resumed reading.

"Why," I wondered, "does a student with his exceptional vocabulary and retention of material, respond so well verbally but refuse to turn in any written assignments?" No answer presented itself, so I sighed and rose to circulate among my students for the remainder of the half hour I allotted each morning for independent study, pleased to find everyone on task. Many worked alone at their desks writing or reading. Near the back of the room, I listened for a moment to five students involved in a science project on the life cycle of butterflies, before moving on to a trio who were drawing and comparing pie graphs for math. Another group was illustrating the second amendment to the constitution for their group project.

Seeing none who needed my help, I returned to my desk, took a sip of the tepid coffee at the bottom of my cup, picked up a red pencil, and began an attack on the endless task of correcting, correcting, correcting. The point of the pencil snapped, so I laid it aside and without looking up, reached for another from the pencil holder at the front of my desk. Instead, I jostled the cowbell sitting in the holder's spot, and it plummeted to the floor.

Along with the kids, I jumped at the resulting cacophony. In the ensuing silence of students too frozen to move, blood pounded in my ears and enflamed my face, and I mumbled an embarrassed, "Sorry," as I bent to retrieve the offending thing. When I straightened up, intending to put the bell back where it should have been, I saw they remained silently immobile, staring at me. "I guess I need to explain," I said, almost stammering. "This morning I slopped coffee all over my desk, and after I cleaned it up, I guess I didn't put everything back where it belonged. That's why I knocked it on the floor. The bell—it was an accident." Still no response. Taking a deep breath, I began again, choosing each word with care. "The bell was not rung. It fell. It was an accident and I'm sorry you were upset. As you can see, it scared the heck out of me, too." I saw Allison whispering to Jody and pointing at the bell. Jody said nothing, but this time I had no trouble interpreting her look. Dismissive looks are unmistakable.

Many students still looked apprehensive, indicative of the importance of the cowbell's symbolic disapproval. Smiles of relief finally appeared when I said, "You are all behaving perfectly and I am very proud of you." Mimicking Lily Tomlin's Edith Ann I added, "And that's the truth." They laughed. Their teacher was back to her weird self. It wasn't important that most of them had no idea who I was mimicking, just that things were back to normal.

For the rest of the hour the cowbell remained silent. Two minutes before the recess bell rang, like thoroughbreds at the starting gate, every kid was waiting in line at the door, straining toward freedom. Their voices were hushed, but their body language was loud and clear. I flung the door open and jumped aside. I watched them scatter about the playground before I nudged the door shut, dropped into my chair, and propped my feet on the clutter on my desk. In the near silence, uninterrupted by kids or parents or intercom, more tired than I expected, I tilted the chair as far back as possible and closed my eyes.

In the trance-like prelude to sleep, I remembered a wet, rainy Saturday a few years ago. I was vacuuming the living room while my four kids read or played quietly in their rooms. They always played quietly out of sight when there was housework to do. There was a knock at the door, and I opened it to see Cal's kindergarten teacher, Mrs. Kristol, standing there. Her cheeks were nearly as bright as her rain-soaked red raincoat. Standing on the step, she didn't say anything as she studied my face without smiling. "Hi," I said, wondering why she had come. "Won't you come in?" When she did, I said, "Let me have your coat. Would you like some coffee? Or tea?" I pushed the vacuum cleaner hose out of her way.

"Thank you, coffee, black, would be nice." She shrugged out of her dripping raincoat, handed it to me and sank gracefully onto the sofa. I draped her coat over a chair on my way to the kitchen.

"So, what's Cal done now?" I asked, returning to hand her a cup of coffee and taking a sip of mine as I sat at the other end of the sofa. I couldn't imagine any other reason she'd be at my door in that weather.

"Well, nothing, really. It's just that I'm worried, and before I made an appointment for him with the district psychologist, I wanted to talk with you." She looked so ill-at-ease I was tempted to pat her on the shoulder.

"A psychologist? Good grief, why?" I demanded.

"It's his artwork. Everything he draws is scary and spidery and black. I know he has a complete box of crayons, but he refuses to use any of them. He does everything in black pencil."

"Never? He never uses any colors?" I asked, dumbfounded as I thought of the drawings he'd taped to the refrigerator, and a few he'd left on my walls. They included every color in his 64 crayon box.

"Well," she hesitated, took a breath and said, "he splashes all the colors available in the poster paints at the easel, it's just what he draws at his desk that's always black. Black, and spidery. In pencil."

I leaned my head on the back of the sofa, thinking. This was a new one, and I'd long ago discovered that trying to figure out what was going on in Cal's mind was an exercise in futility. With a shrug I asked, "What did he say when you asked him why?"

"I didn't want him to think I was criticizing him, so I haven't asked him," she said.

In my usual tactful way I yelled, "Cal!"

"Yeah? What?" he yelled back from behind his closed door, probably figuring I wanted him to help with the cleaning. Getting no response, he opened his door and yelled, "Yeah?" again, then stared in surprise at his teacher as he came reluctantly into the room. "Yeah?" he said again, more to her than me.

"Hi, Cal," she said, smiling.

"Hi," he said with more suspicion than warmth.

I came right to the point. "Cal, Mrs. Kristol and I are curious why you only use a black pencil when you draw at your desk."

With pure exasperation in a voice one would use with a mentally defective chimpanzee, he said, "Mom, I'm not a little kid anymore. I'm in school now, and I get to use really sharp pencils, like you and Lissa. I don't have to use those baby crayons any more like Cabot and Risa. Can I go now?"

I nodded, unable to speak. When the bedroom door closed behind him, Mrs. Kristol and I doubled over in stifled laughter. "When all else fails, go to the source, and ask," she said.

The nerve-jangling bell signaling the end of recess blasted me back to the present. Mrs. Kristol was gone, but not her final words. Smiling, I opened the door.

Roark took his best shot, but with a class as great as mine, his effect was short-lived. Jody was behaving well, probably thanks, in part, to extra recess minutes and peer pressure, but I knew better than to forget her dismissive look. Between no problems with Jody and a plan for Derek, it was a wonderful morning.

At noon, finished eating, each student quietly watched the clock until I opened the door. I watched as the last one raced to the playground before I reluctantly turned from the beckoning sunlight, and returned to my desk. Derek's steady stare followed me as he waited at his seat.

"Let's talk over here, Derek," I said, hoping it sounded like an invitation and not an order. He shambled over, pulled a chair next to me and sat without speaking, letting me know the ball was in my court.

Turning my chair to face him, I said, "Derek, you've been in my class for nearly two months and I still have no papers from you."

"I know," he answered, with neither insolence nor arrogance—just a simple statement of fact.

Taken off guard by this unexpected answer, a few seconds elapsed before I asked, "Do you understand how to do the assignments?"

"Yes," he answered.

This time I expected his brevity. "You're sure they're not too difficult?" I asked.

"No."

"In that case," I said, "will you do this much? So I'll know you've heard and understood the assignments, will you head a paper for each assignment and hand it in with everyone else's?"

"OK," he agreed.

It was time to put the ball in his court—time for me to go to the source. "Derek, if the work isn't too hard and you understand it, why won't you do the assignments?"

For a long while he stared at me in silence. I waited. He looked away. With his body rigid, in a nearly inaudible monotone he answered, "You wouldn't understand."

I thought about this a moment before I said, "Maybe I would. I already understand that this is something very important to you."

Stony faced, he studied me before he answered, in a voice so choked with anger it was a whisper, "You want to know why I don't give you my work?" He took a deep hoarse breath. "Why I don't give *anybody* my work?" No longer in a whisper, he flared, "It's because I can't stand having people writing on my papers!"

I stared at him, speechless. While his answer surprised me, the unrestrained passion startled me. So far as I knew, Derek had never before exhibited anger, or even irritation, toward me or anyone else. Other teachers referred to him as self-contained or withdrawn. Now, defiant and angry, he glared at me, immobile, waiting for my reaction. I knew now that beneath his impassive exterior, anger raged; what I didn't know was why, and I had to wait for him to tell me.

When I regained my composure, I said, "You were right, Derek. I don't understand. But maybe I will, if you'll help me. I need you to explain it to me." To reach this complicated child, to understand him, to understand what he was telling me, I needed more time, more information, and most of all, I needed his trust. The bell signaled the end of recess. "I can't lose him now!" I thought in desperation. Impulsively, I touched his arm, "Oh, no. We're out of time, Derek. Please come in again tomorrow."

He waited, scrutinizing me, before he gave a small nod and stood. He returned his borrowed chair, sat down at his desk and opened his book. I began breathing again.

"Good afternoon," I greeted my class with enthusiasm as they trooped in.

When my contract day ended, I checked one last time for any messages left in my box. On a pink, deckle edged note, I read, "Madam LaZonga wishes to remind you that she is expecting your company at dinner tomorrow night."

As if I'd forget Ethel and our monthly dinner together.

Chapter Twelve

In my message box the next morning was a note from Roger's mother saying he had the flu and would be out of school for at least a week. Beneath it lay another of Ethel's pink, deckle-edged notes. This one had what looked kind of like a drawing of a knife and fork and the words "Do Not Forget!!!" printed in red crayon. Me? Forget? Not likely. Of course Ethel had no way of knowing that before I left home this morning I'd assembled my kids in the kitchen to bribe them into behaving in my absence, if not well, at least no worse than usual, with the promise of a dinner out tomorrow night.

"What do you mean by "dinner out?" Cal asked suspiciously.

"It's up to you," I replied as I tossed a sandwich and an apple into my lunch bag and tore off a paper towel for a napkin.

"You mean like cheeseburgers?" Cabot demanded.

"I don't want any yukkie veggies." Cal saw no point in leaving anything to chance.

"OK, OK, all right, cheese burgers, no veggies," I agreed, hopping around trying to get my other shoe on.

They were relentless. They knew I dreaded being late to work, so they kept adding provisos: French fries, soda pop, that euphemism for sugar water, and banana cream pie. They ran the clock out, leaving me no time to negotiate and soon their menu looked like the heart-attack special. "Yes, yes, yes," I agreed to Cal's, "Can I bring my burger and French fries home instead of eating them there?" knowing from past experience he intended smearing one with peanut butter and dip the other in his concoction of tartar sauce, ketchup and mayo. So far he hadn't found an additive for the soda pop, but he was young still.

"Anything, just behave yourselves and it's all yours," I yelled, flying out the door and into my car, trusting I was completely dressed, or at least that nothing vital was missing. I slammed the car door, rammed into reverse gear and shot the car up the driveway. From the top I looked back as I streaked up the hill to the arterial. All four were high fiving each other in the doorway. Laddie lay at their feet, his tail thumping.

The day passed with no out-of-the-ordinary occurrences, so by four o'clock I finished all I intended to do. With great deliberation, I stacked all my work-in-progress into a pile in the center of my desk— and left it there. No way was I transporting it home where it would give me a guilt trip when I ignored it. I switched out of my sensible flats into dressy black pumps, scooped up my thermos and my purse, checked I had the two-for-one coupon book and made a fast exit. I had a couple of errands to run and being late meeting Ethel might mean another guilt trip. Something she's really good at.

It was dark by the time I reached the restaurant, relieved its smoothly paved parking lot was well lit by multiple lights that flickered and flashed across the building's façade. I walked swiftly toward the imposing entryway, where a tall man in a black and red uniform, reminiscent of the Buckingham Royal Guards, held the door open. At my, "McCall, dinner for two," with a silent nod, he motioned that I should follow him. He stepped aside when we reached an archway of carved wood as dark as teak, opening onto a discretely dimmed dining room. I turned to ask if I was the first to arrive, but my elegant guide had vanished. *Now what am I supposed to do? Trot around on my own hunting for Ethel? Peek at strangers eating dinner?*

The room was imposing—as big as a Boeing hangar, but with delusions of grandeur. Red fabric covered the walls, its gold embroidery catching the light of the crystal chandeliers. Massive high backed chairs upholstered in red velvet ensured the privacy of their occupants. I discarded any thought of trotting and peeking about. Patrons here would probably dismember me with one of their foot-long steak knives. My heart sank. "Oh, Ethel, I may never see you again," I lamented. I enjoy being melodramatic, since it doesn't require an audience to be pleasurable.

"Your table is ready." A low voice interrupted my big scene. Another member of the Royal Guards stood at my elbow. He swept away and I swept after him, assuming an air of regal hauteur—a difficult maneuver in three inch heels on six inch thick carpets. The pretense ended when we reached the table. The waiter held my chair out, but slid it back in time to catch me, when both I and my jaw dropped, at the intimidating array of heavy silver cutlery and crystal stemware. The thought flashed through my mind that maybe this wasn't a restaurant; it was the bridal registry at Nordstrom's.

A crisp snap followed by a light breeze brushed my face as a napkin the size of my kids' pup tent floated into my lap. The maitre 'd or waiter or whatever he was, propped a shoji screen sized menu on the table in front of me, and without a sound slipped away across the deep carpet, leaving me to hope he, or one of his cadre, hadn't misplaced Ethel. I heard a rustling and peeked around the menu to see that a second menu now faced me from across the table. "That you, Ethel?" I stage-whispered.

After a long silence, I heard, "Yes. Shhh, I'm counting the forks. How many do you think I'm supposed to use?" She closed her monster menu. "Can you believe these things?" she asked and began wafting it up and down, chanting, "A one and a two, and a. . .you know, I bet I could build great biceps doing this twice a day."

"Stop it," I said laughing, "you're ruining my hair-do."

"Oh, sorry. Is that your hair? I thought you accidentally stuck that bunch of autumn leaves on your head and I was trying to blow them away."

I didn't dignify this with a response.

A waiter, identifiable by his black and red uniform, discreetly cleared his throat, a reminder it was time to order. We gave him what we hoped were our penitent looks, and obediently began reading our menus. I gulped as I skimmed the right hand column and gave silent thanks for our two-for-one coupons. Just the entrees, sans salad, beverage, tax and tip, would pay for all four of my kids' junk food outings for a month. Since the two-fers didn't cover beverages, we opted for ice water with a twist of lemon. I could always drain my thermos on the way home for a caffeine jolt. But my attempt at frugality died when I saw the hors d' oeuvres featured escargot in herbed butter and wine.

Ethel appeared to be in a hypnotic trance breathing the words, "Exotic fruit compote drenched in apricot brandy."

"Ethel," I said, determined not to go into bankruptcy alone, "it's only money. You can't take it with you." I leaned toward her to deliver my big argument, "And just remember this: if I can't take my money with me, then I can't take any excess fat, either." Hors d' oeuvres were ordered.

"Besides," I rationalized as the waiter left for wherever they keep hors d' ôeuvres, "we didn't order a salad or tea or coffee or dessert, and we just won't eat any rolls, ergo, both cost and calories are canceled out."

"Ergo?' Ethel asked with lifted eyebrow.

I shrugged. It worked for me.

The waiter returned on little cat feet, not with brandied apricots and escargot, but a basket of warm rolls and butter which he placed between us. One deep breath of the yeasty fragrance blasted what was left of my will power. I closed my eyes and for a couple of blissful moments just inhaled. Opening my eyes I said, "Let's really go on a starvation diet tomorrow," then howled, "Hey, no fair!" Ethel was chewing, even as she reached for a second roll. By the time our hors d' oeuvres arrived, the bread basket was empty. Soon only dirty dishes remained and we raised our menus to begin our entrée selections. It was several minutes before I told the waiter, "I'd like the lobster Newberg." I looked longingly at the baked potato with all the trimmings, but figured the cream and butter in the Newburg had enough calories and cholesterol for one meal.

"I'm going with prime rib—super rare, with Yorkshire pudding." Ethel smiled in ecstatic anticipation as she added, "And chilled asparagus spears with Hollandaise sauce, since we've decided against a dessert."

Relaxing from the strain of all this decision making, I set the menu aside and glanced about the room to see if I could see what others were eating.

I jumped at Ethel's suddenly hiss, followed by, "Look! Look at that couple who just came in!" She was pointing over my shoulder. I twisted around, but couldn't see beyond my chair which was both high and wide. There was a wicked smile on her lips as she tilted her head for a better view of whatever was behind me. "Quick, before they sit down. That table over in the corner." I had to hang over the armrest and lean halfway out of my chair to see anything, but I knew from Ethel's conspiratorial expression, I couldn't afford to miss whatever it was. "Isn't that the father of your newest student?" she asked.

Forgetting dignity, I rose up on my knees to look over the back of my chair to see who she meant and saw Jamison Kerr, the father of my newest student, Jody Kerr. But the woman with him was at least fifteen calendar years younger and light years prettier than the woman I'd seen in the hall. I felt a smile tugging at my mouth. This man had made life miserable for Nick, and fate was about to even the score. Remembering Jody's dismissive look made me wonder if I was about to receive an equal number of unwelcome visits from Daddy Kerr.

I watched as he leaned toward his pretty dinner companion, smiling as he held her chair. He laid his hand on her shoulder as he straightened up, and stood for a moment facing my direction, so I made it a moment to remember.

I couldn't help it. I backed out of my chair so quickly, I had to grab the table to maintain my balance before I stepped alongside it. "Hi, Mr. Kerr," I called cheerfully, maybe a little louder than necessary, before I gave a Queen Elizabeth wave and flashed them what Cal called my snake look. My greeting was not returned. "I doubt I'll see much more of Jody's daddy this year," I told a startled Ethel as I plopped back down.

"I can't believe you did that," she croaked.

"Did what?" I asked, feigning an innocent tone that didn't fool Ethel for a second. "All I did was say hi."

At that moment our waiter materialized with our entrees, but I thought his hands shook slightly as he set them before us and I wondered if my greeting to Kerr had anything to do with this. Was it possible that Kerr was a regular here? But the fragrance of the lobster Newberg, bubbling in front of me, made everything else irrelevant. "This is so good," I said with a mouth full of lobster. Ethel merely nodded so as not to interrupt the rhythm of her chewing. And for the next few moments, silence reigned.

Declining desserts, we waited while the waiter cleared away our empty plates to begin the real purpose of the evening: catching up on each other's families, especially my four offspring and Ethel's two granddaughters, and realized anew how blessed we each were to be part of such perfection. The waiter refilled our water glasses, and forgetting we'd refused desserts, handed us dessert menus and waited a moment before asking if we were going to order dessert or after dinner drinks. My body quivered as I summoned all my will power to forego the dark chocolate mousse with raspberry sauce, (my favorite) and the key lime pie, (Ethel's favorite) from among the many temptations. Just as I was about to cave, Ethel took one look at the right hand column and said, "No, thank you," rescuing me. The waiter nodded, took back his menus and left.

A few minutes later, finished for the moment with family doings, we began discussing our classes and I asked, "Ethel, you've been in this school for over eight years haven't you?"

"Almost nine," she replied.

"Then you may have had one of my students in your kindergarten class. Do you remember Derek Hall?"

"Yes, I remember him very clearly, as well as his twin sister."

I stared at her. "What twin sister?" I asked.

Chapter Thirteen

Taken by surprise, it took me a moment to get my voice back. "Twin? You said he had a twin sister? What happened to her? How come I never heard about her? Where is she? Ethel lifted her hand facing the palm toward me, signaling she wanted to get a word in. I took a deep breath and held it.

"I had no idea you didn't know." Her voice and face left no doubt she was serious. "I assumed it was in his student folder or that his parents told you he had a sister. Her name is Dierdre. "

"Dierdre? Of course I remember his older sister Dierdre. She was in my class last year. I seldom look at student folders except for parent/guardian information. And no one, including Dierdre, ever mentioned she was his sister or that he had a twin. Come to think of it, no one ever mentioned Derek last year. That's why, until he entered my class this year, I kind of assumed that Dierdre was an only child. Did something awful happen to his twin" I knew I was babbling, so I paused before Ethel could hold her hand up again.

She frowned, thinking, measuring each word, "No, Dierdre is Derek's twin."

"No way," I interrupted.

With an exasperated sigh, Ethel ignored the interruption. "Will you just let me explain! Since I taught the only kindergarten class at that time, I had both of them. Besides being smart, they were twins, so they got a lot of attention from the other kids, which they enjoyed. It was impossible not to like them. But talk about different. That old cliché *as different as night and day* could have been coined for them."

Alerted by my sudden intake of breath, Ethel's hand shot up before I could interrupt. She laughed, but it sounded more rueful than amused. "It's funny, but I remember thinking how clearly the divergence in their personalities expressed itself in their art, especially finger painting. Dierdre's were exuberant splashes of vivid colors running into each other all over the page. She usually ended up with more paint on her face and in her hair than on the paper. Derek's art looked as if the paper contained invisible geometric forms only he could see—lines he had to stay within. And except for what was on his fingers, all the paint was inside those lines." She paused, smiling at the memory, but I knew better than to interrupt. "With his height and reserved manner, Derek was occasionally mistaken for older than he was, and even I tended to expect more of him than I did of tiny Dierdre. She was a sugarplum fairy; he was the man in the gray flannel suit."

We looked up as the waiter placed our bill on the table with practiced discretion, and I leaned forward to see if an X or something marked the exact half-way point between us. He left and we went into our usual routine of trying to figure out how much tip to leave, and how much each had to ante up for our separate shares after deducting the half-off coupon. We could probably do it faster if we didn't giggle so much and exclaim at how much it cost even using a coupon. We had to add and subtract more than once to get everything just right, after which, of course, neither of us had the right change.

The waiter, who had long since returned, was both wise and experienced and waited with non-committal patience. Good strategy, since this gave us a guilt trip that we assuaged by increasing his tip. He slipped the black leather folder holding our money off the table, and I looked at my watch and realized my kids had been left alone a little too long. "I have to leave," I said. "Can you meet me for lunch tomorrow? I'll ask an aide to sit with my students while they eat. I need more information on Derek before I meet with him during recess."

"You mean brown bagging in the lounge?" she asked.

"Right," I said, rising. I took one last look around, absorbing the almost hedonistic ambiance and only incidentally noticing that the corner table had new occupants. I sighed, "I really hate to leave all this gorgeous luxury. It's been a wonderful evening—but then all my times with you are. I can hardly wait for next time." I gave Ethel a quick hug.

She smiled, knowing I meant it. "Just don't lose the two-fers," she said and followed me out.

Chapter Fourteen

Throughout the following morning even the chilly rain that drizzled from a gray cloud cover couldn't dampen my spirit. My students were attentive and caught on quickly in both the math and the spelling assignments. Just before morning recess, Roger said, "I didn't hear the story you were reading while I had the flu. Would you tell me what I missed?" Before I could answer, hands flew up all over the room to a chorus of, "I'll tell him," and "Let me tell him." Their enthusiasm for story time vindicated my assessment of their intelligence when, against the advice of a couple of their previous teachers, I chose to read _The Hobbit_. I felt a sense of pride seeing the eagerness with which they vied to tell their least favorite classmate, Roger, about it.

"That would be a nice thing to do," I told them, my pleasure evident in my voice. The bell rang and Roger found himself surrounded by half a dozen boys, all giving their versions of the story as they jostled their way out. The day was drizzly, dark and overcast, but no one seemed to mind.

Adventuring no further than the doorway to avoid any random drops from landing on my hair, I watched them for a moment before scanning the area for Alice, the playground aide. I spotted her talking with four or five laughing girls, while keeping a vigilant watch on the students in her assigned section. Her ready smile and fair-mindedness made her a favorite adult among the students.

"Hey, there, BJ," she called when she saw me watching her, "planning on taking over my playground duties?"

"Eeyuck. No way, especially not on a day like this. You, at least, took time to grab a jacket. Wish I had. I'm freezing." Still surrounded by the girls, she walked toward me, and I said, "Actually, I was hoping you'd take over one of *my* duties. Would you consider supervising my class during their lunch today? It's important, and I promise on my next paycheck that I'll be back before you have to report for playground duty."

"Yeah, right." She laughed. "Some pledge. I know what your paycheck looks like, but I'll do it." Scanning her territory, she turned away and, without saying goodbye, hurried to where some boys seemed to be forming a circle.

"Thanks," I called, backing into my classroom before I froze, but not before the wind shifted and rearranged some of my hair. The room was warm and I settled for just being thawed out, shrugging off my messed up hair. The rest of the morning was uneventful except for a visit from Roark who opened and stood for a moment just inside the door to the hallway, but left without coming in or speaking.

As the door closed behind him, Billy raised his hand and asked, "Why was Mr. Roark in our room?"

"Wish I knew, but I'm sure it wasn't for anything good," I thought, but what I said was, "I really don't know."

As the lunch hour approached, I told the students to put their science materials on their desks when they finished eating, explaining, "I have a meeting I have to go to and Alice has agreed to be here and I expect perfect behavior from each one of you. While you know I'd never, ever, threaten you," I flashed them my wicked smile, "let's just say that if you aren't totally perfect, I'll have to lecture you on good behavior and school rules and every boring thing I can think of instead of reading *The Hobbit* when I come back." The ensuing groans assured me I'd made my point. The door opened.

"Good afternoon, Alice," my perfect class sing-songed in unison, as she came into the room. Smiling, I scooped up my purse, brown bag lunch, thermos and coffee cup.

"Good afternoon," she answered them with a smile and took her place at my desk. From the door, I turned and waited until I caught Derek's eye. With an almost imperceptible nod he indicated he remembered our meeting.

Hurrying into the lounge, I shoved my purse under the ugly black chair, plopped my brown bag on the brown Formica table, and mentally compared today's tan walls with last night's lush red ones and accepted the fact I wasn't in Oz any more. Only the heady fragrance of my coffee as I poured it from my thermos was comparable.

Ethel wasn't there yet, but Mary Johnson was, in a lime green pants suit and dark green earrings so flattering I felt a pang of envy. I knew I looked good in my navy blue outfit, but not as good as she looked in her lime green. I smiled at her and surprised myself when I dropped my voice to a whispered, "Hi." We were the only ones in the lounge and it seemed too quiet, like it needed more than two occupants to come alive.

Mary answered in her normal voice, so maybe she didn't feel the emptiness. "Ethel told me you wanted information about Derek Hall."

Still whispering, I said, "That's right." Vic in his flashy red sweatshirt and Mark in his unflashy blue and white overalls came in, bantering about something, filled their coffee cups, waved at Mary and me and went to sit on the sofa. With four in the room, I said in my normal voice, "She's supposed to meet me here for lunch."

Mary nodded, "I know, but something came up. She said that she'll get here as soon as possible. She said you were concerned about Derek and that you'd be interested in what I could tell you." Checking that she had my attention, she said, "Were you aware that he was in my third grade class the year his parents separated?"

I shook my head. "No. I saw in his folder they were separated and they have joint custody, but that's about all I know."

Mary nodded. "Derek took it really hard. I'm not sure about Dierdre. She was in Paul Martin's class. He teaches somewhere in Oregon now, but at that time he felt Dierdre just took it in stride,"

I interrupted, "When you say Derek took it hard, what did he do?"

She thought a moment, then said, "Well, at first, he just looked kind of sad and sort of withdrew from the other kids. This seemed like a normal reaction, so I didn't push him. And the other kids, being kids, went on as usual. They still asked him to join them at recess, but he usually didn't."

With a lot of noise, the chair next to me was scraped back and Mary and I were interrupted by Ethel, who, feigning great surprise, exclaimed, "Oh, no. Don't tell me you didn't wait for me before you began eating," and sighing pathetically, sagged into a chair across from us. Gaping at me, she exclaimed, "What happened to your hair? Last night's pile of leaves looks like today's compost."

Flabbergasted, I opened my mouth to retaliate, but she cut me off, adding, "Oh, well, no matter. Let's eat." She opened her brown bag and pulled out some carrots and celery. "Sorry I'm late, but I'm glad to see you two are talking as well as eating without me."

I made a face at her rabbit food and asked, "You call that eating? Doesn't even have dip to go with it. I think I prefer my ham and cheese sandwich." I bit into it, pleased to note Mary was enjoying real food, too. Of course, unlike Ethel and me, she probably hadn't seriously over-caloried last night.

I realized how concerned I was about Derek when I saw there was a plate of lemon cookies at the far end of the table and I hadn't noticed it until now. Missing a plate of cookies was not part of my m.o. I stood to reach across Mary and the empty chair next to her and could barely got hold of the cookie nearest me.

"Hey, BJ, I'd have been happy to pass them," Ethel protested.

"Couldn't take the chance you hadn't seen them yet and then how many would be left?" I took another when she set the plate in front of me. My sandwich forgotten, I swallowed cookie number one before I asked Mary, "Was exhibiting sadness the extent of his reaction?"

She looked pensive and I thought her green eyes turned a little grayer. I'd heard moods influence eye color. "No," she said, "that was just the beginning. He began turning in assignments late, then missing some. By Christmas he wasn't turning in any assignments. He refused to participate in class activities, just sat or stood looking into space. At recess he'd lean against a wall and simply wait for the bell to ring."

"Was any professional help brought in? The school counselor or the district psychologist? Were his parents even aware of his withdrawal?" I prodded.

"Yes to all of the above. We all did what we could, but nothing changed. He just withdrew more. It was like his body was in class, but he wasn't. By June, district policy dictated I couldn't pass him into fourth grade. He was assigned to Paul Martin's third grade the following year." Mary sat silent, then, "I didn't have a choice, but I never felt right about it."

I couldn't think of anything to say, so I bit into my sandwich, remembering Dierdre, so bright, so vivacious so popular. She had eyes the same shade of blue as Derek's, but hers were never still, and like her, they danced over everything, missed nothing, a well coordinated bundle of energy. She was elected fifth grade student council representative as well as class secretary and brought the house down with her dance routine in the talent show. It was fun just being around her.

Derek would be in my classroom in a few short moments and I wondered how I should approach this hurting, angry youngster. I remembered watching him as he shambled into my classroom for the first time, avoiding looking at anyone by keeping his eyes on the floor. He was so tall and gangly and moved so awkwardly, I had the feeling that if there was a piece of string on the floor he'd trip over it.

When I tried to visualize Derek two years ago, my throat constricted and my eyes stung. I saw an eight year old boy moving from one parent to the other, and felt his helpless loneliness as his twin sister and all his peers advanced, leaving him behind. I couldn't repress a shudder imagining his humiliation as he came to school day after day to sit among younger, smaller classmates.

I stood, stuffed my thermos under my arm, drained my cup, squashed my lunch bag, pitched it into the trash, flung my purse strap over my shoulder and scooped up another cookie. "How's that for multitasking?" I asked, grinning at Ethel. "And I really appreciate your asking Mary to give me some background on Derek."

"I hope it helps." She picked up another carrot, waved it at me with a wry look before she crunched it saying, "My penance for last night's heavenly over indulgence."

"Thank you so much, Mary. You've been invaluable," I said.

Derek was waiting. I had no idea how I was going to help him, only that I had to try. "No," I thought, shaking my head, "trying isn't good enough. I have to succeed!"

Chapter Fifteen

I came into the room just as Alice finished buttoning up the dark brown cardigan that matched her slacks and was pulling the door closed to follow the last student racing out for lunch recess. Only the lingering smell of spaghetti, the waste basket overflowing with paper towels, and the flashlight batteries and pieces of wire from the science project aligned at the top of each desk, indicated the room had been filled with students. Before the door closed completely, I called out, "Thank you."

Alice pushed the door back open far enough to say, "BJ, you have the most wonderful class! You've no idea how lucky you are—how much they've calmed down since last year." Laughing, she added, "You are so lucky you didn't have them then. Well, playground duty calls. Bye."

"Oh, yes," I thought, "I certainly do know how lucky I am."

The door clicked shut and I looked to the back of the room to where an arm in a pale blue sweater angled out from behind a tall book. I assumed it belonged to Derek. Still undecided how to begin, I sat down at an adjoining student desk and looked toward him, unsure whether or not to smile. He offered me no clues, just waited, impassive and silent, his book now lying open in front of him. I said, "Hi, Derek," figuring this was a safe beginning.

With slow deliberation he inserted a paper in the book, closed it, placed it in the center of his desk, and initiating eye contact, nodded. And waited.

I could see the waiting game wasn't going to resolve itself, so I ended it. "Derek, I need your help. I need to know what you want from me." His expression remained impassive. Not hostile or angry or wary, even. Just impassive. I leaned across the aisle and rested my hands on his desk and said, "I want to help you succeed in school, but I don't know where to begin."

He raised one eyebrow, more questioning than distrustful I thought, so I said, "I remember you once told me you hated having people write on your papers. Why is that so important to you?"

For a long while, he sat, immobile, his face revealing nothing, watching me. A sense of loss swept through me as I thought, "I've lost him. He's retreated back behind his wall of silence, and I have no idea of what to do next."

With an abruptness that caught me off guard, his demeanor changed. His eyes became angry slits, his voice, so low it was almost a whisper, had the tension of controlled anger, as he leaned toward me. "You ask me why that's important? Having people write on my papers? Why shouldn't I hate having people write on MY papers? Because they ARE my papers and only I should write on them."

Numbly, I looked at his angry, set face, now drained of color, making his nearly invisible freckles and pale blue eyes stand out. I understood his words, but not the intense anger. I shook my head as if that would shake away some of my confusion and asked, "But I don't understand. Why does having someone write on your papers make you so angry?"

He glared at me. "Why?" He almost spat the word at me. "Because I work and work on my papers and then someone else messes it all up. They make it ugly." He took a deep shuddering breath. "And nobody cares."

I stared at him, too stunned to speak, while his last three words echoed and re-echoed in my mind.

"And you want to know what else?" he demanded. Without waiting for my response, he lashed out, "All they ever do is write what's wrong. Always wrong, wrong, wrong. They use big check marks to show how stupid they think I am. 'This is wrong.' 'That is wrong.' They never write, 'This is good.' And at the top of my papers they write how much I got wrong so everybody can see it. And they do it in big sloppy red ink that looks like they were bleeding all over my paper. I don't even want to touch my papers after that."

The realization washed over me that much of what I saw as anger was primarily pain. Although he hadn't turned in any papers for me to deface, waves of guilt engulfed me. For him, the markings on his work were worse than graffiti—comments, even positive ones were intrusions on his personal property, and by extension, on him. "But," I thought defensively, "It's always been done that way. I didn't invent the system. That's just the way it's always been done. Always been done?" The self-serving excuse made me cringe. "The way it's always been done? How many times have those words been used to avoid responsibility? Those were the words of the mob absolving itself in Shirley Jackson's *The Lottery*. Derek is right. So now, the question is, what am I going to do?

"You're right, Derek," I said. "I'm sorry. I never thought of it like that." Then words failed me and we sat facing each other in an uncomfortable silence. I thought of Ethel's description of his finger painting: so precise, so neat, so contained, and I knew instinctively that she had never defaced his work.

Then, just like in the movies, an idea like a light bulb flashed. I had it—the revelation, the answer, the win-win solution. "Derek, listen. I've got it." I was almost incoherent in my excitement. Since his face registered skepticism, not anger, I continued talking. "What if I wrote my corrections and comments on another piece of paper. You know, one I could staple to your paper. Or even a paper clip if the staple bothers you."

He looked at me speculatively, thinking this over. Then, his voice no longer angry, said, "I guess the staple would be OK." After a moment he asked, "Would you staple it so other people couldn't read it? You know, folded over or with the writing facing in?"

"Of course," I said, relieved and delighted and excited at the prospect. "That's a good idea. No, it's a great idea. Derek, you're a genius!"

"Yeah, right." He heaved a loud dramatic sigh, "So, OK. If you do that, I'll turn in the assignments you want."

Now I was an emotional mess. I wanted to laugh. I wanted to hug him. Mostly I wanted to be able to hold back the tears burning behind my eyes until I was alone.

"You know what, Derek," I said, standing and turning away toward my desk for a tissue, "I think your idea is really good. So good, in fact, I'm going to use it for all my students. There is no reason in the world why anyone needs to write all over someone else's work." I took a deep breath and turned back toward him. "You need a break, so grab the few minutes left of recess, but I'd like to talk about this a little more. Can you give me another recess soon?"

"I'll consider it," he answered with an impish half smile. And disappeared out the door.

Chapter Sixteen

It was one of those days dreams are made of, I thought, hurrying to the lounge before my break ended: no insurmountable hassles with my kids before I left home; traffic less hectic than usual; a productive meeting with Derek; and lemon bars in the lounge.

When the signal ending lunch recess sounded, I hurried back to my classroom, brushing away the powdered sugar decorating my blouse and, with a light heart, opened the door and greeted my returning class with an enthusiastic, "Good afternoon. Come in. Come in." A few students flashed me quizzical looks, but most accepted this as their teacher acting weird again. Story time was the highlight of their classroom day and it took only seconds for them to sit in a semi-circle on the floor, eager for me to continue the adventures of the hobbit Bilbo Baggins.

Earlier in the year I established story time protocol. "I always wanted to be an actor," I told them. "When I was a kid, I used to write my own plays so I could always be the star, and I'd make my younger brothers and sisters be everything else—lesser actors, audience, even props, like trees or toads. As a parent, I discovered reading out loud to my children was almost as much fun as acting. But it's fun only when the audience is interested. So," I paused and looked around making eye contact, "if you appear disinterested by talking or looking around, then I get frustrated. And I just have to stop."

Sarah raised her hand, looking up at me with luminous her gray eyes, enhanced by her sea green tee shirt. In her usual serious manner she asked, "Is it OK if we color while we listen? My last year's teacher always let us."

"I know," I answered, matching her seriousness, "lots of teachers do it that way, but I prefer it if you just relax and listen. That's one reason I have you sit on the carpet." Her look told me she was disappointed at this answer and the brief buzz among the students indicated she wasn't the only one. "I'll try to explain it to you since, as I just told you, it's very important to me that you enjoy what I read to you. How can I tell if you are enjoying the story unless you are looking at me and I can see your faces? If your expressions tell me you are enjoying the story, then I'll read for the full fifteen minutes before you go back to your assignments." They got it, but there weren't any high fives.

In the following months on only two occasions were the fifteen minutes cut short. I loved inventing voices for Tolkien's superbly created characters and I think my joy in story-telling was contagious. They sat as if mesmerized, responding to the story's events with gasps or wide-eyed wonder and sometimes laughter. When I related this to their previous teachers, they accused me of exaggerating, refusing to believe this group that had, ever since kindergarten, been notorious for its inability to sit still, stop talking and listen now sat attentively for fifteen minutes or more. Maybe someday I'd invite them to come see for themselves.

After story time yesterday, my class made me smile as they returned to their seats mimicking my interpretation of Gollum's hissing, "Yessssssss, my Preciousssss," before beginning their assignments.

Today, about ten minutes into the story, the door opened. Holding its knob, so the door didn't quite close, Roark stood in the entry observing us and after a moment, left without speaking. This did not give me a good feeling, although I was elated that I was the only one who looked toward the door. Not one student risked appearing distracted and thus responsible for story time ending prematurely. Or maybe they really were too involved in the story to notice the door had opened. Either way I was proud of them.

Story time over, the kids organized themselves into their assigned teams to continue their project in Health but with less enthusiasm than usual. This unit on nutrition involved handling four lab rats in order to weigh and feed them, often followed by animated discussions punctuated with laughter of what they observed and then recorded in their lab notebooks. Today I heard little laughter. No one asked about Roark's unexpected visit and I worried they were reacting to my apprehension.

I walked among them, observing the variety of opinions under discussion and the quiet civility with which each idea was met. The room was too quiet and, illogically, this nettled me. "What," I thought ironically, "would some of their previous teachers think if I told them I was bothered because these kids were too quiet." Same answer as before—they wouldn't believe me.

"Lighten up," I told myself. "Roark's gone. The kids hardly noticed him." But the nagging feeling persisted. The science project involving live rats was never meant to be passive. What good is discovery that doesn't engender a spark, excitement, electricity? It was time to investigate. Pasting on a smile, I stopped by a group making notations in their notebooks and asked, "Which of you wants to tell me what you did and what you discovered?" Uncharacteristically, they jumped at the sound of my voice, evidence they were on edge. For a moment no one answered, then they all began at once. The instantaneous cacophony, made me laugh. The pall cast by Roark dissipated and I had my class was back, my noisy, energetic, full of life kids.

But for me, hidden I hoped, from my students, the tension remained. Unexpected visits from Hatchet Man had that effect.

"OK, kids. Clean-up time," I called moments before the end of the day. Allison was near the rats' cage and I said, "Allison, will you please take the litter from the cage and dump it in the garbage can?"

Involved in reaching for his jacket, Billy heard my request and unaware Allison had already opened the cage door and pulled the tray of litter out, he yelled from across the room, "I'll do it. Let me do it." With his eyes only on the cage, in his eager race to help, he plowed headlong into Allison, who stood transfixed, watching him approach. She, along with the rest of the class, could only watch in alarm mixed with the desire to laugh, as the tray flew from her hands, over Billy's head, flipped and scattered litter on desks, students and the floor before it fell. "I'm sorry. I'm sorry. I'll pick it up," he said, dropping to his knees.

"Just leave it alone!" I yelled, running toward the mess as students shook the litter from their hair and shoulders. Forcing myself to speak calmly, I said, "Each of you grab a paper towel, dampen it and wipe off your desks and books. Then wash your hands. Joey, give Billy a damp towel. Billy, just go sit at your desk and stay out of the way! We're out of time and the buses are coming. I hope no one misses their ride thanks to you!" Billy slunk to his desk and I sent Jody to find Mark Smyth and his vacuum cleaner.

She returned quickly saying Mr. Smyth would come in after the students left. When the school day ended, I guided my students carefully around the piles of litter and out of the building, grateful they responded quickly, and no bus rides were missed. With one last irritated look at Billy, waiting silently in line, I returned to my room and sank exhausted into my chair. Billy tired me, but recalling Roark's odd behavior drained my emotions and made remaining upbeat difficult. But I was darned if I'd ever let him know.

I poured myself a half cup of coffee, grateful for the solitude, and leaned back intending to plan what I needed to do next. It wasn't to be. I set my cup down so quickly that, although only half full, it splashed coffee on my desk as the door opened and for the third time that day Roark's presence darkened my day. Not wasting time on niceties, he strode to the front of my desk, where he stood stony faced looking down on me, and came straight to the point. "Children in fifth grade are too old to be read to. They should be reading independently. Silently. On their own."

Recovering my voice, I began, "I agree they should read independently, but. . ."

Before I could explain that we had independent reading at the beginning of the day, I was cut off with, "Furthermore, '*The Hobbit*' is far above their intellectual level. You should select something more appropriate." He turned and left the room. I wondered if he practiced his exit lines in front of a mirror. It was somewhat of a disappointment that Mark had vacuumed up the litter while I took the kids to the buses, since imagining Roark skidding in it made me smile.

"Well, isn't that precioussss," I thought as Roark's words replayed themselves in my mind. "First Roark says they are too old to be read to, then he says I should select something more elementary to read to them. Wonder if he'd care to put that in writing." I got to my feet, shook my fist toward Roark's office and quoting Scarlett O'Hara's, "I'll think about that tomorrow," snatched up my cup, gulped the last, now tepid, dregs of my coffee, traded the cup for my purse and thermos and hurried to my car, muttering, "I'm going home. I need some peace and quiet."

Where did I get the idea a house with four kids and a shaggy dog equal peace and quiet?

Chapter Seventeen

Outside, the world was cold, drizzly and dark. It wasn't enough that Roark interfered with story time and Billy scattered rat litter, used rat litter, all over, now nature dripped her icy rain drops down my neck and those darn politicians chose today to take away my beloved daylight saving time. So now I had to drive home in the dark, engaged in a relentless struggle to peer through smeary arcs left by windshield wipers emitting a monotonous click, scrape, click, scrape that set my nerves on edge. My lousy frame of mind wasn't improved by bumper to bumper traffic. Why couldn't they all just get out of my way, preferably by staying home.

Roark's intrusion, like an irritating song that won't go away, with the appropriate name, ear-worm, kept replaying itself. As if that weren't bad enough, *now* I thought of the brilliant repartees I wish I'd said, like, *How come the librarian says every copy of what I'm reading to my class is instantly checked out?'* Or, switching from hot sarcasm to cold sarcasm, *Could it be some of my incapable students are actually reading those over their intellectual level books?* Followed by, *And why do you suppose so many parents have told me their kids begged them to buy The Hobbit so they could read it at home on their own? Huh? Huh?*

I smiled with smug satisfaction at myself in the rearview mirror as more, equally brilliant phrases, flourished in my imagination: *And how come my students' attention spans have gone from a minute and a half to over fifteen minutes—and not just for story time? Just answer that Mr. They're Too Old to Be Read to Roark.* It was too bad Roark wasn't there to be devastated by my blistering intellect, but remembering his 'open door policy', I figured he'd probably insist it was just coincidence. "I'll go to the union rep tomorrow. Let him figure out what I can or cannot do."

With that decision, Roark vanished from my mind and I concentrated on driving in the inky darkness, blinded by idiots too rude to dim their headlights and accepted the fact that I was just one more insignificant component in a vehicular pack train, each of us trailing one after the other in nose to rump formation. It wasn't a pretty picture.

By the time I broke free of the freeway onto the hushed side road to my house, my mood had gone from frustrated to thoroughly nasty. With an angry twist of the wheel, I made the sharp U-turn onto my sixty foot long driveway and roared into the carport. I jerked to a stop, jumped out, slammed the car door, and stomped to the porch. Through the locked door I heard scurrying sounds and frantic, "Mom's home. Hurry up."

Ordinarily I dawdled collecting my things from the car before sauntering to the house. Sometimes I even bumped the horn before turning onto the driveway. Accidentally, of course. That way, if the kids were doing something I could live without knowing about, they'd have time to get it out of sight.

Tonight, however, I unlocked the door with a vicious twist of the key and flung the door open, nearly tripping over the broom lying across the threshold. I kicked it aside. The scritching sound my feet made grinding grit into the slate entry way told me two things: 1. Laddie, our Australian sheepdog, was inside, and no one had swept up after him, and 2. Now the slate had to be swept as well as washed, waxed and buffed—not even close to any of my favorite activities. "All right!" I yelled, "Who let the dog in? And where is he now?"

The house was eerily quiet. Eerie because my house is quiet only when it's empty. Where were my kids? Or more to the point, what were they doing? "Lissa? Cal? Cabot? Risa?" I called. Then called all their names again, but only Lissa responded, hurrying from the bathroom toward me.

"OK, that's one, only three to go," I said, softening my tone. Even frustration with Roark couldn't stem the rush of love I felt for my kids, even when I was mad. And I was still mad—at Roark, at traffic and now at the gritty floor left by the dog.

Expecting to hear," Sorry, Mom, I meant to sweep the floor," or even, "Laddie is in the basement," what I actually heard was, "It's not my job to sweep the floor. Cabot's the one who brought Laddie in. But you're so late we have to hurry to get to the yard-goods store before it closes. I have to have a pattern for a skirt and the cloth and thread and stuff by tomorrow or I fail home-ec." She threw all this at me in one breath. Just what every parent loves to hear the minute they enter the house.

I blinked, shook my head and hoped I'd heard wrong as I repeated, "Tomorrow? Your teacher waited until now to tell you? Is she out of her tree?"

"Uh, well. I knew about it last Wednesday, but you had dinner with Mrs. Holmes that night, and the next night you had to help the boys with their math and Friday I stayed overnight with Patty and I guess I kind of forgot to tell you after that." She mumbled the words, and having used up her store of courage, her whole body drooped. She knew I hated being hit with 'right now' demands. Especially those that required getting back in the car and driving some place. And doubly so when it was raining.

"Just what I wanted," I thought, "I get to load four hungry kids into the car, drive to the shopping center, drag three of them protesting into a yard goods store, and THEN come home and fix dinner. Even Roark couldn't top that."

I looked around. "Where are the other three?" I asked. "And Laddie?"

Before she could answer, Risa opened her bedroom door a crack and peered out at me.

"Come on out," I said, hoping for a better response this time.

"Hi, Mom," she mumbled, staring at the floor. Instead of her usual impetuous rush for a hug, she came toward me hesitantly. I put my arm around her as and moved close enough to hug Lissa as well.

Ignoring for the moment the mysterious disappearance of the boys and Laddie, I went into the kitchen and found the linoleum was sticky as well as gritty and had brown spots of what looked like cocoa dotting it. But the sink and counters were clean, clear of breakfast dishes and whatever they'd fixed for snacks, ready to prepare dinner on. "Come help me," I told the girls, setting the oven to preheat. "I want to put a roast in, so it will be ready when we get home. Lissa, get some potatoes peeled and covered with cold water in the sauce pan. Risa, set the table."

The girls shot each other nervous looks and neither moved.

Irritated, I snapped, "Now!" I glared at Risa and said, "Go and get the silverware from the silverware drawer and start setting the table."

Reluctantly, she crossed to the drawer, opened it, and looked back at me. Except for a couple of bent forks we used for picnics, it was empty.

"Well, you'll just have to take the dirty silver out of the dishwasher and hand wash it," I told her, yanking it open. It was empty. "Where is the silverware? In fact, where are the dishes?" I asked, my voice rising to a level not far from hysteria after I turned away from the empty dishwasher to open the door of the dish cupboard and found it, too, was nearly empty.

Lissa was looking at the ceiling and Risa looked near tears. What in heaven's name was going on?

"Mom!" Lissa demanded frantically, "Look at the clock. We have to go now, or the store will be closed and I'll get an F and it will be all your fault!"

She was two-thirds right. The store would soon close, and she'd probably get an F. Whose fault that would be we could discuss later, along with the missing silverware and dishes.

I dumped some seasoning on the roast and shoved it into the oven, setting the automatic timer for 90 minutes. Heaving an exasperated sigh at the unset table and unpeeled potatoes I yelled, "Calvin! Cabot! Get in here this minute!"

"Hi, Mom. You called?" Cal asked with the nonchalance that warned me to beware. He flashed me a smile as he stepped back into the house through the sliding glass door that opened onto the deck. I hadn't thought to look on the deck since its lights weren't turned on.

"What on earth were you doing on the deck? It's freezing out there and why didn't you have the light on?" This definitely was not normal behavior. Cal complained of hypothermia when I turned the thermostat below 70. Not only was he dripping wet, but he'd been out there in the dark, in the rain and with no jacket. My 'Mom Alert' was on full throttle. As Cal sidled around me, shaking the rain from his hair and splattering water in all directions worse than Laddie, I detected a strange smell emanating from him. It seemed to be part chemical and part smoke-like.

I sniffed, leaning toward him. "Get a towel, a dry sweat shirt, your jacket and get in the car," I ordered. "And what is that awful smell?"

Shivering, but assuming his macho persona, he swaggered past me to his bedroom. "What smell?" he asked.

Now I was on high alert. When Cal answered a question with a question, something was up. Further interrogation was blocked when Lissa swooped after him with the towel from the kitchen, but before she reached him he ducked into his room and slammed the door. "Just hurry up, you idiot," she yelled at the closed door. When it opened, she was waiting to grab him to drape a towel on his head and begin rubbing his hair none too gently.

"Leave me alone. And you're a double idiot!" he howled, snatching the towel from her.

Angrily, Lissa grabbed all their jackets from the hall closet, got behind Cal, who was dabbing at his drenched hair with the towel, and began pushing him, as well as Risa, toward the door.

"Get your hands off me," he snapped. Turning to me, he planted his feet on the floor and demanded, "Why should I get in the car? Where are we going? I'm hungry, so we better be going for hamburgers."

Through clenched teeth but enunciating each word with care, I answered, "You're going to get in the car because I told you to. We are going to the shopping center to buy cloth for Lissa. And we are not going out to eat. Any more questions?"

"I'm not going to any store to buy cloth!" he howled. "That's boring. What if someone sees me? They'll think I'm a weenie."

I said nothing, just gave him 'the snake eye'. Casting a malevolent look at Lissa, he opened the door and went out, followed by Lissa and Risa.

Three down and one to go. "Cabot!" I yelled. "I told you to get out here!"

There was no answer, but there were sounds of movement coming from his bedroom. I stalked over and flung the door open and was knocked to one side as Laddie bounded off Cabot's bed and fled to the basement. Long haired dogs have a unique aroma when they're wet and the smell from Cabot's room nearly gagged me.

"Oh, Mom, you scared him," Cabot wailed, attempting to go after him.

Blocking his way I asked, "Was Laddie in your bed?"

"He was cold, and I wanted him to get warm," Cabot explained, still angry with me for frightening Laddie.

Now I could look forward to a load of laundry before sending Cabot to bed tonight. "Go in the bathroom and change into these clean clothes," I said, handing him fresh pants and shirt I grabbed from the laundry basket still sitting in the dining room. Obviously someone had forgotten to put them away. "And hurry!" I ordered, picturing the growing rebellion in the car. "Or I'll send your sister in to help you."

He balked. "Why do I have to change?"

"So we can stand being in the car with you," I said.

"Why do I have to get in the car?"

"Just do it," I snapped.

With an air of pure martyrdom and the alacrity of a turtle with an injured leg, he inched his way toward the bathroom. "I still don't see why I have to," he complained.

The front door crashed open. "Mom," Lissa yelled. "Where are you? The store's going to close."

At his sister's voice, Cabot bolted into the bathroom.

"We have to wait for Cabot," I said. "He smelled too awful to have in the car and I sent him into the bathroom to change. I don't think he'll be much longer."

Pounding on the bathroom door, Lissa yelled, "Cabot, get out here right now or I'm going to kill you."

With surprising speed, Cabot burst from the bathroom and ran past Lissa. "I still don't see why I have to get in the car. Is it OK if we take Laddie?"

"No way," I answered, grabbing my coat and purse to charge after them before one of the four escaped. Back in my car once more, I satisfied myself it held four live bodies, none of them happy, no dog, and all seatbelts fastened. And I could still smell Cabot.

As I drove to the store, I wondered how I'd find time to launder the bedding. I knew it wouldn't make any difference to Cabot. He liked everything about Laddie, including his smell. Not so the rest of us, and his room *was* near the kitchen.

"Cabot," I said, "how many times have I told you to keep Laddie out of doors or in the basement?"

"But Mom," he argued, sounding as forlorn as if Laddie had died, "we were playing in the ravine and he went in the stream and got wet and he was cold."

"He was also covered in pine needles and leaves and grit," I answered. "And he smelled. You should have taken him to the basement and dried him with a towel and brushed him."

"Well, I would have. Is it my fault you drove in so fast I didn't have time? I don't see why you had to drive in so fast," he finished accusingly. Then he brightened. "If I brush him when we get home, then can I take him in my room?"

"Not until you bathe him. He still stinks." I figured this gave me a short reprieve. Laddie hates baths and the boys have their hands full just catching him, never mind getting him into the tub.

"Can't you drive any faster, Mom?" Lissa interrupted.

"No," I snapped. "Getting stopped for speeding won't get us there any faster."

Scowling, she crossed her arms over her chest and heaved several heavy sighs of martyrdom. Martyrdom must be catching.

When we pulled into the shopping center, I found a parking space close to the yard goods store. Almost before I stopped, Lissa leaped from the car and tore inside. The other three sat motionless.

"I'm not going in there," Cal announced, pressing defiantly back in his seat, his feet dangling.

"Me, either," both younger siblings parroted, pressing back in their seats, but with their feet sticking straight out.

"Want to bet?" I asked in my most menacing voice.

Casting dirty looks in my direction, they piled from the car and, following Cal's lead, slouched their way to the store.

Our sojourn in the yard goods store was, to put it euphemistically, challenging. Hungry and bored, Cal and Cabot flung each other rancorous insults that threatened to escalate into physical encounters. "Cut it out," I snarled. They shut up and wandered off to handle bolts of material, making loud comments as off color as they dared, while I struggled to convince Lissa that a lined jacket of faux leather, albeit a great addition to the assigned skirt, was a little above her skill level. She wasn't happy, but she acquiesced. Throughout, Risa remained by my side, demanding and touching nothing. It was nearly closing time and Lissa and I were the final customers. The boys, sensing their imminent parole, were waiting quietly near us at the check stand. When a loud speaker blared that the store was closed, I jumped and could barely stop shaking enough to write a check for the materials. I thanked the clerk, who watched apprehensively as I herded the kids to the exit.

Outside, before I could release the door handle, the wind wrenched it from my hand and slammed the door against wall.

Rain pelted in. "Run!" I yelled at the kids as I fought to close the door before racing through the downpour to unlock the car. It was gratifying to see they were capable of obeying instantly. Before all doors were locked and seatbelts in place, I had the motor running and the heater on. Instantly steam clouded the windows and the still powerful aroma of Laddie emanating from Cabot filled the car.

"Okay, everybody take a handful of tissues and wipe the windows," I ordered, holding one over my nose and passing around the box every parent learns to keep handy. "Cabot, the minute we get home you get in the shower while I finish dinner." This elicited giggles, teasing, and indignant responses from the back seat.

The word 'dinner' reminded me and I said, "We can't eat dinner without dishes. What happened to all the dishes?"

There was that eerie silence again.

"I asked you, where are the dishes? Somebody answer me." Irritation, along with my voice, was rising. In the dark and the rain, I didn't dare turn around. I tried to see them in the rear view mirror, but they were ducked down out of sight. Next to me, Lissa had her nose pressed against the passenger window.

Preoccupied with the kids, I didn't see the red light soon enough. I slammed on the brakes. Terror shot through me as we skidded to a stop in the middle of the intersection. Other drivers, more alert than I, waited until my car was no longer moving before creeping around us. The last car drove away, the light turned green, and I moved forward. My voice shaking, I said, "We'll talk about the dishes when we get home."

Edgy and exhausted, just thinking about dinner was more than I could handle. The roast was in the oven, but the potatoes weren't peeled, the dishes were missing, the table wasn't set and it was nine o'clock. I saw a MacDonald's on our right and sighed, knowing when I was licked. I swung into the take-out window line.

"Before you get too excited," I informed the celebrants in the back seat, "this is instead of the end-of-the-month dinner out." They knew which dinner I meant—the dinner that every Friday following payday that they got to choose, as long as it was inexpensive and local. They loved ordering from a menu and being waited on.

"You mean we get to eat a hamburger at home, and that's it?" Cal protested.

"Hey, it's not my fault we're out here in the rain in the middle of the night, and I'm too tired to cook. Besides, now you'll have time to clean the floor, brush Laddie, find the dishes and put the laundry away before bed."

"Five Big Macs. No drinks," I told the voice on the loud speaker. It was a quiet ride home.

No sooner was the front door unlocked, than Cabot raced past me shouting, "Laddie, we're home. I'll take a shower, Mom, just as soon as I see if Laddie's OK," he called from the bottom of the stairs.

"Fine," I muttered. Reminded by the garlic and roast beef fragrance from the kitchen, I checked that the oven was turned off.

"Lissa," I demanded as she came through the door, "Where are the dishes?"

"Ask Risa," she said, scurrying past me, carrying her bag of sewing supplies to her room.

"Yeah, ask Risa," Cal mimicked, adding, "I have to go to the bathroom. Now." It was a challenge I chose to ignore. He ducked around me and I heard the simultaneous slamming and locking of the bathroom door.

"Well?" I said to the only child remaining. The rain dripping from her hair added to the utter pathos of her expression.

"It's like this," she gave me a beseeching look, "you know how you told us you hate coming home and seeing the kitchen full of dirty dishes?" She stopped, waiting to see if I remembered.

"Yes," I answered, wondering where this was going.

"You said if we had the kitchen clean and you didn't see any dirty dishes lying around and the floor swept, you wouldn't look in our bedrooms or bathroom until Saturday. Didn't you?"

"Yes," I said again.

"Well, Cabot was supposed to sweep the floor, but he wanted to get Laddie warm first, and then you drove in too fast and he didn't have time. And that's why the broom was lying on the floor."

A sense of guilt swept over me. How did all of this become my fault? I shook my head, thinking I really must remember to drive in more slowly in the future. "But what does all this have to do with the missing dishes?" I asked, getting back on track.

She looked miserable. "I wanted to surprise you, so I was making cookies and when they were done, my favorite cartoon was starting and I forgot it was my day to put the dishes in the dishwasher and then you drove in so fast and that's when Lissa reminded me and I couldn't stack them in there the right way so they wouldn't get broken."

I must never, never drive in that fast again, I thought. Aloud I asked, "So what happened to the dishes?"

Without answering, she walked across the floor and into her bedroom. "Risa," I called, "get back out here."

Shoulders slumped, she came out, carrying our big plastic picnic tray. It was filled with dirty dishes.

"Why in the world were those in your bedroom?" I asked.

"I didn't want you to see them, so I put them under my bed," she explained. "I was going to put them in the dishwasher tomorrow after you went to work."

"You put them under your bed? Why under your bed?" I asked, dumbfounded.

"Because if you couldn't see them, then you wouldn't say they were lying around. That's what you said, "You didn't want to SEE them lying around. You never said they had to be in the dishwasher."

"You're right," I said. Then burst into laughter at her ridiculous literal ingenuity. So literal, so caring, and so ingenious. I love ingenuity. It beats unimaginative every time.

For a moment the kids stared, then began to laugh with me, making the only storm the one outside.

"It's late," I said when I finally stopped laughing. "Those dishes have waited this long, they can wait till morning. But in the sink, not under the bed." Then added, "Risa, you need to wash five glasses for milk." While she washed them, I plopped five burgers on the counter along with catsup, mustard and mayo. "Dinner's ready. Come and get it," I called. When you're hungry, even a big Mac looks good. And we were all hungry.

It wasn't long before we tossed the MacDonald's bags and wrappers in the trash and the kids sat dunking Risa's cookies in their milk. I prefer dunking them in coffee. Somewhere around 11, with Laddie brushed and in the basement, the floor swept and less sticky, although not exactly spotless, and both Cabot and his bedding clean, I kissed each kid goodnight and got ready for bed.

Soon, chuckling over Risa and the missing dishes, I fell asleep, forgetting about Cal's strange behavior and unidentified smell. It didn't seem important.

Chapter Eighteen

I t was morning—early morning—and somewhere the uproar of an out of sync cement mixer shattered the silence, and stole my sleep. I burrowed my head under my pillow in a vain attempt to regain oblivion. As my sleep fogged brain began to clear, I recognized the unholy racket was that of my ancient dish washer. I rolled out from under the comforting warmth of my down comforter, shuddering when a gust of icy wind from my open window slithered up under my nightgown. Shoving my feet into the slippers beside the bed, I felt my way in the dark to the kitchen, wondering how in heaven's name the dishwasher got turned on.

The kitchen's light forced me to squeeze my eyes shut, but I opened them to narrow slits at Risa's triumphant shout, "See, Mom! I told you I'd put them in the dishwasher before you got up today. I got every single dish in. And I even turned it on so we'd have clean dishes for breakfast."

"What time is it?" I mumbled squinting toward the clock.

"It's almost 4:30. I knew I had to start early or I might not finish before you woke up and I wanted to be sure and keep my word. Are you happy with me now?"

My head hurt, my eyes burned, and my nightgown was not designed for warmth. But none of these mattered. "Yes, I'm happy with you now," I told her, "but let's go back to bed."

"I love you, Mom," she said, hugging me before dancing to her room. From her door she called, "I put the leftover cookies in a bag for you to take to school." Even nearly numb from the cold, I laughed as I shuffled back to bed. I really must start saving for a new dishwasher," I thought as I fell asleep to the old one's syncopated rattles.

An hour later in the predawn dark, the dishwasher was silent, but my alarm wasn't. In one smooth motion I punched its off button and swung my legs over the side of the bed, and shock waves shot all the way to my scalp when I missed my slippers and my feet hit the icy floor. I swung them around until they located the fleecy scuffs. I slammed the window shut before shuffling my way through the house, flipping on lights. First stop, Cabot who could sleep through any sound except that of a sibling touching his stuff. I pounded on his door, opened it cautiously and leaped aside to avoid being head-butted by Laddie.

"OK, Cabot, time to get up," I called. "Hurry and open the front door so Laddie can go out." Careful not to breathe, I ran to open his window, leaned out, inhaled twice and turned, scooping up the scattered smelly clothes littering his floor. I thrust the dirty laundry at him and said, "Take all this downstairs to the utility room after you let Laddie out."

Muttering unintelligible sounds, he kicked his blankets aside and rolled to his feet, scowling first at the open window then at me, snatched the grungy clothes and left his room. "Hi, Laddie, good boy," he said lovingly. Maybe he'd say good morning to me later on. The front door slammed and I assumed Cabot's non-reappearance meant Laddie was out and Cabot was headed down the stairs to the laundry room.

As if on cue, Cal and Lissa's doors flew open and they raced each other for the bathroom. Lissa' s room was closer and her legs were longer. She won and slammed and locked the door in Cal's face. "You better hurry," he threatened. "You know I can't hold it very long and if I can't, I'm going to stand right outside your bedroom!" With that he stormed into his room and slammed his door.

The Keystone Kops were in out in force. Another door flew open. Risa giggled, enjoying the confrontation. Why not? She wasn't in the middle of it. Cabot, empty-armed and minus Laddie strode past me, glared at the closed bathroom door, and stomped to his room and slammed his door.

With everyone awake and on their feet, I returned to my room to get ready for work. I did not slam my door.

Back in the kitchen half an hour later, I assumed the open bathroom door meant the boys had followed their speedy get in and get out procedure, hoping they'd included teeth brushing and, after toilet use, hand washing. I'd check it out later. Sitting at the counter, Lissa was smiling as she smoothed the polished cotton material spread out before her, enjoying its rich turquoise sheen. "I'm sorry I waited so long to tell you I needed this," she said, looking up at me. I smiled and nodded an OK. She folded and slipped the material into her backpack before reaching into the dishwasher for a clean cereal bowl.

Cal sauntered from his room, stepped around me and brushed against Lissa, riling her as he intended. Stretching, he lifted his jar of peanut butter from the cupboard, bent to reach in the fridge for the container of milk he'd scrawled his name on, and turned and set them both on the counter where the material had recently lay. "Mmmm. This is really good," he drawled, leaning with studied insouciance against the sink, and shoved one hand into the peanut butter jar. With slow deliberation, he extracted his hand, fingers curled, then extended one finger at a time to lick it. He gazed from lowered lids at his sister when one insulting finger remained extended a little longer than the others. Delighted with her look of anger and revulsion, he used the same hand, now shiny with saliva, to lift his container of milk to his mouth, and guzzled noisily.

I shook my head, acceding to albeit amused at his audaciousness.

"Gross." Lissa shuddered in disgust.

Getting exactly the reaction he hoped for, Cal laughed. With a quick look at me, he ostentatiously used his uncontaminated hand to open the refrigerator door to return his unfinished milk, then hastily washed his hand in the sink and wiped it on his jeans. Only one hand had peanut butter on it—no point in washing both. "Well,

I'm full," he said, ducking past me and racing into his room. He wasn't sure what Lissa planned to do, but knew he'd be safer on his own turf.

Risa came into the kitchen, wrinkled her nose when she saw the brown smudge she hoped was peanut butter, on the edge of the fridge. She tore a paper towel from the roll and gave the entire area, including the handle, a thorough wipe-down before pulling the door open and reaching in. "This is for you, Mom," she said, holding up a wax-paper wrapped sandwich. She put it, along with some of her homemade cookies, into a sack with "MOM" printed on one side in big black letters. "It's bologna, with just a little bit of mayo and mustard." She watched for my reaction.

"Perfect," I said, adding an apple to the bag. She smiled.

"I want lots of mayo and ketchup on mine. No mustard," Cal ordered, leaving the safety of his room.

"Me, too," echoed Cabot as he searched the cupboard for any cereal containing more sugar than grain.

"Yuck, not me. I want mine like Mom's," Lissa said, giving a theatrical shudder.

"I know, I already did all that," Risa answered, dumping three wrapped sandwiches into paper sacks. "If you want cookies, get your own. I only have to do sandwiches." She picked up a sack that obviously held more than a sandwich, and placed it carefully in her backpack.

"Come eat breakfast, kids," I said to those not already eating. "Here's your orange juice and milk." I placed both alongside some boxes of cereal.

"I only want juice," Cal said, splashing some into a glass. "The peanut butter filled me up and I already had my milk."

"Fine," I said. "Whatever."

When my coffee pot stopped dripping, I poured some coffee in my travel mug, dumped the hot water out of my thermos before filling it, and inhaled the rising steam's fragrance.

I hugged each kid and checked to see that their clothes were clean and reasonably well coordinated. "Don't forget to brush your teeth," I reminded them while avoiding a look into their bedrooms. With my purse, lunch, coffee mug and thermos, I left the warmth of my home for the cold darkness of the carport, stepping over the prone body of Laddie lying across the doorway. He kept his pathetic brown eyes trained on me as I leaned back over him to pull the door shut. "Forget it," I told him. "Besides, you know as well as I do Cabot is going to let you in the minute my car is out of sight." Still watching me, he laid his head on his paws and whimpered, unable to control his thumping tail. He was a lousy actor.

I backed out of the carport, knowing that tonight the floor would be swept, the dishes in the dishwasher and everything in order. But just to be sure, I'd remember to hit the horn before coasting very slowly down the driveway.

Chapter Nineteen

The rain left the black macadam slippery and shiny enough to reflect the overhead street lights and I drove with extra caution the short distance to the freeway entrance. Remembering last night's scare still sent shivers skittering down my spine. Nearing the end of the on-ramp to I-405, I flicked the signal indicator, and waved a thank-you to the driver who slowed to make room for me in the rush hour conga line. During the mind-numbing creep south, unwelcome thoughts of Hatchet Man, slithered in making me wonder what real agenda lay behind his objection to *The Hobbit*. Was it simple harassment or ammunition for a bad evaluation or something else entirely?

Further concerns regarding Roark died when from my left a clunky old beater car whipped in front of me before veering right, onto the off-ramp on two wheels. I hit the brake hard, grateful my seatbelt kept me from an encounter of the worst kind with the steering wheel, but I held my breath until the screech of tires from the car behind me ended, and I knew there would be no jarring rear-end crash. Relieved, but shaky, I moved forward, and waved a second thank you to the driver—this time for not hitting me. The blood red tail lights of the clunker disappeared down the ramp, and I hoped whatever its driver was hurrying toward was worth it.

Taking deep breaths, I struggled to relax and groaned as I remembered the white board still covered with yesterday's assignments. I'd have to clean it before I wrote today's assignments and I couldn't remember anything I planned to do today. My frustration level rose as traffic vacillated from a sluggish creep to a stop and go two-step. Back-up on the exit ramp demanded my full attention as I alternated between the brake and the accelerator down the ramp to the surface road where reasonable speed resumed and I could think about my plans for the day. I needed to meet with Roger, redo the whiteboard, organize the student papers scattered across my desk and begin correcting them. There probably wouldn't be time to finish many, but I could begin reducing the number I'd have to take home tonight.

Swinging onto school property, I saw my parking space waiting for me to fill its dark emptiness. It was irrelevant only two vehicles, barely discernible through the mist, were in the lot—my space was mine to claim. Locking my car, I smiled with pleasure in the moist opaque whiteness barely penetrated by the school's outdoor lighting, but kept my eyes on the ground to avoid skidding on the slimy leaves littering the concrete walkway. Standing in the shelter of the overhang, I reached to open the door, just as it swung outward, throwing me momentarily off balance.

"Hi, BJ, sorry about that, didn't mean to knock you off your feet," Mark said, laughing apologetically as he held the door open and ushered me in with a sweeping bow. Brandishing a wide broom he said, "I was just on my way out to clear the leaves off the walk. Think it's necessary?" Without waiting for an answer, he and his broom disappeared into the misty dark and for the second time this morning, I took a deep, shaky breath. Noting the light was on in Roark's office and the outer office, I hurried quietly to my classroom. I'd check for any messages in my box later.

The silence of the semi-dark hallway reminded me that with Mark out of doors, I was alone in the building with Hatchet Man. I was sure he would never do me physical harm, but I felt a sudden chill and cast a furtive glance over my shoulder as I approached the psychological safety of my room. I flipped on the lights and I opened the draperies. The mist had lifted, revealing a pale silver moon backlighting clouds drifting like ragged scraps of lace across the black sky. For a moment or two I gazed in mesmerized wonder, truly moon-struck.

Returning to the tasks at hand, on a sheet of notebook paper I listed:

1. *write memo regarding Roger*
2. *erase board and write today's assignments*
3. *organize papers scattered on desk*
4. *re-pin lopsided pictures on bulletin board*
5. *begin correcting papers*
6. *sit, relax in chair, pour small amount of coffee into cup, inhale and sip*
7. *call Union Rep Vern Clayton*
8. *Do number 6 first*

Soon most of the tension oozed out of me and I was ready to face the day.

An hour and a half later, with my lesson plans under control, class assignments on the white board, student papers organized, with a few even corrected, and the pictures properly aligned, it was time to call Vern Clayton. Taking one last sip of coffee, I traded my cup for my purse, picked up the bag of Risa's cookies and went to the phone in the nurse's office, by-passing the voices and laughter from the lounge, hoping there would be time to join in.

When I repeated Roark's comments that *The Hobbit* was too advanced for my students, followed by his statement that fifth graders were too old to be read aloud to, Vern interrupted to ask, "Did he order you not to read to the kids?"

I had to think for a moment, then said, "No, he just said they were too old to be read to and that the *Hobbit* was too sophisticated for their age."

"Well, then," he said after a moment, "as I see it, you can reasonably assume that he was not issuing an order but simply stating an opinion. I'll check district policy further, but it seems to me that you can continue to read to your class, but call me if anything further develops."

I thanked him and hung up. Relieved, I left the room, eager to share my cookies and saw Roark ahead of me at the lounge door. Before entering, he glanced back, hesitated a moment when he saw me, and made an abrupt about face, brushing past me without speaking. I shrugged and joined my friends.

At fifteen minutes before the bell, I returned to my room. At two minutes before the bell I looked outside and saw the moon was gone, replaced by western Washington's famous, or infamous, rain. Fat drops squiggled down my window, transforming the multi-hued jackets and raingear of students huddling under the eaves into mobile works of modern art. When I opened the door, the colors scattered and reformed themselves into a vivid line that wound its way past me into the room. Let the museums keep their art, I'll take mine any day.

Bringing up the rear was Billy McGuire, who stopped in the doorway facing me. "Hey, guess what, Ms. McCall," he said in a stage whisper that carried across the room. Bouncing up and down as he tugged on my arm, I knew he was trying to keep his voice down so as not to jeopardize the silence required for extra recess minutes, but whatever was exploding inside him was stronger than his control.

"Guess what! You'll never guess. But guess what. My gramma is taking me to Disneyland this summer. She really, really is." Every inch of him was in motion from his shock of red curls to his hip hop feet. His face glowed, every freckle threw out light rays and his hand tugged on my arm as if I were a giant salmon he was reeling in.

As I tried to extricate my arm while keeping an eye on the class, I responded with a banal, "That's wonderful, Billy."

He recognized the triteness of my words. "Ms McCall, you're not listening." His voice was aggrieved. "It's really important."

I glanced down at him, hoping the class understood the assignment on the board and concerned that Billy's news was keeping the class from their extra recess minutes.

He dropped his hold on my arm and his animation drained away. "My mom says when I do that when she talks to me, I'm acting like she's just a piece of cellophane." I couldn't miss the pain in his voice.

I stared at him. "What does that mean?" The expression was new to me.

"It means you only look where I am but you aren't looking at me—like you're looking through me at something behind me, because I'm just a piece of cellophane. She says cellophane is stuff they used in the olden days before they invented that new stuff." He paused to see if I understood.

I understood, all right. For the third time, a student I cared about accused me of not listening, and I wasn't proud of the pattern.

Giving him my full attention, I said, "Billy, you're right and I'm sorry. You are not made of cellophane and going to Disneyland is very important. I'd like to hear all about it, but if you tell me now, everyone will lose their recess minutes."

It came as no surprise that my students were paying more attention to Billy than to the assignment on the board. But I was surprised by the enthusiastic burst of voices calling out, "It's OK." "Let Billy tell us about his trip." "We can have extra recess tomorrow." Wondering if this was a majority opinion, I scanned the room and saw from the smiles and nods it was. These kids never ceased to amaze me.

It took less than three minutes for Billy to share his wonderful news, bow in acknowledgement of his classmates' applause, and beaming, take his seat, pausing to return a few high fives along the way.

I was eager to share his description of cellophane, especially the olden-days part, with Ethel. A lightness of spirit permeated the morning and when recess time came, almost before they were out the door, I heard Billy answering his classmates' questions. The happiness in his voice was evident and I heard no regrets over the lost extra minutes. Not lost, really. Just taken sooner.

Smiling, I scooped up the new batch of spelling papers scattered on my desk to put them in order. I caught my breath when I saw

Derek's name on one and pulled it out. His words, written with care, were precisely aligned. Sure I would discover no errors, but knowing I couldn't afford to be wrong, I read the paper in minute detail, before reaching for my black pen, the one with the extra fine tip, and printed 100% on the sticky side of a sticky note, and stuck it at the top of his paper. "Sticky notes, sticky notes, how I love my sticky notes," I hummed as I worked. Unable to think of a rhyme to finish my poem, I found repetition worked just fine. I continued humming as I wrote the same grade on most of my sticky notes. I love writing 100%. I thought it looked better in red, but red was out and black was in.

Morning recess ended and my kids returned, still filled with buoyant good will, making me glad today's spelling assignment was short and I'd finished correcting all of them. Prior to handing them back, I said, "I have a new way of putting your grades on your papers. Derek thought you would like more privacy and we agreed that rather than writing on your papers, I'd use sticky notes and write how many you got right which is more important than the number of errors." Walking among my students as I handed back their work, I watched Derek from the corner of my eye and was delighted with his look of pleasure as he turned his sticky note over, and I knew I'd passed an important test. Some of the class looked puzzled, but pleased. I gave them a couple of minutes, then asked, "So, did Derek have a good idea or not?" The response was overwhelming—they loved it. More than one classmate called out, "Way to go, Derek."

"Teaching this class sure is easy," I thought. "Or maybe it's just that these kids are so much fun, they make it feel easy."

Later, while the first group of students clustered around the sink to wash for lunch, I walked over to Roger and rested my hand on his desk. He looked up and nodded that he remembered our meeting.

Finished eating and their desks cleared, my class tumbled out the door, eager to begin running, jumping or hanging from the monkey-bars. Some brought out jumping ropes, some headed for the baseball diamond and some started a game of tag before clearing the doorway.

Roger waited at his desk, watching me.

I walked to stand by his desk, his words, "Nobody listens to me," pricking my conscience at every step. Turning the seat from the desk in front of him, I sat down. "I remember what you said, Roger. And it was true, then, but it isn't now. Now, today, I want to listen to you.

"Why?" he asked.

Caught off guard, I knew my answer had to be the right one—chances for a 'do-over' were slim. I said, "Give me a couple of minutes, Roger, I'm not entirely sure how to answer that."

He gave a noncommittal shrug.

"I think," I said slowly, searching for what I hoped would be the right words, "that school has become your enemy. That you see us as always ignoring you and criticizing you, and when no one listens to you, you see this as proof you are right." I stopped.

Still wary, he dipped his head without answering. He raised his head, his look, direct and challenging.

"I am not your enemy, but you are the only who knows what I need to do to prove it to you. So if I listen, will you tell me what you want? How I can help you like being in school?" I shifted a fraction away from him, giving him space, but without losing eye contact.

Still wary, but I sensed less so, he leaned toward me. "I want someone to like me," he whispered. "Last year I had a friend. We were in the same class. His name is Petey. This year they put us in different rooms. I don't know why. We asked everybody to let us be together. Even our parents asked if we could have the same teacher. Now on the days one of us gets in trouble and has to stay in for recess I don't get to see him at all."

I waited, but he sat without speaking, misery in his eyes and sagging shoulders. Praying I could keep the ache in my throat under control, I broke the silence, "Is that it?"

"No!" Anger edged out the sadness. "I want the kids to stop making fun of me at recess. And I want the playground aides to listen to my side of it when I get in fights." Anger and sadness abated as he said, "I used to be glad when it rained, because we had to stay in for recess and Petey and I could play chess. And I liked lunch time because sometimes we could sit together to eat. But when we had to go outdoors, the other kids would pick on Petey because he's little, and when I got mad they told the playground aides, and they made me go to the principal's office. I really hate recess."

"You play chess?" I asked. After all he'd told me, I was startled that this was my initial reaction.

"Yes, and I'm good, too." A smile flickered as he said, "So is Petey. Sometimes he beats me, and sometimes I beat him. But neither of us ever gets mad. We just say, 'Good game.' and we play again."

My spirits lifted. I smelled peanut butter.

"You know, Roger, I think I might have a way for you to have lunch with Petey." I paused, "But it has a price tag. There are things I want, too." I gave him my 'go ahead, test me' smile.

"Like what?" he asked, curiosity overcoming wariness.

"It will be really tough. You know those passes all the teachers hand out as rewards for various things?"

"Yeah," he said unimpressed, unsure where this was going.

"You know they can be used for extra time in the library, or to work on a fun project. Sometimes the kids use these as lunch passes so they can go to another classroom to eat with their friends."

"Yeah, I know, but I never get one." He said this in matter of fact resignation.

"Would you like one?" I asked. "Or what if I changed one a little bit and asked Petey's teacher to let Petey use it to come here for lunch?" I knew Petey's teacher would be only too glad to send Petey to me rather than have me send Roger to her.

"You already know I'd like that." He looked at me with unveiled suspicion before adding, "But you didn't tell me what you want."

"How about that. OK, are you ready? Here's what I want. For you to earn a pass, you have to turn in every math paper, on time, with all mistakes corrected, for a week." I held my breath and waited.

Suspicious, he muttered, "That's it? Yeah, I guess I could do that."

"Good," I said, and smiled, "then it's a deal?" I paused before, like one of Columbo's afterthoughts, I added, "Of course, the following week you'd have to turn in all your math papers as well as your spelling assignments to get another one. Still interested?"

"You mean for a second pass I'd have to turn in a whole week of papers in two subjects?" Leaving nothing to chance, he was nailing down the details.

"That's right," I answered. "If eating with Petey is worth it to you." I stopped and put on an expression I hope looked like I was in deep thought before saying, "Of course, by the third week. . ." I never got to finish the thought. He'd found the hook in the peanut butter.

"OK, OK, OK, I get it. You're going to add science and social studies and everything, aren't you?" he demanded.

I flashed him my innocent look. "Well, it's what the other students are required to do."

He leaned back and laughed. "You're really cool," he said.

I joined him, laughing with relief and pleasure. If I'd won the Oscar, a pay raise and the Congressional Medal of Honor, I'd trade them all for those words. Well maybe not the pay raise.

Still laughing, I said, "Would you believe I have more?"

"Like what?" he asked. I was pleased his tone indicated more interest than wariness.

"Like, what if I give you permission to leave the playground and come into my classroom when you feel angry and want to fight someone?"

"Can you do that?"

"Well, it means I can't leave and go eat or be with my friends. I have to be in the room as long as you are. But on really bad days, you're worth it."

"I could clean the boards and empty the waste baskets," he offered. "Or I could just be real quiet and read. I love to read. I could play chess with you. Do you like to play chess?"

"No," I admitted, "I never learned, but if you were really quiet, you could bring Petey in with you sometimes, if you wanted to."

He sat a long time, staring into space. "You know what," he said, "I'll just start with the final deal."

It took me a moment to figure out what he was referring to. "You mean turn in all your assignments the first week?" I asked in astonishment.

"Why not?" He shrugged, enjoying the effect of his words, "I'm not stupid, you know. I just never thought it was worth it before."

Chapter Twenty

With Halloween over and Thanksgiving fast approaching, I had little patience for anything that pressured me, and I scowled at the dirty green pick-up truck tailgating me. "Get back, you moron," I ordered its reflection in my rear-view mirror. "I have better things to think about than you on my way to work." I flipped the mirror skyward, and voila! ugly pickup vanished. Too bad it wasn't that easy with Roark. When the harmony of *The Magic Flute,* floated from my radio, I sang along, paraphrasing Roger's "I'm not stupid as you know" to improve Mozart's "Let us hurry, let us run." Mozart might not have approved, but what the heck, he's dead and Roger isn't.

To the west, light from Boeing Field revealed the nearby area and flickers of low-flying planes, but little else. Only after I passed beyond its aurora, could I see the moon and stars still shared the distant sky. In the east, an ethereal silhouette of the Cascade Mountains rose as the sun's first rays gilded Mt. Rainier's peak and sent flashes of gold from the hood of my car. No fairyland could be more wonderful.

Soon I left the freeway and the obnoxious tailgater, to curve my way down the exit ramp, returning my mirror to its original position. Mozart's *Flute* ended and I turned the radio off. I needed to concentrate without distraction on a plan for my upcoming meeting with Derek. Most especially, I planned to tell him of the enthusiastic responses from the other teachers when they heard his sticky note idea. One suggested I inform the inventor of sticky notes of Derek's great idea. Most of us agreed there should be a required course for teachers called, *Respect for Students' Privacy 101*. But I probably wouldn't tell him how long it took me to realize I could save myself a lot of folding if I wrote on the sticky side to begin with.

A spatter of raindrops splashed across my windshield just as I coasted into the parking lot. What else would one expect in November in western Washington? Stepping out of my car, I opened my umbrella, spun it around over my head a couple of times and ascertaining I was alone, belted out, *"I'm singing in the rain..."* The really short version, since those were the only words I remembered. I hurried to the building, glad my umbrella protected my hair, but wishing it did as much for my shoes.

"Good morning, Mark," I said, flapping my purse in greeting as I passed him in the hallway. Since my car was the only one in the lot, other than Mark's pickup, and he seldom brought goodies, I saw no point in checking the lounge. From the well lit hallway, I took one step into the dark shadows of my room and quickly flipped the light switch. Hugging my thermos under my arm, I dropped everything else on my desk and opened the drapes to admit the weak gray light that barely penetrated the rain streaked windows.

Steadying my banged up thermos from its inclination to topple, I grimaced at the unappetizing dark brown scum covering the bottom of the cup I forgot to rinse out yesterday. Using only my index finger and thumb, I carried the disgusting thing to the sink and waited for what seemed like forever for the water to warm up. But even sipping coffee from the sanitized cup didn't relax me.

I picked up the list of supplies requested by Mrs. James who'd volunteered to design and create a new bulletin board display for me. I expected her shortly to discuss it with me. I'd admired the work she had done for other teachers in the past. Today I'd be the lucky one. Maybe she'd like me and come again. Maybe even on a regular basis. I could hope. To me, a dependable volunteer is a treasure on a par with the hot fudge on ice cream, and I loved hot fudge sundaes. I looked again at her list and left for the art supply closet. In its musty atmosphere, I gazed with longing at everything needed to create works of art, but, unless there was a package labeled *talent* on one of the shelves, not by me. With a sigh, I gathered the requested materials and left.

Through the open door to my classroom, I saw Mrs. James, her hands on her hips and her head tilted to the side, scrutinizing the bulletin boards. At her desk, Chris was stashing her books and supplies. With Chris's golden red curls and Mrs. James's auburn ones, no one could miss their obvious relationship. I was pleased they were early, giving us time to plan without interruption.

"Hi," I called, extending my hand, the one not holding the art supplies, toward Mrs. James.

Chris looked up with a smile and said, "Hi, Ms. McCall."

"Good morning," her mother said, taking my hand before reaching for the supplies. "When are you planning to have the kids make their stained glass designs?" she asked. "If it's today, I can go ahead with the bulletin board background for them this morning and start the designs this afternoon. Is that OK with you?"

"More than OK," I thought, but, "Yes, on both accounts," is what I said. "I plan to give you, and them, an hour and a half this afternoon."

Chris wiggled with excitement. "My mom's really good. She showed me how to do really pretty stained glass. But it's really silver foil and some clear plastic that I painted a design on."

"In that case, Chris, since you already know how to do it, would you consider being our assistant this afternoon?"

"I can do that. But I have a question. You said that if I brought a grown-up from home, and I did—I brought my mom—then I could eat lunch at the round table with my friends." She pointed to the round table at the back of the room that was used for projects and small group instruction. Without waiting for my response she added, "And you said if I brought a note I could have a cookie. She can write you a note now if you want her to." She looked from her mother to me.

"Bringing your mom, who also does bulletin boards, counts for both, Chris, especially if she stays and eats with you." I walked to my file cabinet for Chris's Oreo. "I'd love to have you stay, Mrs. James. Chris will enjoy introducing you to her best friends. Shall I order an adult lunch for you? It's the same as the one for the students, but twice as expensive, and unlike the kids', doesn't include milk. Coffee is in the lounge, and it's free." I was getting almost as good as my kids at getting a lot said in one breath.

"I accept, so I'd better get started," Mrs. James said, walking toward the nearest bulletin board.

"I have to go invite my friends," Chris called from halfway out the door, a small bit of chocolate at the corner of her mouth.

"Now I have a question," Mrs. James said, as the door slammed behind her daughter, "I don't understand what kind of note you want her to bring from home. She's asked me several times to write a note to you, but I have no idea what you want me to say."

I laughed. "I guess it does sound weird. It's something I thought up awhile back. So many parents are nervous or uncomfortable coming into the school, I was trying to find a way to make it easier." I paused, searching for the words to make myself clear. "I thought if they got in the habit of sending me little messages, like, "Hi, have a nice day," or "I'm not sure if you want me to help with this homework," or "I have no idea what this means," then dropping in might be the next step and it would be less formal than parent-teacher conferences. We'd get a chance to know each other a little. Does this make sense to you?"

Puzzled, Mrs. James asked, "Do you mean just send a note for no reason?"

"Exactly," I said. "And then I thought if parents dropped in at lunch time, they could eat with their kids and they could meet and see for themselves who their children's friends are. Kind of a bonus." I stopped.

"And let's not forget the bonus for you—you'd have the parents on your turf where you could ask them to be volunteers," she said with a sly smile that made me laugh. This woman was going to be fun and I looked forward to having her in my classroom.

"Maybe you didn't know this," I told her, "but the kids win, too. Having a parent in the classroom is a status thing at this grade level. And they like winning a cookie for bringing a note from home."

With a toss of her head that set her red curls bobbing, she whispered in mock awe, "Wow! A whole cookie." Laughing, she turned and ripped a long strip of green butcher paper off my less than lovely attempt at bulletin board design.

Recognizing a dismissal when I saw one, I said, "I'll be right here at my desk if you need me," and pulled a stack of the never-ending paper work toward me.

Mrs. James' presence in the classroom prompted some comments and speculation from my students when they entered. After they were seated, I said, "Chris, why don't you introduce your mother and tell the class why she's here."

Almost skipping to the front of the room, Chris faced her classmates and proudly announced, "This is my mother, Mrs. James. She's a really good artist and she's making a new bulletin board for the stained glass windows we're going to make this afternoon." Her brown eyes glowed and a huge grin nearly reached her ears, at the ensuing chorus of approval. Their curiosity satisfied, they settled down to begin work.

At noon, Mrs. James gathered up her materials and stood surveying her handiwork. On a background of blue, white clouds and snowflakes seemed to dance. I visualized how wonderful they would look when the kids' artwork was added. All I could say was, "It's beautiful. Thank you."

Almost before the last student finished washing up, the familiar squeaking of the wheels of the lunch cart announced it had begun its roll down the hall. After it stopped at two classrooms before ours, students who'd ordered hot lunches were lined up behind Joey Allendez, this week's designated milk monitor. He left the room first, and soon returned with a plastic serving tray holding small cartons of milk, which he placed on a front desk. The other students returned, carrying foil-covered metal TV trays emitting the aroma of pizza, and filed past Joey to pick up their milk. Chris returned with two lunches, handing one to her mother before picking up her milk and leading her mother to the round table. She introduced the four girls she'd honored with an invitation, among them Jody Kerr, whose attitude and behavior had greatly improved. I smiled, musing how some parents enliven a classroom by coming into it, others by staying out.

Even with all the giggling and the noisy conversations, the lunches got eaten. Chris's animation and bursts of laughter indicated she basked in the limelight of her mother's acceptance and popularity. Some of the boys at nearby desks turned their chairs so they could ask Mrs. James questions. The recess bell rang and within two minutes trash was in the garbage cans and desks were wiped. Chris gave her mother a quick hug and ran outside with her friends, leaving Mrs. James and me alone in the room.

"I really liked that," Mrs. James said. "I meant to leave earlier, but it was so much fun, I kept staying just a little bit longer." She looked again at the bulletin boards, satisfied with what she saw. "They came out well, don't you think?" she asked.

"They're great!" I said. "Thank you so much. I can hardly wait to see their artwork added this afternoon. I really hope you'll come back."

"I have to. The stained glass won't be ready to hang today and no one else is allowed to put the kids' work up. They might do it wrong. Besides, I have to call a few women I know. I'm afraid if I don't convince some of them to be volunteers, I'll be the only one on your list. And saying no is really hard for me." With a smile, she waved and hurried out.

Chapter Twenty One

Not much time remained of my lunch break, so I stuffed my purse under my arm and walked a little faster than usual to the lounge, hoping for something sweet to go with my coffee. What awaited me wasn't sweet. It was the intercom squawking, "Ms. McCall, please come to Mr. Roark's Office," before I got through the door.

"Oh crap!" I muttered *sottovoce*, "what does Hatchet Man want now?" I was pretty sure that whatever it was, it wasn't something I'd like. But, like an obedient minion, I about-faced and followed orders. From her desk, Marla shrugged and raised her eyebrows, waving me toward his open door. I scanned his office, about the size of a double-wide closet, or, more accurately, a double-long one, and equally inviting, As usual, the lamp that stood on Roark's desk was unlit, and the window above it was hidden by drawn drapes that matched the beige walls. Dim light from an overhead fixture revealed a middle-aged man in a gray suit next to a blond woman in a brown sweater, sitting stiffly next to Roark. Four chairs were arranged around the oval table that filled most of the space in his office. They sat in a row on the right facing an empty chair on the left.

Everyone looked at me without smiling as I waited in the doorway. When Roark pointed to the empty chair, I walked to it and sat. Breaking the silence, Roark said, "Ms. McCall, these are Mr. and Mrs. McGuire, Billy's parents." I nodded at them. My nod was not returned and I wondered why they were here and why they looked like the before picture in an ad for acid stomach remedies.

His face expressing the epitome of regretful disapproval and in a voice somewhere between that of a judge and an undertaker, Roark intoned, "Ms. McCall, you have been asked to come here so that I can inform you that Mr. and Mrs. McGuire have asked me to remove Billy from your classroom." He let this sink in before saying, "They and I agree that your unprofessional treatment of Billy caused him embarrassment and humiliation." Out of their line of vision, he flashed me the hooded triumphant look often associated with the twirling of a skinny black mustache. The McGuires appeared mesmerized by the grain of the oak veneer of the table.

"Unprofessional treatment?" I asked.

Ignoring my question, Roark said, "I sent a student runner to find Billy and tell him to come here so we can tell him what has been decided." I got the hooded look again.

The McGuires, who hadn't looked at me since I sat down, continued studying the table's veneer. Their preoccupation ended when, in his usual fashion, Billy burst into the office. Seeing his parents, he skidded to a stop and, a little louder than necessary said, "Hi, Mom, hi Dad. What are you doing here?" He looked around the table and added, "Hi, Ms. McCall."

I wondered if I was the only one who noticed he hadn't addressed Roark. I smiled at Billy, but remained silent.

Without preamble, Roark said, "Billy, we have decided you will not have to stay in Ms. McCall's class any longer. You are being transferred to Mr. Archer's class today."

"Huh?" Billy said. "How come?"

Roark must not have anticipated the question, because it was a moment before he answered, "Because she embarrassed you when you spilled the litter. She shouldn't have yelled at you."

"But I wasn't embarrassed, so I don't need to leave her class," Billie announced as if this settled the question. He looked from Roark to his parents. When no one responded, he took a John

Wayne stance, with his hands of his hips, and stated, "She's my favorite teacher, and I'm not leaving."

"But Billy, you told me she yelled at you. In front of everyone," his mother said.

"Yeah, I know. But I deserved to be yelled at. I made a mess." Having so informed them, he looked expectantly from one parent to the other, but they remained silent. "And I am not getting transferred," Billy repeated, with emphasis on the not.

His dad flashed a puzzled look at his mother, who shrugged.

In an attempt to regain control of the situation, Roark said, "You need to return to your classroom." He didn't look at me, but it was obvious whom he was addressing.

"Me, too?" Billy asked.

With a quick look at the McGuires, Roark nodded.

I didn't dare smile as I stood and, followed by Billy, strode from the room. "Who," I thought, "would have guessed Billie would be the one to take control of the situation? Sometimes he surprises me." We walked without speaking until, halfway down the hall, Billy stopped and tugged on my arm.

He looked sad, almost near tears. "I'm sorry Ms. McCall. I shouldn't have told them. Next time I won't."

Hugging students is a no-no, but giving them huge smiles isn't. Then, cognizant of possible future consequences, I said, "No, Billy, telling them was the right thing to do. It is always OK for you to tell your parents everything that happens to you. No one knows what may happen next time."

I hoped there wouldn't be a next time, at least not one involving me, but knowing Billy, all bets were off.

Chapter Twenty Two

Okay, just because I was born here and proud of being a Washingtonian didn't mean I didn't get tired of dull, damp, drizzle, especially after yesterday's meeting with Roark, et al. This morning I was more than tired of trucks throwing mucky water on my windshield, obliterating what little visibility I had in the predawn fog. Drained of energy and enthusiasm, I dragged myself from the parking lot, passed the uninviting lounge and pulled my classroom drapes aside. In true Western Washington fashion, everything had changed. Hardly able to breathe, I gazed in awe as the dreary rain-drenched world turned bright in the emerging sunrise. The wet gaunt branches of leafless trees shone as if polished, the chain link fence flashed silver, and matted clumps of grass rose out of the mud, washed and green. "What a great place to live," I thought. "How could anyone get tired of living here?"

As if presenting a slide show just for me, the rising sun threw shadow patterns around the room, before slowly filling the room with light, pale and still. Sounds from the playground and the hall brought me back into the waiting world. I reached for the math book and leafed through it. There was so much we'd covered. "How can Derek possibly catch up without missing anything of importance in the time we have left?" I so wanted him to succeed, but the reality left me dispirited.

I shoved the math book aside and reached for my empty cup, half filled it, and leaned back. Outside, it was still a nice day, as

November days go, but the glow was gone. With the hope that a change of scene might stimulate my creative thought processes, I picked up my purse, and left to find companionship and, if I was lucky, something to go with my coffee.

Vic stood blocking the door to the lounge, so I circled around him and made a bee-line toward the sprinkle of sugar sparkling on the one remaining cookie. Seeing John moving slowly toward it, I sprinted across the room, snatched it and shoved it toward, but unfortunately not in, my mouth. His howl of protest turned to howls of laughter when crumbs scattered over my face, in my nose, and across my blouse. I felt rewarded as I licked the few crumbs sticking to my lips. John, being John, forgave me. But it cost me two Oreos.

At the required five minutes before the bell, I gulped the last of my coffee, brushed any remaining cookie crumbs off my face and blouse and raced to my classroom. When I opened the door for my students I wasn't even breathing hard. I guess there's lots of energy in sugar cookie crumbs.

With the attendance taken, lunch orders tallied, and the class engaged in the board assignment, I reached for two unsealed envelopes lying on my desk. I laughed when I read the top one. "Dear Ms. McCall, Sarah insisted you wanted me to write you a note. I can't think of anything to say, but here it is. Sincerely, Mrs. Marston." I looked up and smiled at Sarah standing next to Kevin. The second note read, "Kevin says he'll get a cookie for this. Thank you. Mrs. Kwan." What a wonderful golden day this was. With both children watching for my reaction, I signaled them to come to my desk. "I love the notes your moms sent," I said, holding out the container of Oreos. My promise of a cookie in trade for un-required notes from home seemed to be catching on. These were the fourth and fifth notes this week. I reread them with pleasure, opened my desk drawer and added them to my growing stash. But my questions regarding Derek's math continued to plague me. An idea, an untested one, seemed possible, so I thought I'd suggest it.

When their lunch period ended, I waited until the door closed behind the last student before I turned to Derek. From the drinking fountain at the back of the room, he nodded at me and walked with smooth assurance toward my desk. I stared in surprise. It was as if he'd been reassembled. Both the slouch and the shambling gait were gone.

He caught me staring and smiled. "Is this where you want me to sit?" he asked, indicating the chair near my desk.

"Yes, here by my desk," I hoped I didn't look as dumbfounded as I felt. "Derek, I've been so pleased with the quality of work you've been turning in—especially in English and Social Studies. I've known from the start that you read at a very high level, but now you're conveying this in your written work."

He nodded, but didn't say anything.

"I'm concerned about your math, though. You're doing well in the current assignments, but there was a lot we covered earlier and it's possible there may be areas you missed." At his quizzical look, I added, "I'm referring to the concepts that may be unrelated to what we're doing now and I need confirmation you're familiar with them." I sighed. How had I let myself lapse into that pompous teacher jargon?

Was there just a hint of condescension when he asked, "Are you saying you want me to do all the problems I missed?"

I shuddered at the thought. "Absolutely not! That would be a horrible waste of both your time and mine. You'd be filling up pages and pages and I'd have to correct all those pages. I think there's a better solution."

Mimicking my shudder, he uttered a heartfelt, "Oh, good! Please elucidate."

"Elucidate?" I repeated, staring at him again. Was this the withdrawn monosyllabic boy of three months ago? The grin he couldn't hold back confirmed my suspicion that he'd deliberately thrown me off-guard.

"Fine. I shall now e-lu-ci-date," I replied, my pronunciation making us both laugh. "Ready?" I asked.

He nodded, but with some of the old wariness.

"What if," I began, "you start on math page one."

His wary look remained as I continued, "After you read the directions, you work a couple of problems. If they're easy and you understand what you're doing, you go on to the next page and do the same. You do this for no more than an hour or so a night until you're caught up." I paused, waiting for his response.

"You mean you only want me to do a few of the problems? Not all of them?" I could tell he was surprised—since he didn't use any words of more than two syllables.

"Right," I replied. "Just until you're sure you really understand them. Maybe four or five, however many it takes."

"Then what?" he asked.

"Then," I said, as if it were obvious, "every morning you come to class a few minutes early. I'll leave the teacher's manual on my desk and you use it to correct your work. You write *OK* or *Done* or something at the top of the page, put the papers in the book, and leave it on my desk and I'll record them in the grade book."

He thought about this a moment, then asked, "But what if I wasn't right? What if I made some mistakes?"

This kid leaves nothing to chance," I thought with satisfaction. "Well, if you made a mistake, it's up to you to figure out why and fix it before you leave it on my desk."

He still looked troubled. "Well, what if I can't figure it out? What if I just don't understand it? Then what?" Not waiting for an answer, he leaned forward, and said hesitantly, "I think maybe I have an idea."

"You do? What is it?" I asked, hoping it was the same one I had.

"Well, maybe, if it isn't too much bother, I could show you and ask you to help me, you know, to explain it." He looked at me, waiting.

I wanted to hug him. "What?" I asked. "You want me to earn what they pay me for being a teacher?" I laughed. "That's a great idea. That's the best idea yet. Then you fix it and leave it for me to record. That way all I have to put in the grade book will be marks to show you've understood and done the work." Oops, now I was the one who saw a small glitch. I asked him, "How do I let you know I've recorded a page? Could I put an OK at the top of the page if I do it lightly in pencil?"

To my great delight he flashed me another impish grin, "Yeah, I'd consider that within the realm of tolerance. An OK would be AOK," and joined me when I erupted in an unrestrained whoop of laughter. The three syllable words were back.

I looked beyond him and could swear the noonday sun had cast another mantle of gold across my world.

Chapter Twenty Three

Since becoming road-kill was not on my to-do list, I had to drive with more care than usual. I hunched over the steering wheel, squinting through a windshield smeared with rain and highway gunk being slapped back and forth by the wipers. Oily pools of water left by two days of nonstop November rain made the early morning darkness especially treacherous. Ever the optimist, I pushed the button that squirted solution onto the windshield, and watched the wipers swipe it through the ooze with little effect. Any hope for a glimpse of my mountain I knew was unrealistic. "Oh, well," I thought, "tomorrow is another day. Muck is temporary, the mountain is forever."

"I could make that into a song," I thought. "Muck comes, muck goes, muck is forgotten. The mountain waits." I thought about that for a minute before adding, "Sunlight comes, sunlight goes. Sunlight is remembered. The mountain waits." This led to the happy thought that since the Billy McGuire incident, Roark seemed to have forgotten about me. Maybe his attacks had come and now were gone. I knocked on wood. Since the dashboard was faux wood, I added an extra knock.

It must have worked, because my parking space was available. "I'm happy and I intend to enjoy every second of my *joie de vivre*, therefore any thoughts of Roark are hereby relegated to oblivion," and with a defiant head toss, I left the car. I had no trouble protecting my hair, but holding my umbrella so it sheltered my usual supplies and my good shoes balanced on top of them as well, took some doing. Satisfied everything balanced, I sloshed and splashed and stomped through every puddle between me and the entrance, thoroughly soaking my beat-up old Keds of summer. Opening the door, I tossed my umbrella in and quickly followed it.

Before the door closed, Roark's icily precise voice fractured my euphoria. "BJ, come to my office at 8:30 this morning." It was an order, not a request. Startled at his unexpected appearance in the entry way, I jumped, dropping everything: papers, purse, lunch, thermos and shoes. Squatting, I closed my umbrella, gathered everything up and stood, struggling to regain some semblance of dignity. Roark was gone, a clear indication there'd be no explanation. I didn't move until the staccato clicking of his heels on the tile floor died away and the empty halls were silent.

"Well," I thought, "if he can make my *joie de vivre* pass, then I can make his *mal de vivre* pass, and I don't care if there isn't any such phrase. I know what I mean." But the apprehension creeping over me did not pass. I tried repeating, "Roark's *mal de vivre* shall also pass. Roark's *mal de vivre* shall also pass." It was fruitless. I had the words and the rhythm, but there wasn't any music. I squished my way to my classroom, hearing only the faint, sodden squeak of my rubber-soled shoes on the tile floor, kind of wishing they'd make an echo.

My room smelled musty and the air felt dank and cold. Warmth would come when the furnace fired to life. I opened the drapes to the still dark sky, looking for signs of daylight, but knowing that for three more months the dark would linger a little longer each day. With a soft hiss the radiators began to warm and I forgot the dark and remembered summer would return. At my desk, I bent to exchange my sodden tennis shoes for the black leather ones that were more appropriate with my navy blue Nordstrom's pants suit.

"Why does Roark want me in his office?" I wondered, automatically organizing the stacks of corrected papers waiting to be entered in the grade book. "Probably nothing. Could be just a follow-up of my evaluation." I picked up a pen, and laid it back down. "Get real. I've already had my evaluation follow-up and this obsessing isn't getting me anywhere." I poured some coffee. As the hot liquid warmed my hands and relaxed my throat, I reached for the pen. Although several papers remained in the stack, I set them aside and my reviewed the plans for the day. At 8:29 I considered taking my remaining quarter cup of coffee with me, but it was cold, so, taking only my purse, I left.

"Hey, hey, hey, good buddy, BJ," John called out as I opened my door. "How do you like my new shirt?"

I struggled to respond with enthusiasm. "It's a lovely shade of red—very similar to the one you wore last week."

"I know. My wife had to really search for one she knew I'd like." He winked at me, and with his infectious laugh, asked, "So, where are you headed? No point in going to the lounge. I just left there and no one brought treats."

"What? No treats?" I struck my forehead in mock tragedy. Then shrugged and as nonchalantly as possible added, "Gotta see Hatchet Man—orders."

John's smile disappeared. "Oh." His one word response told me he understood. "I'll look for you at morning break." He lifted his hand in a half wave as I walked past him toward the office. Along the way I smiled and responded to everyone I met, but made no further stops until I entered Roark's outer lair.

"He's waiting for you," Marla said, putting her hand over the phone she held to her ear, and nodding toward Roark's office.

"Thanks, Marla," I said. Since his door was open, I knew he heard us, so I waited a moment before knocking on the frame. Seated at his desk, he did not look up from the papers in front of him as he said, "Come in and shut the door." It was an order, not an invitation.

I followed his instructions, but for a moment I kept hold of the handle. "Good morn. . ." I began.

"Sit there," he interrupted, pointing at the chair opposite him.

I perched on the edge of the chair, hugging my purse like a shield, between us. "You asked me. . ." I began.

"You're here," he interrupted in a voice as stony as his face, "because I'm not pleased with your teaching."

Speechless, I sat staring at him. He remained silent, watching me. After what seemed like forever, I regained my voice and choked out, "You're not? In what. . .?"

"Your humor is inappropriate. You think you're being funny, but you're not."

The direction of his attack was so unexpected, I had trouble processing it. "I don't understand. Are you referring to my teaching or my personality? Has someone compl. . .?"

"You are being deliberately obtuse." His voice, while remaining low, became sarcastic. "You need to reevaluate your classroom demeanor as well as your teaching methods."

"My teaching methods? What methods are you referring to?" I asked, unable to make sense of what he was saying.

"Just what I said," he replied as if talking to an obstinate four-year old. "You need to upgrade your teaching strategies and take a good look at your infantile sense of humor."

Embarrassment competed with frustration. When a sudden fiery heat swept through me, making my face flush and tears sting my eyes, I gritted my teeth. No way was I going to let him undermine my self-control. With rigid determination, I kept my voice neutral. "I don't know exactly what you mean by upgrading my teaching strategies. What is it you. . .?"

He rose slowly, splaying his hands on his desk for balance as he bent toward me. "Since you said you don't know what I mean, it's obvious you either need to pay closer attention, or, worse, realize you're in the wrong profession." He stopped.

Stunned, I groped blindly in my purse for a tissue to blot my running nose.

The morning bell sounded, followed by the clamor of slamming doors, footsteps pounding on the tile floors and voices echoing in the hollow halls. "You should be in your classroom." Roark pointed to the door, dismissing me.

My face flaming, my emotions in turmoil and with no idea what Roark was demanding, I left. "Well," I thought as I approached my classroom, "at least that, whatever it was, is over." I took several deep breaths wishing I had time to go to the restroom and splash my face with cold water.

My perceptive class knew instantly that all was not well, and responded by being so well behaved it was scary. Nearly an hour passed before my face cooled, my eyes quit smarting, and my nose quit running. By then my class had shed their perfection routine and returned to normal—good but no longer perfect.

That night my own kids were equally perceptive. Without a word they headed for the great outdoors with Laddie after my purse flew across my bedroom followed by my shoes, both pairs. Only Lissa, carrying four jackets, remained when I stormed to the kitchen, but when the cast iron skillet slammed onto the stove, I heard the door click shut behind her, too. I hadn't yelled at any of them, but they weren't in any big hurry to find out why I was so steamed. They preferred to let me do my venting on the potatoes and hamburger patties.

Chapter Twenty Four

The following morning I drove to work on autopilot, oblivious to the weather, the traffic or my mountain. I dreaded going to work, dreaded running into Roark, dreaded a day of spinning my wheels wondering what Roark's agenda was and what he planned next.

Even so, I wasn't prepared to find him waiting for me in the hall, exactly as before. I felt trapped in a rerun of a bad movie when he ordered me to be in his office at 8:30, turned and exited left.

"What next?" I fumed. I contemplated pitching my thermos at his door, but doubted it would survive many more dents. Besides, what had my thermos ever done to me? When my attempt to stomp loudly down the hall was thwarted by my soggy Keds making gentle squish, squish, squish sounds, I accepted that this definitely was not an auspicious beginning to a great day.

Outside it was still dark when I yanked the classroom drapes open and I was confronted by the distorted reflection of my angry face in the rain streaked window. With a shudder, I turned to glare at the clock. "Well," I thought, " I've got an hour and a half before my meeting with Hatchet Man and I don't intend to sit here mooning about it." I straightened my spine, took a deep breath, picked up my pen and began putting the names and dates on the progress reports I sent home with each student every Friday. Names and dates I could do from memory. The comments took a little longer.

I struggled to keep a tight rein on my thoughts, but still, like the wings of a vampire bat, the question returned, "What does Roark want now?" It beat in ceaseless circles in my mind until my head felt bruised and sore. I rubbed my temples, hoping to fend off an incipient headache until, recognizing defeat, I reached for the aspirin in my purse, but changed my mind, reaching instead for my thermos. Soon my throat muscles relaxed, the vampire bat slowed down, and with a second half cup, life seemed to grow brighter. Leaning back, I cradled the warm cup in both hands and closed my eyes. Without warning, tears began trickling down my cheeks and dripping onto my blouse.

I jerked upright. "What is the matter with me? No way is Hatchet Man going to make me cry!" I shook my head, fighting for self control. I gulped the last of my coffee and snatched up my pen. But everything blurred and swam about. I dropped the pen and laid my head on my arms. "I'm scared," I realized with surprise. "But why? Roark's not liking me isn't reason enough to be scared. He's never liked me, and that's never scared me before." I raised my head and stared numbly at a bleak gray dawn. And then it hit me. The memory of Roark's escalating attacks on Edna sent a burning itch down my spine followed by a sharp cramp that had me running for the restroom.

When I returned, it was 8:28, time to meet with Roark. I swung my purse over my shoulder, closed the door to my room quietly, and still shaky, walked to his office, relieved not to meet anyone along the way.

I nodded silently to Marla and stood waiting at Roark's open door. He let me wait. When he figured enough time elapsed, he looked up, said nothing, just pointed to the empty chair. I shut the door, walked with military precision to the chair and without a word, sat, hugging my purse.

After a minute or two, he asked, "Do you know why I told you to be here this morning?" He sounded like a TV cop.

"No," I replied, deliberately brief. It's hard to interrupt a single syllable answer.

"I should think it would be clear, even to you, after your evaluation. Or maybe you didn't understand it." His tone as insulting as his words.

"I asked you for clarification on why my evaluations weren't better, but you. . ."

He cut me off. "You asked for examples of what I considered needed improvement. I'm not required to give you examples. I told you that you needed to improve. I do not consider you an outstanding teacher in any way. It is up to you to bring your teaching up to higher standards. It is my job to see that only outstanding teachers remain in the profession."

It was out in the open. He intended to destroy my career. A long silence ensued, our body language making our mutual hostility evident.

As the shrill of the morning bell subsided he ordered, "Be here again tomorrow at 8:30," and, like yesterday, pointed to the door.

It was time for plan B. On my lunch break, with the door to the empty nurse's office closed, I telephoned my brothers' law office and asked which of them would be available to see me that night after school.

.

Chapter Twenty Five

That afternoon as the last student left, I hurried to the office to call home before driving to meet my brothers. After two rings, Lissa answered. "Honey, it's Mom," I said.

"Oh, hi, Mom. Is something wrong?" she asked. I seldom called home from work, so her concern was normal.

"No, not really, but I may be a little late. I have to see your uncles before I come home and I didn't want you to worry."

"Does that mean I have to fix dinner?" she asked with just a touch of hostility.

Thinking fast I said, "Oh, no. I won't be too terribly late, so if you can hold out, I'll pick up hamburgers and stuff on my way home. You can all snack on peanut butter and crackers if you like."

"Cal's is almost gone. Do we have to share ours with him? We don't have a whole lot left, either."

What I'd thought would be a quick FYI home was turning into a contract negotiation. "Why not take out enough for the three of you and hand the rest of the jar to Cal. I'll stop and pick up two new jars on the way home. OK?"

"Yeah, I guess." She heaved a loud martyred sigh.

"Bye, I love you," I said before she added more perks.

"Yeah, bye, love you, too," she said.

I hung up, thanked Marla, waved goodbye and ran to my car.

Traffic was light until I reached the jam-packed on-ramp to the freeway. Finally reaching the head of the line, like a bird of prey,

I waited for a slow-moving driver I could swoop in front of, and join the vehicles that, like a flock of geese, were honking their way north. Ever the optimist, I hoped I'd reach the law office shared by my brothers before dark. I didn't. I parked under a light, noted my gas gauge hovered just above empty, so I scribbled "gas" on a sticky note and stuck it on the dash board.

My stiff cramped muscles creaked as I unwound myself from behind the wheel and as I opened the door, heard the muted sounds of distant traffic. The cool air felt good as I stretched and took several deep breaths, waiting for my eyes to adjust so I could look around carefully before crossing to the building. Once inside, I saw them waiting at the second floor landing. "Are you all right?" they asked in unison.

"Well, yes and no," I answered as I climbed. "Physically, I'm fine. Mentally I'm a mess."

"Well, if that's all, then I'm leaving. Unless you need both of us, I have a client I've already kept waiting," my younger brother, Jason, said, pulling on his coat.

"Go, go. Nobody needs two lawyers." I laughed and nudged him toward the stairs.

When the outer door closed, my brother Norman and I walked to his desk and before my butt hit the seat I blurted out, "I didn't mean to frighten you and I know I probably sounded melodramatic, but the truth is, I'm scared and I don't know what to do next. Roark is trying to fire me." I stopped because I ran out of breath.

"Slow down, BJ," he cut in quickly, "and tell me what he's done to make you think so." He sounded just like a lawyer. Irritating, but probably a good thing.

"He harasses me. Every day. And makes me cry and I hate him!"

"You say he harasses you," my brother said in his calm lawyer voice. "What exactly does he do?"

I described the encounters as chronologically and unemotionally as I could. That is, I kept my voice under control, but I'd have had to tie my arms down to stop their waving about. My brother, the lawyer, listened, jotting a few notes as I talked. "And," I finished, "he told me to be in his office at 8:30 again tomorrow."

He nodded. "I agree, this does sound like harassment. Now what we need to do is devise a plan to stop him. Our counter-offensive, you might say."

"And then I want to sue him and I want him fired," I said getting mad all over again.

"Um hum. I understand. Suing him would make you feel better. But it could be difficult," the lawyer who used to be my brother said. "If we take him to court, it comes down to he said/she said testimony, and judges tend to give extra credence to the administrator."

"So what do I do? Just let him harass me until I have a nervous breakdown?" I howled.

"Well, if you could stand not suing him," he grinned at me, "and you'd settle for making him stop, I think we have a chance for success." The grin widened into the wicked smile I'd seen as a teen-ager—the one that preceded his practical jokes. I should have guessed years ago he'd become a lawyer. "So," he said, "I'll leave it up to you: sue him or stop him. Your call."

I was still mad and the idea of attacking and suing Roark felt really good. But the less volatile, more intellectual side of my brain realized that this was probably not the better option. As my brother's devilish grin returned, I felt a twinge of pity for Roark— just a small one. But it didn't last long.

"OK," I conceded, not too graciously, "so what's plan B?"

"As I see it, your real problem is the secrecy he's established. He's gambling on a 'he said/you said,' situation and thinks he holds all the cards."

"Right," I agreed. "So?"

"So that makes the solution easy: you don't fold, you raise and call him, after we put just one more chip in the pot." He flashed me a wolfish smile. "You've always been good at improvisation—here's your chance to see just how good you are."

When I heard his plan, a momentary wave of sympathy for Roark returned. But it passed quickly.

Chapter Twenty Six

On the surface, all was as usual this Wednesday morning. I arrived. Roark pointed. I sat. Beneath the surface, all was not as usual: I was no longer terrified.

"I assume you have been working on improving your skills," Roark said, with more than a touch of irony.

Resisting the impulse to say, "You've no idea," I held my purse closer and politely answered, "No, not really, since I still don't know exactly what it is you want from me."

"Must you always pretend ignorance?" he asked. The irony had escalated to sarcasm.

"But I am ignorant. I have no idea what you are talking about. I've asked you repeatedly for specific ways in which you think I need to improve and you won't tell me." It wasn't easy, but I kept my voice neutral, not whiny or accusing.

"You're an adult. Figure it out." He kept his voice too low for it to carry beyond his office.

I was sure this was how he wore Edna down—repetition, sarcasm and secrecy, chipping away her confidence and dignity.

"I'm sorry. I just don't know where to begin." I sat up straighter, holding my purse close to my chest like a shield, and initiating eye contact. "In fact, I'm beginning to suspect these morning discussions are more harassment than attempts to improve my teaching," I said, raising my voice.

He looked as if his trained poodle suddenly bit him. After all, I'd never challenged him before, at least not since the first day. As far as I knew, no one had. Certainly not Edna.

"Yes," I said, "I think maybe I should call the union rep and ask his advice."

"Please. Do that," Roark said. "What are you going to tell him? That your principal doesn't think you're performing adequately? That he's been trying to help you improve your performance? That you can't handle criticism?"

"How are you trying to improve my performance? All you've done is say I need to improve, but when I ask for specifics you tell me to figure it out. You've done this for three days and so far you've given me nothing to begin working on. You don't like my sense of humor. What has that to do with being a good teacher?"

"I warned you a long time ago that not cooperating with a principal was foolhardy. You laugh at inappropriate times. You ignored my opinion that reading aloud to fifth graders was unnecessary." His voice dropped, "I do not like you. Maybe now you're beginning to see what that can mean."

"Are you saying that all of this is retaliation rather than attempts to improve my teaching?" I asked, my voice rising in astonishment. "That it really is harassment?"

"Is that how you see it? As I see it, I'm a conscientious principal trying to help an inadequate teacher improve." The sarcasm in his voice was loud and clear.

Whatever he might have added was drowned out by the morning bell. For the first time he held the door for me, indicating I should leave. Above the clamor of the students, he said, "Tomorrow, 8:30."

Still holding my purse tight against my chest, I faced him. "Whatever you say," I said in my sweetest voice, smiled warmly at Marla, and left the office.

My footsteps were the only sound in the now empty hallway. I stopped outside my closed classroom door long enough to remove the tiny tape recorder in my purse and turn it off. With a smile, I returned it to my purse and with a new lightness in my step, entered the room.

Chapter Twenty Seven

Thursday morning there was no mist and no rain. It was cold, but not cold enough to wear a jacket, so I left mine in the back seat. Soon my tail lights joined the glittering ruby line snake-dancing its way south.

Above, the full moon outshining the stars, briefly backlit a spiky row of trees on a nearby hill before creating a glowing halo above Mt. Rainier. When the freeway curved, both mountain and moon disappeared.

Seeing only Mark's old pickup in the parking lot, I laughed out loud as I scooped up my jacket along with my usual paraphernalia. It was a lovely day. Although the rumble of the furnace was unmistakable, my room was still a few degrees below comfortable, so I put my jacket over my shoulders. By the time I finished the Friday reports to parents, fleshed out my lesson plans for the following week and set out the paints and supplies for the afternoon craft project, it was a little after eight and the building was warm, so I transferred my jacket to the back of my chair. Seeking something sweet to go with my coffee, the lounge seemed a likely destination. The closer I got, the faster I walked. John stood at the door, holding out a sticky lemon bar on a napkin. "Your favorite," he said, grinning.

"Have you been waiting long?" I asked licking the powdered sugar off the top, any good intention of nibbling slowly instantly gone. "I don't know which is sweeter, you or the lemon bar," I said, looking hopefully to see if there were more on the table. There were.

John laughed, "You look perkier today, and that powdered sugar on your chin is so *tres chic*." Lowering his voice he asked, "Are you meeting with Roark this morning?"

His concern nearly brought me to tears. Afraid of embarrassing both of us, I gave a forced laugh and attempted my mysterious smile, the one that Ethel says reminds her of Alice's Cheshire Cat with gas, and said, "He ordered me to, but—maybe. Maybe not. Time will tell. By the way, would you like to see the gift my brother gave me a couple of days ago?"

Without waiting for an answer, I lifted out the tiny tape recorder running in my purse.. "You'll never believe how powerful this thing is," I said, turning the volume to high. "Just listen to this." Several teachers standing nearby stopped talking as they recognized their voices.

"Isn't this a remarkable little machine? It's hard to believe how well it tapes through my purse. My brother gave it to me with two tapes, but I left the other one home today." John seemed to be speechless. I looked around the room, but no one was in a talkative mood. Some of them even left. After a few minutes I said, "Well, guess I'd better go—it's 8:30. Time to go see Roark." I put the recorder back in my purse. From some of their less than appreciative looks, I figured it might be in my best interests to let them watch me erase the tape during mid-morning break. I wondered who, if anyone, had reported to Roark.

A puzzled Marla stopped me as I entered the outer office. "BJ, Rick said to tell you he has a meeting this morning and won't be able to meet with you."

"Thanks, Marla," I said, awed at how fast news traveled. I smiled nonchalantly at her from the door and hurried back to the lounge. Maybe there would be some lemon bars left. There were. Well, actually there was one on the plate John held toward me. "Want half?" I asked.

Always the gentleman, John shook his head and waited until I'd swallowed the last bite before demanding, "OK, BJ, what going on?"

I scanned the almost, but not quite, empty room. "I'll tell you about it later, John, I promise, but not in here. Have you seen Ethel this morning?"

"She was here, but stayed just long enough to get a lemon bar, saying she had too much to do."

"Thanks, John, I need to see her before school starts." I smiled, looked hopefully at the empty plate, but it remained empty, so I left.

Ethel's door was closed. A good thing, judging by the reek of poster paint, glue and enamel that nearly asphyxiated me when I opened it. Along the wall were a few cornstalks and scarecrows left over from Halloween, but no Pilgrims, Indians or Mayflowers yet. Ethel was at her desk, the only one in the room not covered by a turkey with a glorious tail. With their poster paint still wet, turkeys were spread out everywhere—on counters, on window ledges and on the floor, everywhere except for a zigzag path from Ethel's desk to the door. I remembered tracing around my spread out fingers to create turkey tails in kindergarten.

"Hey, Ethel, your kids really dig holidays," I called from her doorway, not yet sure it was safe to enter.

"You spoke?" Ethel asked, looking up from the stacks of magazines on her desk.

"Yeah, but I don't want to interrupt your reading."

"Feel free." She sighed. "I'm just going through the magazines the kids brought for the collage we're working on. I go through them very carefully these days." She gave a rueful half laugh. "Ever since one of my boys brought in an armload of his dad's *Playboys* and I didn't realize it until I looked over his shoulder at the centerfold he was pasting on his page. We were making an alphabet book and he was on the letter N."

"Oh, no, what did you do?" I asked, stepping with great care along the path through the art work to her desk. I picked up some magazines and flipped through them. No *Playboys*. Darn. But a

Cosmopolitan looked promising. I'd heard it was the female answer to *Playboy*.

Ethel grinned, retrieved the magazines I'd scooped up, including the *Cosmopolitan,* and shoved them out of my reach. "Well," she said, "as you can imagine, not a lot of options presented themselves, so very casually, I said, That's very interesting, Jonathan. What in your picture starts with the letter N? and he looked at me as if I weren't quite bright and answered, *Navel, of course.* "

We laughed. Nothing pulls you up short like a literal kid.

Still laughing, Ethel shook her head and added, "The worst part was when I met with his mother and told her these were inappropriate for her to have sent and handed her the ragged remains of what was left. She looked stunned, and when she got her voice back, she told me her husband had collected every issue of *Playboy Magazine* and, because there were none missing, was convinced they were quite valuable.

As a parent, I empathized, but couldn't help laughing. "Anyone who thinks teaching is dull has never spent time in a kindergarten class. But I am here on serious business, Ethel. I want to invite you to go for our monthly dinner, but a week early—like tonight. Dutch treat," I hastened to add, lest she get the wrong idea. "Can you make it?"

Pulling her calendar toward her, she studied it a moment. "You're in luck. The mayor and the governor just canceled on me and the night is open. You're on. Where do you want to go?"

I'd already looked through my two-fers and held up the one I liked best. "How does this seafood restaurant, *The Clam Shell*, look to you? Everyone's been raving about it."

"Sounds fishy to me," she said, ignoring the coupon. I gave her the requisite groan, muttered, "Reservations at five OK?" and left when she nodded.

⌇◎◎⌇

While we waited to be shown to a table, we read the specials posted on the wall above the reservation desk, so by the time we sank into the well padded leather chairs by the window overlooking Puget Sound, we were ready. I looked out over the water, and, mesmerized by its darkening shades of blue, its whitecaps flashing in the sunset's final rays, I lost track of time or place.

"Earth to BJ. Earth to BJ. You're not alone at this table." Ethel's unexpected bad imitation of a robot snapped me back to the present and made me laugh, slightly louder than was lady-like. A staid waiter silently flicked a napkin into each of our laps before standing two attached planks of brown wood encasing the menus on the table in front of each of us. Mine had a carving of a fish on it.

"Ethel," I asked, "what does this carving look like to you?"

"Hmmm," she hmmed judiciously, staring at it, "I would say it is a salmon leaping over a clamshell. Yes, I'm sure that's what it is." Laying hers on the table, she studied it, squinting and turning her head from side to side, before proclaiming pompously, "Mine is a whale leaping over a clamshell. I do believe we have entered the training arena of the aquatic circus performers."

"You know what, Ethel, without the carving, these look just like the planks of cedar the man in the fish market sold me to grill salmon on."

"You know better than to end a sentence with a preposition," she admonished as she flipped her planks open and exclaimed, "Oh, look! This menu must have a dozen pages. You know, if it said entries instead of entrees I'd think it was the Seattle phone directory."

I laughed, tickled by her exaggeration. "Oh, Ethel, I'm so glad you're here."

"Fine. Now I expect you to tell me what is going on." Ethel kept her priorities straight..

I wondered if I should point out she'd just ended her sentence with a preposition. Probably not. Instead, I said, "I will. I promise, but let's eat first." Just then I caught the fragrance of burning maple logs and looked toward a massive stone fireplace at the end of the room. Its flames lit the rough textured cedar walls and cast flickering shadows among the high roof beams. "Oh, Ethel, don't you love the way a fire brings life as well as warmth to a room?"

A big sigh told me Ethel figured it was time to stop talking and order. Her sigh hadn't escaped the notice of the waiter, either, who now stood next to her, pencil and pad in hand. We skipped cocktails and salads and went straight to a house specialty, oyster bisque, and gave him our entrée choices. Silent as Carl Sandburg's fog, he soon returned, placing a royal blue bowl before each of us so deftly there was no disturbance of their creamy contents. "A toast, Ethel, to a good future, good friends and good food." I raised my water goblet. We clinked and sipped, savoring the flavor of local water, lightly iced and with just a hint of lemon. The perfect vintage with oyster bisque.

After removing our empty bowls and refilling our water goblets, the waiter set a warm blend of melted butter, garlic, wine, and a bunch of herbs I couldn't identify alongside my bucket of steamed clams. When he set a basket of warm, crusty sour dough bread on the table near me, I lifted the napkin covering it, releasing a tantalizing aroma. I broke off a chunk and dipped it in the nectar in the bottom of my bowl. One chunk followed another, until even Ethel's share, was gone. "It was her own fault," I rationalized, "she eats too slow."

Ethel, slowly savoring every bite of her sole almandine, finally finished. She studied the empty bread basket, cocked one eyebrow, and asked, "BJ, would you like some of my bread?"

"Thank you, no, I've had enough," I answered sweetly. "I'm ready for dessert." Before she could respond, our attentive waiter placed a fresh basket of bread on the table next to Ethel and out of my reach.

Our dinners tonight tallied slightly less than those on our previous night out, so with reckless abandon, Ethel ordered tea and I had coffee with our raspberry cheesecake. Between taking dainty bites and tiny sips, we prolonged as long as possible this caffeinated and calorie laden heaven. I gazed so hopefully at my plate on which not a crumb remained, that Ethel, afraid I might pick it up and lick it, signaled the waiter to remove it.

"OK," she demanded, leaning toward me. "You've been up to something, and I want to know what it is."

She's not only perceptive, she's intimidating and I figured I'd better start talking.

"Once upon a time a wicked ogre set out to destroy an innocent young maiden," I began.

"Cut to the chase, not so innocent young maiden," Ethel interrupted. "Not so young, either," she added.

Put that way, it seemed like a good idea to forget the embellishments. "You want just the facts, Ma'am, just the facts? So, OK. Do you remember a couple of years back when the teachers were eating lunch in the lounge and someone sneaked in and stole a bunch of purses out of their desks?" She nodded, but her expression said to get on with it, so I said, "I guess in a way, I should thank that thief. I was so psyched, I started hauling my purse with me all the time."

Ethel gave a sudden snort of laughter.

"What's so funny?" I demanded, miffed at the interruption of my enthralling tale.

Still laughing, she answered, "It's been kind of a faculty joke—BJ and her ubiquitous purse."

"Well, it paid off." I told her of my meeting with Roark with the tape recorder in my purse. "And it paid off, not only yesterday, but you may have noticed," I paused before adding haughtily, "*my* purse has never been stolen."

Suddenly serious, Ethel leaned across the table to lay her hand on my arm. "BJ, you got lucky this time. But it wouldn't hurt to walk softly and watch your back. Roark doesn't like to lose. He doesn't like you. And he really won't like losing to you. Just because he lost this round, don't count him out."

Chapter Twenty Eight

"Come on, come on, come on," I prodded Cabot, although I knew from long experience that telling Cabot to hurry was about as effective as telling repairmen what time to arrive.

"I'm going as fast as I can," he called from his room where he was searching for his hiking boots.

"Cabot. . ." I yelled again, louder.

"OK. OK. I found them," he interrupted without leaving his room.

"You can put them on in the car, just get out here." My frustration was reaching boil-over level. The first snow of the season fell during the night, and I anticipated a commute filled with black ice, inexperienced drivers and idiots fish-tailing on their bald tires. But all those goodies had to wait until I dropped Cabot off at his school. He'd barely recovered from a nasty cold and a relapse meant he'd be out of class for another week and I didn't want to risk a long wait for the school bus.

"No, I can't. I'll get my socks wet," he yelled back. Seconds later he clonked out to the entryway. "But I'll wait to till I'm in the car to tie them." He smiled tentatively, hoping his compromise would defuse me. It did.

I handed him his favorite winter jacket, the dark green one with a hood, and waited while he zipped it up before I handed him his lunch and black ski gloves. "I can't put my gloves on until I tie my boots," he said, opening the door and letting in a gust of icy air. It remained open as he raced Laddie out to the snow.

"Make sure Risa zips her jacket," I told Lissa, hugging each of them before descending with care the two slippery steps to where Cabot was doing some kind of snow dance in the driveway with the dog. One look at my expression and Cabot scooted into the car while Laddie made a beeline for the house before the door closed. I made the covered bowl of sugared nuts as secure as possible on the backseat before I tossed my jacket alongside it, followed by my purse and lunch. I put the thermos on the floor.

The wind whipping through the carport tore through my wool pantsuit and I jumped into the driver's seat and started the engine before checking Cabot's seatbelt or fastening mine. I backed up the 50 foot driveway slowly, leaving deep tracks in the pristine snow and checking the brakes twice to assess the traction. At the street, I shifted into second gear, turned the heater to high, and was relieved to see tire tracks all the way to the top of the hill.

"Hey, Cabot, look at those tracks," I said, "if someone else made it, I can, too. Piece of cake. All the manuals say I just have to keep the acceleration steady."

He gave me a quizzical look, tightened his seatbelt, and said nothing as we started up the hill.

Whenever my new snow tires lost traction or slithered on a patch of ice, I maintained a constant acceleration. With only a half a dozen or so such episodes, we reached the top. I laughed exultantly. "See? I told you that whatever someone else can do, I can do!"

"Mom," he said gently, "I didn't want to tell you this sooner, but those tire tracks were on the other side of the street, so I think that other car was going down the hill."

I looked back. He was right.

Snow filled and obliterated the edges of the drainage ditches that bordered the narrow road to his school. Unwilling to find myself nose down in one of them, I drove slowly, leaving lots of distance between me and the car ahead. I eased to a stop behind three other cars when an approaching school bus, followed by a long line of cars, turned on its warning flashers as it slowed. In my mirror I saw another long line of cars behind me. Ahead, in the safety zone on my left, a group of children waited, huddled against the cold.

Cheering, they inched forward, impatient for the bus to come to a full stop and open its doors. I stared in stunned disbelief when a gray pick-up abruptly pulled out of the long line of cars behind the bus and used the safety zone as a passing lane. The bus's door opened and the kids surged forward, scrambling up its steps to safety.

Reflexively, I yanked the steering wheel hard left, and slid, almost in a skid, across the center line, barely missing the front of the bus, and stopped, nose to nose with the pick-up just beyond the spot where the children had been seconds earlier. The scowl that replaced the shocked expression of the pick-up's driver indicated he was less than delighted to see me.

I looked up through the windshield of the bus just as the driver put a notebook into the breast pocket of her uniform and I assumed she had the license number she needed. With a huge grin she gave me a one-handed thumbs up as she turned off the warning lights, retracted the safety signs and moved forward, followed by the long stream of slow moving cars. When, at last the road was free of traffic and the gray pick-up and I had the street to ourselves, I responded to his furious glare with a gracious smile and flashed him the peace sign. He returned neither.

"Oh, well," I told Cabot with a shrug, "you can't please them all." I pulled back onto the street and only then realized that Cabot was crouched on the floor. "What in the world are you doing down there?" I asked. "Did you fall when I turned so fast?"

He shook his head. "I didn't want anyone on the bus to see me. That was embarrassing," he mumbled, climbing back onto the seat and refastening his seatbelt.

We drove in silence to his school. It was early and we were the first to disturb the snow covering the ground and parking area. I was relieved to see lights on inside the building indicating the janitor was there. Cabot pulled his gloves on, unfastened his seatbelt and picked up his lunch, but before getting out of the car, said, "I love you Mom. But sometimes being your kid can sure be scary or embarrassing." Then he grinned and mimicked my earlier shrug, "Oh, well." He walked away, leaving perfect footprints in the snow.

"Oh, well," I echoed, knowing he was right. Again.

I continued to the freeway without exceeding eighteen miles per hour. Once on the freeway, I was still constrained to eighteen miles per hour. All the way to my parking space.

Slip sliding my way along the icy sidewalk to the school door, my breath made tiny puffs of steam in the gray light of not-yet dawn. Bordering the walk, only the shadowy outlines of the dormant shrubs were visible. As I passed the kindergarten, light from its windows caught the threads of frost lacing the shrubs, so they flashed and sparkled, just like the glitter-covered collage of paper snowflakes stapled to the room's far wall. In one corner, multicolored lights blinked on a tiny tree. Since my DNA did not include polar bear blood, I hurried past, foregoing all that beauty for the warm, but far less beautiful, entry hall.

A rush of warm pine-fragrant air enveloped me when I opened the door and the hundreds of flashing lights on the ten foot tree filling the entryway left me dizzy. I circled it twice before leaving to peer into the shadowed lounge. Its empty table looked less pathetic after I placed my red poinsettia bowl filled with sugared nuts in the center and arranged matching paper napkins around it. I filled the coffee urn and set it perking, and left. Figuring Mark was in the furnace room and I was alone, I raised my voice in joyous song. "The Twelve Days of Christmas" echoed off the walls of the empty hallway whose acoustics were better than those in my shower. What did it matter that the only gifts I could remember were the five gold rings. I knew there were a bunch of dancing maids and leaping men and some pigeons in a pear tree, but I couldn't remember how many.

My singing faded in the muffled acoustics of my classroom and died completely when the glare of my classroom lights revealed that Santa had ignored my wish list and hadn't sent his elves creeping in during the night to whittle down the stacks of paperwork covering my desk. "Oh, well, even elves can get stuck on the freeway." With coffee, sticky notes and a black pen at hand, I dug in.

I checked my watch when voices and laughter interrupted my concentration, amazed that over an hour had passed. I sighed that while the *in* box now held lots fewer papers and my *out* box lots more, I couldn't help wondering if I'd ever see the bottom of the *in* box. A nasty little voice whispered, "Not in this life time." "Well, if that's the case, I might just as well go see what's going on in the lounge." I shoved everything aside and leaned down to retrieve my purse. Straightening up, I was surprised to see Sarah Marston watching me from the door.

None of the buses came this early, and I wondered how Sarah got here, as well as why she was here. "Hi, Sarah," I said smiling at her. "Come on in."

She remained in the doorway, silently staring at the floor. This was more than her usual quiet, self-contained demeanor—she looked miserable.

Thinking she hadn't heard me, I repeated my invitation, "Come on in. I'm happy to see you."

Agitated, she hurried to my desk and thrust an envelope at me. Shaking and pale, she continued to stare at the floor as she whispered, "My mother told me I had to give you that."

Puzzled, I took the envelope from her and tore it open to read the short note inside.

Ms. McCall,

Your prejudicial treatment of my daughter and her friends is unacceptable. They are being punished because they are forbidden from taking part in holiday rituals contrary to our religious beliefs. While the rest of your students are enjoying themselves singing and rehearsing, these children are made to sit at the back of the room working on class assignments. This is unfair and humiliating.

Mr. and Mrs. Marston

My stomach lurched at the unexpected attack. Angrily I looked up from the note to Sarah, about to demand, "What in the world have you been telling your parents?" But my voice caught in my throat when I saw Sarah's trapped expression, her face drained of color. Shaken at how close I had come to 'killing the messenger', I needed time to regain my composure. Taking short shallow breaths, I slowly refolded the note. My hands shook as I smoothed the envelope and slipped the note back in it, then opened the drawer where all my notes from parents were piled and added this one. Able finally to take a deep breath, I mustered the best smile I could and said, "Well, you know my rule. If you bring me a note from home, you get a cookie." I pulled the Oreos from my file drawer and watched her face begin to regain its color and lose its look of fear. "It's still recess," I said, "why don't you go outside with your friends?"

As she ran to the door, I shrank into my chair. There would be time enough to reread the note during my lunch break and figure out my response. For now, I just wanted my coffee and solitude. I dropped my purse back in the drawer, cradled the warm cup, and stared into space.

After lunch, as the last student finished eating and hurried out to play in the snow, a lethargic heaviness kept me from rereading the Marston note. I couldn't even open the drawer. "Maybe I'll go get some quick energy in the lounge first." Too tired to lift my thermos, I took only my ubiquitous purse. Wall to wall parents, teachers and aides filled the room, laughing and noisy. And my holiday spirits returned.

"Wow, look at that!" I exclaimed making a beeline across the room. I stopped next to Ethel who sported glitter from her students' paper snowflakes on her nose and sleeve. "How do I choose?" I asked, waving my hand toward the abundance of tempting treats on the table.

Ethel laughed. "You've said the same thing every day this week. And so far your choice has been to eat one of everything."

"Well, no point in breaking a perfect record now," I said, scooping homemade fudge, sugar cookies covered in red or green icing, and a chunk of fruit cake onto one of my red napkins. My poinsettia bowl was empty, so I didn't get any nuts.

Munching and smiling, I linked arms with Ethel and we drifted over to where John, appropriately dressed for the holidays in a red and green plaid flannel shirt, was topping off his cup of coffee with aerosol whipping cream. "Want some?" he asked, aiming the nozzle toward me.

"On what," I asked wryly, "my cookies or my fudge?" A wicked smile as he eyed my blouse answered my question and I ducked behind Ethel.

"Hey! Leave me out of it!" she protested, dodging to one side.

"Sorry, John," Vic said coming up behind John and grabbing the aerosol can, "no food fights on the premises."

"Us grown-ups don't have any fun," John said, trying to look grumpy while wiping away an imaginary tear.

"Thinking of not having any fun, I have to leave," I said. "Got a letter to write." Hoping it might help, I took another piece of fudge before I turned away from the cheerful chatter of the lounge and returned to my classroom.

I'd read and reread and reread again the Marstons' note and continued to feel a sickening heaviness in my stomach along with a flash of anger. I washed the last of the fudge down with some hot coffee before I read the note again, trying to defuse my anger and frustration. "What have I done to make them so angry?" Trying to distance myself, I tried to imagine what John or Ethel would do if the note had been sent to them, and I had my answer. I began to write.

Dear Mr. and Mrs. Marston,

Sarah handed me your note regarding my treatment of the children who do not take part in the winter program. I can understand your concern and appreciate your giving me an opportunity to explain what has happened. I believe it was my failure to communicate with you and with the students.

Are you aware that during the rehearsals, Sarah's group is given time to complete any homework assigned, allowing them free time when they get home? The students involved in the rehearsals have been given the same assignments which they are expected to complete at home that evening.

I would never deliberately hurt or humiliate any of my students and if I have done so, I am deeply sorry. If you have any further concerns, please come in and discuss them with me.

Sincerely,

Ms. McCall

I hoped my response would be understood and accepted by the Marstons. I folded the note and slid it into an envelope and set it on my desk where I would see it and remember to send it home with Sarah that afternoon.

Chapter Twenty Nine

Heavy cloud cover warned of more snow and the pavement remained wet from melt of an earlier flurry, but right now nothing was falling from the dark sky. I felt safe and warm in the cocoon-like solitude of my car, but tense because holiday shoppers added interminable minutes to my reaching home and my kids. When the driver ahead of me mistook his brake pedal for a telegraph key, tapping it repeatedly to send some version of Morse code, my irritation grew with every flash. Gritting my teeth, I slowed to create a long space between us, hoping another driver would cut in front of me. No such luck. Several minutes and gazillions of his dots and dashes later, my self control died. My hands locked themselves in a death grip on the steering wheel, my breathing became wheezing as I leaned forward as far as my seatbelt allowed. Through bared teeth I snarled, "Stop tap dancing on the brake pedal, you moron," while I contemplated sending him a Morse code message with my horn. But I chickened out.

Relieved my kids weren't there to witness my lack of control, I told myself, "Must calm down. Must take a deep breath. Ulcers and heart attacks are not on to-do list." I took a deep breath, then took another, just to be on the safe side and made myself focus on positive things. "One, I'm half way home. Two, my kids will be happy to see me. Three, I only ate four of John's wife's butter cookies, even though I really wanted more." My breathing returned to normal, but sped up again when I remembered my note to the Marstons. "I hope they understand, but from now on I'm going to send out more information on holiday procedures ahead of time." The driver in the car ahead was still in flasher mode, so I slowed even further to create more distance between us. It helped.

At my exit, I gave the flasher a juicy raspberry, figuring cleaning up the windshield was worth it. The remaining trip home was peaceful. Crossing the carport, I climbed to my front door anticipating hugs and enthusiastic welcomes from my kids. "I'm home!" I called, swinging the door wide and gagged as an awful stench enveloped me, just as Laddie knocked me into the doorframe as he bounded past and out the door. Before me in the entry way stood my four-member welcoming committee looking more like anti-war protesters. Their garbled greetings consisted of, "Not my job," "Not my fault," "I didn't do it," words which became clear through repetition in increased volume. So much for love and enthusiasm and peace.

I pushed my way past them to my bedroom, where I dropped my coat and purse on the bed before I carried my thermos and lunch residue to the kitchen where my kids lay in wait. I took a deep breath, almost choking on the stench I earlier attributed to Laddie. "OK," I said facing them, "What is that awful stink?" The cacophony began again. Wrong approach.

"Time out!" I shouted over them. "Lissa, you're the oldest, tell me where that stink is coming from." I saw her mouth open and her lips move, but whatever she was saying was drowned out by Cal yelling, "Don't you dare blame it on me!"

"Blame what on you, Cal," I asked.

"Anything," he responded belligerently.

"It started with Cabot," Lissa interrupted. "He used the toilet and it overflowed and he wouldn't clean it up."

"It's not my week to clean the bathroom," Cabot interjected defensively.

"But you made it overflow," Lissa responded.

"So? It's your week to clean the bathroom," he answered, crossing his arms over his chest.

Staying well out of range, Risa stood silently watching the two antagonists.

"OK," I said, "both of you clean it up. Cabot get the mop, the germy one, and get all the water and whatever else is on the floor mopped up and Lissa, you get the soapy water and Lysol and the clean mop and go over the floor when he's done and get rid of the germs. Cal, get the Drano and the plunger."

"I already got the plunger," he answered.

"Fine. Now get the Drano."

"We don't have any," he replied.

"Yes, we do. It's on the top shelf in the basement storeroom," I told him. "I remember buying a new supply right after the shower plugged up back in September when school started."

"It's gone," he said.

I glowered at him. The room was silent and I realized Lissa, Cabot and Risa were standing motionless staring at Cal who was glaring back at them. It was the defiant look he got when he knew he was wrong and his avenues of escape were blocked.

"Gone?" I asked in my snakiest voice. "The Drano's gone missing? Where has it gone?" For the life of me I couldn't imagine what use anyone would have for a container of Drano, but I was now sure that Cal had found some purpose for it and I intended to find out what it was.

"I needed it." His tone defied me to say otherwise.

"For?" I prompted.

"My science class."

The sudden snorts of laughter from his siblings indicated this was somewhat less than the whole truth.

"Science class?" I asked. "Which one?"

"Chemistry." This response elicited a muffled snort from Lissa and a derisive hoot from Cabot. Risa was backing toward her bedroom.

"Mom," Lissa said, "let me show you something." She started toward the deck. Cabot and Risa started to follow her, but stopped dead in their tracks at Cal's furious look.

"Something wrong?" I asked as I took Cal's arm.

He didn't answer, but the angry set of his shoulders spoke volumes.

On the deck, Lissa pulled a large potted plant away from the wall under Cal's bedroom window and pointed toward a black, blistered area behind it.

"What in the world is that?" I asked.

"Cal's science experiment," Lissa answered.

"Your what?" I asked looking at Cal.

"Just because it wasn't in school doesn't make it not a science experiment," he said. "I read about how to make a bomb using Drano and I wanted to see if it worked. I thought it would just make a lot of noise, but I didn't think it would wreck the paint. You're lucky it didn't break the window, but it sure made it rattle a lot."

I considered interrupting to clear up who the lucky one was, but was stopped by his next words. "When I told Mark about it, he said the one he made set their storage shed on fire, so I guess you really were lucky. Mine only burned some paint off your wall."

Visions of blown off hands, a scorched body and a house reduced to ashes overwhelmed me and I yelled, "I'm lucky? I'm supposed to be glad I have to repaint this wall? I'm supposed to feel good I have a mad bomber for a son?" I knew I was going off the deep end, but the possibilities of what might have happened were too much.

"Furthermore," I shouted, "you don't know how lucky I am. I have a son who is going to repaint that wall and who is going to pay for the paint. And," I dropped my voice to an ominous level as I added the *coup de gras*, "a son who is going to buy two new cans of Drano and empty them down the toilet after right after he cleans the bathroom!"

"Clean the bathroom? No way! It's not my week. That's not fair," he howled.

"I know. But life ain't fair," I agreed, giving him my snake look again.

While the girls and I fixed dinner, Cal snarled his way through the bathroom cleanup. Brushes and mops crashed into walls and

214

fixtures, water sloshed from a pail when it hit the floor and the soap container thudded into the tub. Cabot stayed out of sight in his bedroom, not even suggesting he bring Laddie in with him. The smell from the bathroom wasn't yet gone and the basement was as close as I wanted Laddie's wet hair odor.

"How long ago did Cal make his bomb?" I asked.

"It was that day you came home and Cabot was hiding Laddie in his bedroom," Lissa answered.

I gave her my raised eyebrow look. Some indicator that was. A day Cabot didn't hide Laddie in his bedroom would be more informational.

Lissa thought a moment, then asked, "Do you remember the night Risa hid the dishes under her bed?"

"And you made Mom go out in the rain to buy stuff for your sewing class," Risa added, unwilling to be cast as the bad guy. Or at least not the only one.

It all came back—the weird unexplained smell and Cal shivering in the rain on the deck. I shook my head. Well, that made four for four. I should have known they were saving the worst for last.

But to be fair there was a plus side: they interrupted my obsessing about the Marstons.

Chapter Thirty

The shriek of the alarm shattered the early morning stillness and I woke up bone tired. Last night I waited until my kids were asleep before I crept into their bathroom to finish cleaning it. Cal gave it a good shot, but after all, what are a few grungy spots to a nine year old boy? And what kind of mother would insult her kid's efforts? So, much later I collapsed into bed, satisfied that for now no germs remained in my children's bathroom.

"OK," I groaned punching the clock's off button in mid-shriek, "I hear you. But be warned, Clock, when they invent a kinder, gentler wake-up sound, you will be some clock maker's spare parts." I nudged my sleep deprived body with its frazzled nerves into semi-consciousness and recoiled as questions began a persistent buzz in my brain: "How did the Marston's receive my explanation? Did they even understand what I was trying to say? Is anyone else upset?" Lots of questions, too bad they came without answers and I figured hiding under the blankets wasn't going to produce any.

I swung my legs over the edge of the bed and gasped as icy shock waves shot up them when my feet hit the floor. My gasp shifted to a cough and I thought, "Oh, good, maybe I'm coming down with something and should stay home today." I felt my forehead. It was cool. Except for being tired and hungry, I felt fine, so I dragged myself to the bedroom door and yelled at the kids to wake up. I wondered if Cal would be upset by my follow-up of his bathroom cleaning. Short answer: No. Like his siblings, he was oblivious to what I'd done. I couldn't make up my mind whether to be grateful or insulted.

Two cups of strong coffee later, dressed, and with everything more or less under control, I hugged each kid and lead-footed my way to the carport. I picked up the pace when rain, carried on a chill wind, hit me like icy pin pricks. I leaped into my car and backed out, leaving the gray cover of the carport for the battleship gray cloud cover and rain that covered my windshield like a dirty lace curtain. "It looks like I'm in for a long, sluggish commute," I thought. I was right.

By the time I reached the school the wind driven downpour made me grateful for my chosen parking space. After weighing my options for my dash to the building, I figured my blouse would dry faster than my hair and draped my jacket over my head. With my thermos and purse secured under my right arm, I clutched the arms of my jacket in my left hand and ran. Sheets of water flew from every puddle I hit.

Inside, I snatched the jacket off my head, shook it and squished carefully across the tiles in my soggy shoes. I didn't bother going into the lounge. I could see from the hall that no goodies graced the bare table. "Of course," I shrugged, "what did I expect? Leftovers?" and tossed my dry hair in a dismissive flip.

Once every light in my classroom flared to life, I pulled open the draperies to scan the still leaden sky, hoping for a glimpse of the sun. Seeing no indication that this might be the case any time soon, I sank into my seat and reached for my thermos. "My coffee's probably tepid," I thought as I twisted off the stopper." When hot steam rose to prove me wrong, I shut up and just breathed, thinking that maybe today wouldn't be a total loss after all.

"Oh, darn. Oh doggone, Oh good grief." I stopped muttering only because I couldn't think of any more epithets as I looked at my lesson plan book. "How did I forget the graph paper for math or to run copies of the Bill of Rights?" I looked around, hoping no one heard me talking to myself, saw no one and checked to see what else I probably forgot. When nothing presented itself, I set my empty cup on the desk, grabbed my ubiquitous purse and hurried to the teachers' workroom. "Maybe, by the time I finish running copies, there will be some cookies in the lounge. It never hurts to hope."

"Well, so much for hope." I thought as I passed the empty lounge devoid of cookies, people, warmth and light. But my disappointment was forgotten when I saw Derek waiting at my desk. He stood with his back to me, so focused on some papers in front of him, he didn't hear me come in. He looked up and smiled when I circled around him. I returned his smile before I slipped my supplies onto the desk and stashed my purse before I sat down.

"Look," he said when he had my undivided attention, "I finished 27 pages last night." He held his papers up for my inspection. "I just finished checking, and every single problem was right. By the end of the week I'll be up with the rest of the class." His hazel eyes glowed with pleasure. I hoped the pleasure I felt made mine glow, too.

"What are you going to do when you're all caught up?" I teased, still smiling. "You'll be bored with so much time on your hands."

With a slight frown, he caught his lower lip in his teeth before he said, "I've thought about that." He stepped back to rest one hip on the edge of his desk. "I think I'm pretty good in math, and I wondered if I could do extra. I mean, would you help me? Like get me a book and explain stuff? Would you have time?"

I didn't answer. I couldn't. He'd just offered me every teacher's dream. Struggling to keep my voice under control, I said, "I'd love to help you. Of course, first we have to complete district requirements."

"Yeah, I guess," he went on as if I hadn't spoken. "You know, I was thinking that if I keep going on like I've been doing, I'd probably finish the whole math book in a month." He stated it as a fact and studied my face before adding, "I just thought of something else. My sister's in sixth grade. If she brings her math book home every night, I could start using it. She could help me when I start, but I like doing math better than she does, and I might go past her." He gave me a worried look. "Are you able to do sixth grade math?"

"Oh, I think I could figure it out," I answered with just a touch of irony. But I was still processing his reference to his sister. It was the first time I'd heard him mention her.

"Good," he said straightening up and closing the teachers' manual. He laid his math papers on my desk with the manual on top of them. Later I'd analyze each page before recording it. Considering his plan of action, I had to be sure he understood every concept.

He took a thick book with an uninspiring beige cover from his backpack and laid it on his desk before hanging the backpack on his assigned hook by the door. Pulling on his jacket, he opened the outside door.

Curious, I called out before he could leave, "What's that?" I indicated the book.

"It's a biology book I borrowed from a veterinarian," he answered and the door closed behind him before I could ask why.

As if on cue, Sarah Marston came through the hallway door, holding a white cake box carefully in both hands. She looked back and called, "Thank you," to whoever opened the door for her.

"Hi, Sarah," I said, unsure of what else to say.

Smiling, she crossed the floor and laid the box on top of the math manual. Her luminous gray eyes never left my face as she pulled loose an envelope taped to the top of the box and held it out to me. "My mother told me to give you this," she said. A chill snaked down my spine as I took the envelope wondering whether to open it now or wait until later when I was alone. "You have to open it," Sarah said with a smile that was almost wider than her face.

I took the unsealed envelope and slid out a folded sheet of paper.

"Dear Ms. McCall," I read,

"Yesterday you gave my daughter a cookie. For that I thank you and want to return the favor by sending you this box of cookies—enough I hope for each of your students and a few extra for you.

Last night my husband and I read your explanation to our friends who share our religious beliefs and they were as relieved as we were that our children were not being discriminated against.

Thank you for replying so quickly and for your genuine concern for Sarah and the others.

Sincerely,

Mr. Marston

Mrs. Marston"

Under their signatures were the signatures of eight other couples who were parents not only of my students, but of students in other classrooms.

The lump in my throat interfered with my ability to speak. I lifted the lid off the box and stared with delight at the sugar sparkling off the golden cookies inside. I sniffled and reached for a tissue.

"I told my mom sugar cookies are your favorite," Sarah said.

"And they always will be," I assured her.

She laughed with pleasure and skipped rather than walked toward the door.

"Hey, Sarah," I called. "You brought me a note from your mom—come get your Oreo."

From the window I watched her run toward her friends, Oreo in hand, through the silvery droplets of rain sprinkling down from a sky of polished pewter. What a beautiful day.

I smoothed the note with gentle hands and read it again before laying it across my plan book where I could see and reread it several times more before adding it to the others in my desk drawer.

Chapter Thirty One

If there isn't a word meaning a hatred of alarm clocks, there should be, because I really hated mine, especially on cold mornings like today. Peeking out from under my eider-down comforter where I kept as warm as any eider duck ever did, I saw clues that my room was cold—like the icicles hanging from the eaves outside my window and the cloudy puffs of steam from my breath.

Risking frostbite, I snaked my hand out into the frigid air and punched the off button, and before my nails turned blue, pulled my hand back. The fear of losing my job overcame my fear of frostbite and I flung back my comforter, leapt over the bare floor to the furry sheep skin throw rug that always slid further and further from the bed and fled to the thermostat. I felt several degrees warmer just hearing it click on.

"Up! Everybody up!" I yelled and scooted into the bathroom, slamming the door behind me. Five minutes later I emerged and repeated the order as I opened each bedroom door. "Up! All of you. I mean now. I've turned on the furnace and I don't want the heat to go to waste."

Only Laddie responded by bounding up the basement steps and whining to be let out, whereupon I called, "Hey, Cabot, better let your dog out or any messes are all yours." It worked. One kid up, three more to go.

"Heat does not go to waste," Cal mumbled from under the pillow he'd pulled over his head. "My teacher says nothing is ever gone—it just changes form."

"Fine. So let's see your form change to upright," I answered. The lump beneath the blankets moved slightly and the pillow slid to the floor. I guessed I could count this as halfway. Or at least a start.

With Laddie outside, Cabot headed for the bathroom. Realizing she might not get to use it first, Lissa streaked from her room, beating him by seconds and slamming the door on his irate howl. A realist, he gave the door a half-hearted kick with his bare foot and stomped back to his room. That made two up and one halfway up.

I opened Risa's door, but her room was empty. "I'm out here, Mom," she called from the kitchen. "Nobody ever lets me be first in the bathroom, so I'm making sandwiches. It's my week, you know. And," she added as I joined her in the kitchen, "I put the water in your coffee pot." I smiled and scooped in the grounds.

Lissa opened the bathroom door. Cal, who'd been listening for it, shot from his room, edging Cabot aside and slamming the door. "Fine," Cabot snarled, "I'll just go pee off the deck—right under your window, Cal."

"You'd better not," came a threatening yelp from the bathroom.

And so, another day, much like many others, began.

Just under an hour later, wedged in among more commuters than there are people in Idaho, I drove in the prescribed defensive mode, keeping watch for black ice and screwball drivers. With a tape of Tom Jones titillating my hormones and a setting moon casting light and shadows on my mountain, I anticipated my first class day of the new year with pleasure. I encountered no black ice, no screwballs and just a few nitwits, so the trip to the school seemed shorter than usual.

"Ooops!" I squeaked when my car skidded on black ice before it stopped at an acute angle in my parking space. Relieved that this was the only patch of black ice I'd hit, I maneuvered my car into a more acceptable position with ease since the only other vehicle in sight was Mark's old pickup parked in the far corner.

Navigating the sidewalk proved trickier. The overloaded tote bag of papers and books swung from my arm completely out of sync with my purse dangling from my shoulder. "Amazing how some things never change," I thought as I twisted about, attempting to abort my thermos' slithery escape from under my arm. My plate of cookies and fruitcake tilted without falling, but my brown bag lunch toppled to the pavement.

Standing there in the near dark watching my breath puff into the frozen air and glaring at my fallen lunch, I muttered, "Isn't that just dandy. Let's see, should I pick it up and probably drop everything else, or kick it all the way to the lounge? Guess I'll just let it lie there and hope it doesn't freeze." With an ironic last look at the pathetic little brown sack lying alone on the ground, I said, "Farewell for now. I'll come back for you soon."

Even minus the brown bag lunch, it took creative body language and brute strength to wrestle the heavy front door open one-handed. In the lounge, I slid the plate of goodies to the table, dumped everything else on the sofa and hurried back for my lunch, hoping no hungry squirrels beat me to it.

As expected, my classroom was cold and I knew it would remain so until Mark decided otherwise, so I kept my jacket on and attacked the pile of work on my desk. An hour or so later, I flexed my nearly numb fingers and looked toward the radiator, hearing it begin to hiss a promise of warmth to come. Through the window above the radiator, sunlight struck a sheet of ice hanging from the eave, creating a prism of glittering rays that seconds later vanished. It was time for a coffee break.

I tossed my jacket over the back of my chair and strolled to the lounge, wondering if anyone else loved fruitcake as much as I did. If not, there'd be plenty left for me.

I was puzzled by a subdued atmosphere in the crowded room. People were huddled in isolated groups of three and four, speaking so softly I could hear the coffee perking. I hurried to join Ethel,

Mary and Nick standing near the window. "So who died?" I asked flippantly.

They stared at me silently for a moment. Finally Ethel broke the silence, "No one died, but close to it."

This was hardly the response I expected, so I waited for clarification. Taking my arm, Ethel leaned close to whisper, "Let's go to my room to talk." Nodding agreement, Mary and Nick walked toward the sofa.

"What's going on?" I asked as we walked down the hall.

Putting her finger to her lips, Ethel whispered, "Wait till we're in my room. I don't want to talk where we can be overheard." Once inside, she shut the door with a bang, then turned and in a voice mixed with anger and pain said, "He did it. He finally succeeded."

"Roark?" I asked. It was the only name that came to mind.

She nodded. "He drove her out. Edna finally broke. After she turned in her resignation this morning, she stopped by the lounge to say goodbye. She was in tears."

"This morning?" I repeated. "She was here this morning?"

"Yes, but not for long. He did it again." She took a deep breath. "Edna said that just before she left for vacation he told her not to come back unless she had satisfactory lesson plans." A look of utter disgust crossed Ethel's face, matched by the venom in her voice. "I guess she spent most of her vacation working on them, but when she showed them to him this morning, he told her, I bet without even looking at them, that they didn't meet his standards." I'd never before heard Ethel speak with such contempt.

"Why didn't she go over his head to the curriculum director and get his evaluation?" I flared. "I know. I know," I backtracked at Ethel's withering look. I knew as well as anyone that Edna never challenged authority. "So what happens now? Is she cleaning out her stuff? Should we go down and see if she needs any help?"

Ethel shook her head. "She's gone. Just took her purse and left. All the primary teachers told her they'd get together after school to pack up and deliver her personal belongings."

"That damn Roark must feel really proud. He beat up the most vulnerable woman in the whole district," I said, frustrated and close to tears. "One of these days I'll find a way to let him know what a vile person I think he is."

"I wouldn't be surprised if he's already figured that out," Ethel said, with just a touch of irony, "you aren't exactly the world's most tactful individual. Anyway, there's nothing we can do. At least not today." She took her jacket off a hook and handed it to me. "You have a class that will need you in fifteen minutes. Why don't you take a quick walk in the fresh air?"

She was right. My breathing was ragged and my face burned, which probably meant it was a splotchy red. "He's done it to me again," I thought angrily as I threw her jacket over my shoulders and stormed outside hoping a struggle with cold air and black ice might cool me down a little.

Back in my classroom at five minutes before the bell, with my breathing and skin color close to normal, I stood at the window looking up into the lightening sky. My glittering ice was gone. But I figured it wouldn't have stood a chance against the volume of steam rising from all the noses pressed against the window, anyway. Above the noses all the eyes stared at the clock on the opposite wall, probably counting down the minutes until I'd open the door and rescue them from the cold. Unmoved, I raised my hand in a half wave, but before I could turn away, Kevin and Billy, knowing they'd caught my attention, began leaping about and flapping their arms as if trying to keep warm. Catching on, the others hunched their shoulders, flapped their arms and leaped about as they joined in a wild shivering dance meant to enlist my sympathy. They won. I laughed and opened the door a full minute and a half early.

They tumbled in, all memory of entering quietly forgotten. Coats and jackets were flipped toward hooks, and a few made it, lunches were tossed toward the shelf and most made it, everything else was dumped on desks. I found myself pinioned in a pulsating sea of children spilling over with unrestrained exuberance at the need to tell of Christmas gifts, visits, and activities. My repeated, "Shhh," and "You need to quiet down," fell on deaf ears.

"Well, if I can't stop them, I'd better join them. Why waste all this enthusiasm? I can use today's lesson plans tomorrow. It's for sure they won't create this kind of excitement." I didn't often wing it in my teaching, but something told me this would be a good day to begin. "OK. kids, listen up," I said in my no nonsense—cut the crap voice. They responded as I'd hoped they would and discipline returned.

"In order for me to achieve all I want to this morning, we may have to postpone your spelling pretest until this afternoon." This brought the expected laughter and nods of pleasure. "Instead, I'd like each of you tell the class the one best thing about your vacation. It can be a trip, or a person, or a gift or just sleeping in or no homework—anything that made you happy." The room buzzed. They were ready.

"However," I said, raising my hand for their attention, "I want you to write it first." A chorus of groans followed, and I felt like a traffic cop as I raised my hand again. The groans subsided a little. "As you know, some people forget what they want to say, so by writing it down, nothing important will be left out." I endured their fishy-eyed silence a moment before adding my *coup de grace*, "So just make a list of things you want to include. And spelling and punctuation won't count." I waited for the exaggerated sighs of great relief to fade. "When we're finished listening and telling, you can use your notes to write a story." I stopped talking since no one was listening. They were too involved in their lists.

When most of them had put their pencils down, I said, "Who'd like to go first?" and almost missed the fleeting look of mischief that crossed Joey's face, warning me a caveat was needed—and fast. His disappointment when I added, "And I don't want to see or hear about anybody's underwear," told me I'd guessed right. My years with Cal and Cabot taught me that boys at this age go into paroxysm of unrestrained laughter at the mention of underwear.

"Allison, why don't you go first?" I said, knowing she was eager to model her sky blue jacket and matching purse.

She darted for the coat rack, put on her jacket and pirouetted, saying, "My grandma bought me this because she knows it's my favorite color and my mom and dad bought me the purse to go with it."

"It's really pretty," Chris James said and others nodded in agreement. Allison smiled with pleasure, still wearing her jacket as she took her seat.

I took a breath intending to call on the next child, but before I could, the class surprised me by breaking into spontaneous applause. Each succeeding presentation was met with compliments and applause. Later, looking back on it, I was surprised only that I was surprised. This was a unique class and I should be getting used it.

"Can we start our writing now?" Skye asked after the final presentation.

"Don't you think you should go to recess first?" I answered. Their laughter indicated most of them hadn't noticed the passing of time, either.

Alone, I sketched in my plans for the rest of the morning. I'd collected and scanned the students' notes after each oral presentation, now I'd return them so they could be used as a basis for more formal writing. When recess ended, a silent class hurried to their seats and began writing, some even before receiving their notes, eager to begin.

Well aware of the fallibility of my memory, as each child spoke, I had listened to the affection in their voices and the looks of pleasure as they told of gifts and families and events, and made scribbled notes to include in my student folders for use during my next parent-teacher conference, which promised to be the best one yet.

After a noisier than usual lunch, they left for recess. I retrieved my lunch from the fridge and brought it back to my desk. Holding half a sandwich in my left hand, with my right I turned the pages of the papers I'd just collected, so enrapt I barely heard the outside door open.

"Ms. McCall," Roger called softly.

I looked up. Roger stood in the doorway, waiting for me to respond. "Is it OK if me and Petey come in and play chess?" he asked.

"Petey and I," I corrected automatically.

"Petey and I," he repeated. "Well, can we? A bunch of the kids kind of ganged up on Petey and were making fun of him."

Beside Roger, Petey stood silently watching me.

"And I wanted to knock them down, but I remembered you said I could come in here if I didn't want to get in trouble. And I don't. So can we?" Roger asked again.

"Good decision, Roger," I answered. "Did you bring a chess set with your today?"

He pulled a brown leather box from his back pack. "When my dad started teaching me how to play, my mom bought me this travel set." He held it so I could see it and looked at me seriously, "Sometimes I use it in the car or at Petey's house. I use it a lot."

"He's really good, but I'm catching up with him," Petey said, as Roger smiled at him with pride.

"Then I guess you'd better get started," I said, going back to my lunch and student papers.

In the silent room, I finished my reading and glanced up as I heard Roger whisper, "Petey, you want to know something? You are lots smarter than those other kids, but you don't say things back to make them look dumb." Almost as if thinking out loud he added, "My dad says I should use more self control." He grinned, "And you're way better at that than I am."

Petey thought for a moment, looking down at the chess board. "Check," he said.

"Roger and Petey," I said, as I tossed my lunch sack in the trash, "there are only five minutes left of recess. Let's go out for some fresh air."

Chapter Thirty Two

I thought April was the coolest month. I loved daylight saving time. I loved the pale gold rays of early morning sun that filtered through the lingering mists of night. I loved spring break. But I still hated my alarm clock. After it woke me, I treated myself to five minutes of wake-up time, and lay back looking out my open window. Pink and white cherry blossoms quivered in an impertinent breeze that captured their fragrance and shared it with me. Finally, with a stretch and a yawn, I swung myself out of bed, smiling as I made my way to the bathroom—daylight saving time meant that tonight I'd drive home in sunlight.

My smile vanished as I got closer to the mirror and saw that I appeared to be sporting a halo of fire. "Lenses. I need my lenses. Where are my contact lenses?" I muttered, pawing through cosmetics and brushes and hand soap scattered over the counter. Once normal vision returned, my halo was nothing more than my flame red hair flared out in the night by static electricity into wild spikes. I splashed my face with cold water, ran my wet hands over my hair, and began applying make-up. Finished, I narrowed my mascared eyes to sultry slits and tossed my head, hoping for my hair to flip out sexily, just like in the movies. But it just hung down damply on either side of my head like wiry bloodhound ears. Dousing it with half a can of hairspray and applying a hot curling iron, I cooked it into a less doggy style.

I considered ending my practice of matching my hair colors to the seasons. For this spring so I'd chosen a bottle labeled *Warm Blond Beige,* obviously a euphemism for *Brassy Copper Streaks over Barbie Doll Pink.* But dreams die hard and I couldn't resist giving my head one last toss that might, just maybe shake some life into the rigid strands of copper wire. My hair didn't move, but a flake of mascara fell into my eye making it burn and that made my nose run. A lavish application of eye drops removed the mascara, but it was a couple of minutes before normal eyesight returned. Blinking away the last of the blurriness, in the mirror I saw the reflection of my daughter Risa standing behind me. As often happened, for a second I thought I saw my mother. Risa inherited mom's porcelain complexion, dark hair and blue eyes. Cal's observation that nothing is ever gone, it just changes form made me smile.

"Mom," Risa said, bringing me back to the present. In the mirror her blue, or were they gray, eyes met mine. "Can I go to Erin's after school tonight? Her mom even said I could stay for dinner and I'll call Lissa and let her know I got there OK and you can pick me up later but you have to write me a note this morning so they'll let me ride on Erin's bus." She came up for air, making me laugh. Like her sister, she sure could pack a lot of words into one breath.

Still laughing, I grabbed a handful of toilet paper, wiped my runny nose, and dabbed at the black dribbling down my cheek. With my puffy red eyelids that clashed with my pink hair, and the black streaks and smears, I looked like an animated Picasso. "What a mess," I thought, forgetting Risa's question.

Not getting an instant response, she figured a little buttering up might be in order and added, "Your hair looks really nice, Mom. I like it lots better than the bright green you had for St. Patrick's Day."

After another ineffective swipe, I tossed the wad of toilet paper into the waste basket and turned to face her, delighted with her attempt at diplomacy. Rolling my eyes, I said, "Gee, I never would have guessed you weren't thrilled with the green. Were you giving me a clue when you asked me to tie a scarf or something over my head the day we went shopping together? But don't forget I told you that this was the first time every single parent, fathers and mothers both, showed up for parent conferences. Who knows— maybe green hair on St. Patrick's Day has leprechaun magic."

"Duh," she scoffed, "and maybe they thought their kids were making it up when they said their teacher had green hair."

I gave her my long suffering parent sigh. "Well, the green is gone."

"I know. Now it's pink and orange stripes. It reminds me of that dress you made me wear when I was only four." She gave me an appraising look, "I don't suppose you'd consider ordinary hair color, would you?" I detected a note of hope in her voice.

I hated to dash her hopes, but I had to be honest, "Probably not," then added, "and yes, it's OK for you to go to Erin's tonight. Just be sure you leave her phone number on the counter for Lissa before you leave this morning. And bring me a pad so I can write your note."

She skipped out of the bathroom, no longer interested in my hair. I thought about reminding her to brush some of the tangles out her own hair, but decided it could wait.

I took another look in the mirror and realized that, other than wearing a bag on my head, there was nothing further that could be done with my hair this morning, and a bag, even one with eye holes, might hinder my effectiveness as a teacher. Better just repair the make-up and brazen it out. With any luck, I might not encounter Roark.

❧❧

Carrying the cake I'd baked last night, I called out a cheerful greeting to the half dozen teachers in the lounge, tossed my head for dramatic effect and waited for a reaction. It came. They stared in an eerie silence that made me realize how a criminal in a police line-up must feel.

John waited until I was almost to the table before he gasped, "Oh my God, BJ, I thought your head was on fire. My wife has a kewpie doll with hair that color. We keep it in the closet. It's way cheaper than installing a light." He basked in the ensuing laughter.

With a snarky smile I said, "Gee, thanks, John. Just don't get too close—it gives off sparks. And that's all the warning you're going to get." Although I heard no further comments about my hair, facial expressions told me that some people just take awhile to accept anything new.

I placed my covered cake container in the center of the table, and stood back. John stared from it to me with suspicion until Vic elbowed him aside and lifted the cover. With a theatrical yelp he leaped back. On the chocolate cake's thick topping of fudge, using lots of neon colored icing, I'd designed a glorious ode to daylight saving time—a copper colored sun emitting snakelike rays of blinding pink that nearly matched my hair. Vic snatched up a dinner knife lying on the table, brandished it above the cake before plunging it into the dead center of the sun, snarling, "Die, Medusa, die!" Preferring less mess, Ethel took a larger knife from the drawer and elbowed Vic aside.

Remaining apart from the silliness, Patricia Soames looked on wearing a Queen Victoria *We are not amused* expression. However, as the noise died down, she came toward me, carrying a hefty slice of cake on her plate. "Just before you came in, we were talking about the past few weeks of standardized testing," she said, her serious demeanor keeping me from commenting on the long pink tentacle of icing dangling from her raised fork. In awe of her sharp mind, I waited, wondering where this was going. I didn't have to wait long.

"In my opinion, today's standardized tests are like the carpenter ants that undermine the foundations of buildings." There was an edge to her voice, but I wasn't sure whether it was anger or resentment. "The tests undermine the foundations of learning by chewing up inordinate hours of prepping and testing that should be spent teaching." I nodded and she went on, "I remember when testing was used to pinpoint the kids' strengths and weaknesses instead of bragging rights for administrators of wealthier districts."

Before I could tell her I concurred, John broke in, "But look at the bright side—tests make the test designers rich and generate lots of paper and that makes administrators all the way up to Washington, DC look good. And we all know that's what education's all. . ." he broke off midsentence, looking over my shoulder toward the door.

I turned, figuring Roark had joined us. From the doorway he scanned the room. I thought his eyes narrowed slightly when he looked in my direction. Without speaking, he left. After which, everyone began leaving and I had to hurry to hug Ethel who was nearly out the door. I smiled at John, nodded at Patricia and joined the exodus.

Through dried on spots and streaks left by the spring rains on the windows, I looked past the haphazardly tossed heaps of jackets, backpacks, lunches and other stuff kids bring to school piled against the building like large nests of forgotten Easter eggs, to far out on the playground. Animated figures in blue jeans and white tee shirts dotted the baseball diamonds. Closer in, several more, also in blue and white were jumping rope, whipping down slides, hanging upside down from monkey bars or clustered in small groups. It was like there was an unwritten rule that in the spring all tee shirts had to be white. I thought about the recent furor over a proposal to require student uniforms and wondered how much more uniform there could be than blue jeans and white tee shirts.

The rising sun's warmth released a unique scent of almost dry concrete, crushed grass, and dusty sweat from the kids racing in from the playground when I went out to usher them in. From all directions they came to swirl around me after scooping up items from the piles against the wall and mingling their blue and white non-uniforms with their jackets of many colors.

Of my two rules for entry: straight line and quiet, only the first was being observed. Curiosity beats rules every time. "You changed your hair." "How come you chose pink?" "How long will it be pink?" "I like it better than green." "My parents won't believe me this time either," but I was prepared for these comments. If neither Risa nor John could resist commenting, I certainly didn't expect my students not to, so I remained silent and one by one they fell silent as well, but their upturned faces asked multiple questions as they filed past.

Once inside Skye pitched her jacket toward her coat hook and hurried after me to my desk. "Today's my birthday," she announced, setting a box on my desk. "These are my cookies. I made them myself last night. The recipe only made 24 cookies, so I made half a recipe extra like you showed us in math class. So now I have 36 cookies. But we only need 29 for the class, so I let my family eat four of them and you like sugar cookies so I brought two for you." She gulped a quick breath, watching for my reaction. My initial reaction was that she could teach Risa something about how many words could be spoken in one breath.

But what I said was, "Happy birthday, Skye," and smiled to let her know how pleased I was. "Thank you for my extra cookie, and congratulations on finding a good reason for learning fractions."

She grinned, "I used to think they were really dumb, but now I don't. Can I share my cookies this morning, or do I have to wait until lunch?" Even a mongoose could figure out which she wanted.

"Right after we take attendance and start the board assignment we can enjoy your cookies," I said. Retrieving her cookies, she bounced back to her desk, holding the box carefully. I watched her slide into her seat and from the corner of my eye I saw Joey's hand fly into the air just after he called out, "Do we have to do more of those tests again today?" It was a question I was delighted to answer.

"No, we're finished testing for this year." I allowed my voice to register deep relief.

"Well that's good," Joey announced, "I was getting really tired of them!" If his classmates' high fives were any indication, he wasn't the only one.

"Amen," I added under my breath, wishing I dared join the high fiving.

It was spring, and with the tests over for another year my kids' natural enthusiasm for learning and discussion soared. On such a lovely productive morning I almost resented having to stop for lunch. Watching them leave for recess I thought, "This is what teaching is all about."

As the door closed behind them, Derek stayed inside. He walked to my desk, hesitated a moment, then laid a thick, well worn three ring notebook on my desk.

"What's this?" I asked.

"My notebook."

"I mean, what is it for? Why are you giving it to me?"

Without smiling he said, "I want you to read it." He watched my face for a moment before turning to leave.

"Is it OK if I take it home and read it tonight?"

"Fine," he said and I heard the door click shut behind him.

I slid his notebook into my tote bag, picked up my purse and my cup and joined my co-workers for lunch in the lounge.

Propped up in bed that night, a cup of hot tea within reach, I opened Derek's notebook. If I'd had any idea of its contents I'd have skipped lunch and begun reading immediately. Close to dawn, I was exhausted and my eyes burned, but I had read every word.

Chapter Thirty Three

By the time I set Derek's notebook aside, less than two hours for sleep remained, definitely not enough for someone pushing forty. My muscles ached. My head ached. My eyes ached and leaving my bed created additional aches, something I thought impossible. With my bones protesting at every step, I lurched with all the grace and charm of a rusty robot to the bathroom.

One look in the mirror and I wanted to flee back to bed to hide under the covers, or better yet, under the bed. Instead I brushed my teeth and splashed my face with cold water, jarring my nerves but doing nothing for the dark circles under my eyes. When it turned out slathering on concealer was an exercise in futility, I knew I was once again a victim of deceptive cosmetic advertising. Accepting that the black circles weren't going away, I began a vigorous brushing of my psychedelic hair, but it was still under the control of the bad-hair fairy. Nothing would undo its synthetic Barbie doll style or texture. Conceding defeat with a weak, "Oh, who cares?" I tossed my brush on the counter and headed for the clothes closet.

I flipped the switch, but with a flash and a pop the closet light died. In the dark, I snatched whatever came to hand and pulled it on, figuring no one would notice what I wore after confronting my witchy black eye pouches and coppery-pink spikes poking out of my head.

Tossing the blankets into a semblance of a made bed, I dashed to the kitchen, lured by the irresistible smell of brewing coffee.

Spoons of cereal paused midway from bowls to lips when my kids saw me. Lissa dropped her spoon and spun around to the coffee maker, filled a cup to the brim and handed it to me with a sympathetic smile. I blew her a kiss and took a healthy gulp. All four resumed eating. A couple of gulps later, what I was seeing began to register. Trying hard not to sound critical, I asked, "Cal, why are you putting peanut butter on a pickle?"

"Because you said peanut butter has lots of protein and you said my bones or something need lots of protein and I couldn't get it to mix right with the dry cereal."

He sounded so reasonable, that it was a moment before I rolled my eyes and said, "Of course, how stupid of me not to know that."

Cal nodded, happy I understood. Irony is wasted on children.

"I only put milk and bananas on my cereal," Risa volunteered and added, "I wanted sugar, but Lissa said either sugar or bananas. Besides, I don't like pickles."

"At least not for breakfast," I agreed and nodded my approval at Lissa. From the corner of my eye I saw Cabot take something from under the counter and put it in his mouth. "What," I asked, "are you holding under the counter?"

"Just some dry cereal," he answered, ducking his head to avoid looking at me.

I waited.

"Well, I just couldn't wait till Saturday," he mumbled. "You know I like Capt'n Crunch. If we only get it on Saturdays, you shouldn't have left it in the kitchen." He put the box on the counter.

Lissa snatched it and shoved it in the cupboard. "You better not have eaten any of my share," she warned him. Turning to me she said, "I didn't make lunches today, Mom, it's hotdog day at school. You said we could buy."

I shuddered. I considered hotdogs about as nutritious as candy wrappers, but the kids liked them, so once a month I relented and let them enjoy a nonfood lunch. Besides, I loved the happy expressions this earned me. "OK, hotdogs it is." Laughing, I went to the bedroom for my coat and purse. As I laid their lunch money on the counter, I looked around and seeing no sack with my name on it, figured I'd be eating a school lunch today, too. I kissed the tops of their heads, picked up my purse, thermos and Derek's notebook and opened the door, careful to step aside as Laddie bounded in, delighted to be reunited with his loved ones as he snuffled around searching for spilled food. The threat of a collision over, I reached back to pick up my now half full cup of coffee and went out. Standing in the entry, Lissa watched me get into my car before shutting and locking the door.

A shaft of sunlight flashed off the mirror-like windshield of Mark's pickup as I pulled into the parking lot. Clean glass was as important to Mark as car wax was to me and I smiled with pride at my gleaming red Rebel. A gentle breeze carried a whisper of perfume from the early blooming daphne odora at the corner of the building, reminding me of my mother who always had a daphne shrub near our front door. Nostalgia swept over me and I wondered if people would think I'd gone daft if I gave in to my sudden urge to sit in the flower bed doing nothing but deep breathing, but I resisted the urge once I saw the muddy earth at the shrub's base, and continued inside.

The hallway was dark. The office was dark. Dark can hold promise—maybe Hatchet Man's would stay dark. But where was Mark? He always turned the lights on. I called his name. There was no answer, so I yelled, "Mark, where the heck are you?" Receiving no response, I hurried to my classroom and its light switch. I'd had enough dark.

I opened the drapes and my concern for Mark disappeared. The early morning sun shone through windows so clean they glittered, and I watched clouds stained with sunrise gold and coral, lift, turn to white and drift away. My mind drifted with them, until I drew away from my cloud dreams to reality and the guilt-inducing student papers on my desk.

I debated. With about an hour until the school buses began delivering students, I had a choice: correct some of the never-ending pile of papers in front of me, or re-read Derek's notebook. Remembering my impression of its sophisticated level of information and near perfect composition last night when I was sleepy, I felt it was important that I re-evaluate it in the light of day. With my black pen and a pad of sticky notes nearby, I started reading.

Wincing when the shrill morning bell broke the silence, I stared in disbelief at the clock. An entire hour had passed. Marking my place, I closed the notebook and set it on the corner of my desk. Out the window, instead of clouds, I saw children from every area of the play ground converge, becoming a fast approaching phalanx that splintered off at classroom doors. My own raucous, earthy smelling splinter group, grinning and wiggling, torn between a desire to continue playing or obeying the rules, bumped into each other as some looked back while others shoved forward into the class room.

In the doorway, Derek stopped, blocking those behind him. There was an intensity about him that precluded the usual demands to hurry up or move. "Did you read it?" he asked, but immediately added, "I can come in to see you at lunch today, if that's OK." When I hesitated, he froze, rooted in place while the other students eddied around him into the classroom.

Because I wanted to finish rereading it before discussing it with him, I said, "Maybe not today. . ." I broke off when I followed his gaze and realized I'd laid the notebook in almost the exact spot where he'd placed it yesterday. His stare, a mixture of hurt and disbelief, shook me. Stalling for time, searching for some way to undo my carelessness, I faked a cough before I said, "I meant, yes. I think I can cancel my lunch plans till later. So lunch recess today would be perfect. I can't wait to tell you which parts I liked best." Derek nodded and strode to his seat, while I hoped my clumsy attempt at recovery worked.

After lunch, I propped open the door for my class who fled past me into the sunshine. I waited there a moment, absorbing the warmth and smells of spring before, smiling, I walked toward Derek who was leaning against the front of my desk, watching me and hugging his notebook to his chest. "Did you like it? I mean, did you think it was good?" His voice like his face was apprehensive.

"Did I *like* it? Did I think it was *good*?" I repeated. "I think I would say I was astonished by it and thought it was outstanding." His expression transformed into a smile of unrestrained pleasure and I only hoped that my out-of-control grin didn't make me look too unprofessional. But I couldn't make it go away.

"You liked it? You thought it was good? You really did?" he asked again.

"I really did and I really do, so grab a chair and let's look at it together."

Leaning forward in the chair he hauled a chair over to my desk, he placed his notebook between us.

"This is really well written," I said, nodding at it. "Who worked with you on it?"

"No one," he answered.

"I mean," I clarified, "who helped you organize it?" I was thinking of the sentence structure and vocabulary that were better than some college papers I'd read.

"What do you mean, 'organize' it? I wrote it myself, no one helped me. I just wrote about this bird with a broken wing that I found and I kept a journal of how I fixed it. And no one helped me with it, because I never let anybody read it."

"How did you know what to do?" I asked.

"Like I wrote, I asked my mom, but she said she didn't know what to do and I should call the library. So I did. The librarian told me about a club that trains falcons and I called them and they invited me to come to one of their meetings. I really learned a lot from them. They told me to call the veterinarian, but he said he didn't know much about birds, he mostly worked with animals like cats and dogs. But he let me borrow a book that had a chapter about birds in it." He paused for breath and looked to see if I understood.

I took a breath, too, suddenly realizing I'd been holding it. "Is that the one I saw on your desk a couple of months ago?" I asked, remembering the college textbook I'd seen.

"Yeah, it told me what they eat and how to hold them and how to make a splint for a wing and other stuff."

"I guess that explains the terminology," I said, "and why there were so many words I didn't understand. I was sure someone was telling you what to write and how to spell a lot of it."

"No, besides, except for the veterinarian, nobody knew any of that stuff, and he was kind of busy all the time. I did it all myself." He flashed me the impish grin I loved. "I'm not stupid, you know." Together we burst into laughter.

"And this was an actual log of your capture and efforts to heal a falcon with a broken wing, not a story you made up," I said, wanting to be sure.

"It's real," he answered. "Why would I write a fake journal?"

I was saved from having to figure out an answer to this when the hallway door opened and Roark stood in its entry. He took a step, just one, into the room. A creepy unease triggered a tic attack in my left eye. I stifled a nervous giggle as I thought, "If this were a movie, I'd be hearing scary music about now." Roark frowned and looked pointedly at the open outside door. I ignored the door, looked at him and waited for him to speak first.

Once again I was struck by the difference in our attire. My black slacks and green cotton blouse were clean and serviceable, but not in a league with his well tailored navy suit, crisp white shirt and ice blue tie. And his hair was not pink. With slow deliberation, his eyes shifted from the door toward Derek, ignoring me. He allowed several seconds to pass then demanded, "Why are you in here?"

I resented his intrusion but it was his intimidation of Derek that infuriated me. Feeling my face begin to flame made it worse. I inhaled sharply intending to answer his question, but Roark barely glanced at me, just raised his hand dismissively, making me wish for my tape recorder.

Derek stared in mute bewilderment from Roark to me and Roark snapped, "Well?"

"Because she said I could." Derek's voice was almost a whisper as his head dropped. I felt tears gathering in my throat as the withdrawn look I'd hoped was gone forever returned.

"I've been told you've been in here a lot lately. Are you in trouble?" Roark asked.

"No," Derek answered his voice almost inaudible, hoping his answer was the right one.

Roark shifted his attention to me. I was puzzled when he seemed less angry than triumphant as he said, "I want to be informed if he is."

I stared, silent, wishing my eye would stop twitching and struggling to breath normally. After I heard the door click shut behind him I sat gazing into space, replaying everything in my mind, but unable to make sense of what had just happened.

"What did he mean by that? Did I do something wrong?" Derek's questions snapped me back to the present.

"I have no idea what he meant," I sighed, shaking my head, then used my no nonsense voice added, "and you have done absolutely nothing wrong. Quite the opposite, in fact."

Not completely reassured, Derek studied my face.

"Time to get down to business," I said with an almost normal laugh, "let's talk some more about your notebook." Derek's face lit up, when I said, "It's really remarkable. So remarkable, in fact, I stayed up all night reading it." I gave him my 'would you believe it' look. "In case you hadn't noticed, I've been yawning a lot today."

He joined me in pretending nothing out of the ordinary had just taken place, giving me his mock serious look with its quirky eyebrow lift and said, "Oh, I thought maybe you were just bored."

"Bored!" my voice was almost a squeak. "You thought I was bored? No way was I bored. So let's get back to the journal. I have a few questions." When he gave me the lifted eyebrow again,

I assumed he meant I could begin, so I did. "You didn't say when you found the falcon and all of this began."

"Yes I did, right there on page one. I said I just started fourth grade."

"Oops, sorry. I forgot."

He gave me a look that said he expected better from a teacher and said, "Anything else?"

I laughed. "I think it's time you went out for what's left of recess. I need a rest. Besides, since I don't want any more memory lapses, I need to finish rereading your journal." I closed it and deliberately set it on the corner of my desk. I didn't tell him he would get it back plastered with sticky notes. The good kind.

He rose and strode to the door. Unable to resist one more one-ups-man-ship, with one foot safely out the door he asked, "Did you know falcons are oviparous?" and whooped with delight when I gave him the dumbfounded look I knew he wanted. He loped away to join his friends and I suspected he knew I was already reaching for my dictionary.

Alone in my room, quiet now except for the distant sounds of children, I sank with pleasure into my chair and closed my eyes. When I'd told Derek I needed a rest, I wasn't kidding. Too little sleep and the encounter with Roark had taken their toll and I drifted into that mesmerizing twilight zone between waking and sleeping. As if from a distance, I again heard Derek's voice so matter-of-factly saying the sentence I'd almost missed, but now knew I'd never forget, "No one helped me with it, because *I never let anybody read it.*"

Chapter Thirty Four

There were no further encounters of the Roark kind and I sailed into the house that evening calling, "Who wants to go out to eat?"

The three younger ones launched themselves at me shrieking, "I do. I do." Eschewing such childish theatrics, Lissa gave only a slight nod, but was unable to hide a smile. Caught up in the enthusiasm, Laddie woofed and jumped up on Cabot. "Sorry, dog, you're not invited," I informed him, but he ignored me and continued woofing at Cabot.

"How about fish and chips?" I shouted from my bedroom as I changed into jeans and sneakers.

"I like Chinese better," Cal said, and was immediately seconded by Cabot.

"Yeah," Risa agreed, "that waitress at the Chinese restaurant is really nice to us.

"Which waitress?" I asked, coming into kitchen where Cal was drinking from his milk container.

"You know," he said, "that one that lets us have free refills on our soda pop. The last time we were there I asked her if she had any kids."

"You didn't!" I said, figuring it was probably true, just hoping she hadn't taken offense.

"Yeah, I did. And she said she did, so then I asked her how come she was working in the restaurant instead of staying home with them." He studied my expression a moment before adding, "She said she needed the money to take care of them, and I said that's what my mom did, too. That's OK, isn't it?"

"Oh, absolutely," I replied. Saying more required being able to breathe.

Taking this as encouragement, he happily continued with, "Oh, good. Then I asked her if people gave her tips and she said yes because otherwise her pay wouldn't be enough money to live on and I said I didn't think you got tips. You don't do you?" Without waiting for an answer he said, "All I had with me was a nickel and I gave it to her and she said it was the best tip she got that day. I really like her."

He paused and I grabbed my opportunity. "Time for everybody to get in the car." I wasn't sure I wanted to know if there was more to this story.

"Let's go fast, Mom," the kids beseeched me as we started down the road that edged the side of a ravine. They considered the ride down the steep, twisting road to be their personal roller coaster all the way to the stomach churning dip at the bottom. Seeing neither cars nor pedestrians, I gave a long blast of the horn and yelled, "Here we go!" and roared down the street. They shrieked at every turn while I inwardly marveled at how fast zero to 20 seemed in low gear.

"Hey," I said when we again drove like normal people, "guess the new word one of my students used today." Without waiting for a response, I said, "Ovipara." They loved esoteric words and began chanting, "Ovipara, ovipara, ovipara," until I cut them off, saying, "So, what do you think it means?"

"No fair," Lissa said, "we don't have a dictionary in the car. You always let us use a dictionary."

"Yeah," the others joined the attack, "you always let us use a dictionary."

"Oh, all right. So I'll tell you. It's what we call birds and turtles and fish and anything that lays eggs."

"Does that include Uncle Albert? That's what most of his jokes do," Cabot said, looking at his siblings, delighted with their instant laughter. Unwilling to relinquish center stage, he said, "Guess what. In reading class we're supposed to look for new words and use them in a sentence and I said, 'Jacklyn likes to masticate at lunch time.' I don't like Jacklyn and she got really mad, but Mrs. Bell told her it just meant chewing and said I should stop teasing her."

I figured I'd be hearing from Mrs. Bell. "Where did you find that word?" I asked.

"Cal found it for me in his *Mad Magazine*."

I shot a look at Cal, who gave me his innocent *Who? Me?* look. "What *Mad Magazine*?" I asked. "I haven't seen any *Mad Magazines* in the house."

"It was Steven's."

"Steven's, Cal?" I asked. I knew Steven's mother and doubted Mad Magazine was her kind of humor.

"Well, really his dad's," Cal hedged. "Steven kind of found it in his dad's closet." He stared out the window. "Besides, you should be glad I told Cabot to say masticate instead of calling her mother a thespian."

"Yeah," Cabot said. "I already knew what masticate sounded like, but I had to ask Cal what thespian meant and what it was supposed to sound like, you know, like masticate kind of sounds like mast. . ."

"Yes, I know," I interrupted. "And were there any words *you* felt compelled to share with your class, Cal?"

"Nope," he replied with self-righteous innocence.

I didn't say anything, just kept glancing over at him as I drove.

"Oh, all right," he muttered. "I was going to ask Sharon if she's show me her uvula but

her brother was right there and he's bigger than I am, so I didn't."

I rolled my eyes. Cal may be a daredevil, but he's a daredevil with a strong sense of self- preservation.

I caught Lissa's eye in the rearview mirror. "Don't look at me," she protested. "I kind of like keeping my good reputation."

"I don't get it," Risa complained. "Lissa told me what masticate and thespian mean and that the uvula is the thingy that hangs down in your throat, but I still don't know what's funny about them."

"Yeah," Cabot agreed, "I can't figure out what uvula is supposed to sound like."

I took a breath, wondering where to begin, but was drowned out by Lissa's agonized "Motherrrrrr!"

"You're right. We'll talk about it tonight at home," I said, wondering if raising kids ever got easier and scowled at Cal who was snickering.

I sighed, then brightened—thankful I had only Mrs. Bell to meet with. Steven's mom was on her own.

Barely had we come to a full stop in front of the restaurant than the kids piled out and raced to the door. By the time I closed the back windows and locked the car, they were inside. From the entrance I saw they had cornered the waitress they liked and were in deep conversation with her. That is, they were talking and she was listening. I guess that counts as conversation with kids.

Their backs were to me, and I noticed again how singular each one was. Lissa who loved blue was wearing a car coat in her favorite sapphire shade, while Cal lit up the room in a jacket of flaming orange. Cabot, wearing an identical jacket but in forest green stood near Risa, hooded in vibrant lavender. I thought of how lucky the two younger ones were. Cal was so hard on his clothes they never became hand-me-downs, while a trio of female cousins younger than Lissa but older than Risa latched on to anything Lissa outgrew, so nothing ever made it down to Risa.

The pungent aroma of garlic and ginger and grilled meat over-riding the tobacco stink escaping from the adjoining bar, made my mouth water and my stomach growl. It was time to eat. Families and couples occupied all the booths except the one at the back of the restaurant, which happened to be the one nearest my kids, so

I headed there, the squeaking of my rubber soled sneakers on the dark linoleum tiles inaudible over the din of voices and clattering of dishes and silverware.

Sensing rather than hearing me approach, Lissa turned and called out, "Oh, hi, Mom."

The other three glanced in my direction and waited, wiggling with impatience until I reached them. With a smile, the waitress turned and walked toward the kitchen.

"Hey, let's sit here," Cal called, scrambling into the booth. Since it was the only one available, we joined him, sliding easily over the red plastic seats. It was one of the larger booths, so I wasn't squished when I sat separating the two boys after Lissa, having no intention of getting caught between her brothers, claimed the seat facing Cal and motioned Risa to sit next to her.

Intent on working my way out of my jacket while avoiding jabs in the ribs by Cabot struggling out of his, I looked up, surprised to find our waitress standing by our table. She held a shallow black lacquer bowl filled with fortune cookies in one hand, and a pot of tea in the other. "I thought you'd enjoy these," she said and gave the kids what I could have sworn was a conspiratorial wink before she left.

"That's odd. These are usually served at the end of the meal," I said looking into the bowl. It was more than odd. "She brought way more than five, let's hope they aren't too expensive." I reached for the teapot, but pulled back as the kids converged on the bowl. Each one seized a cookie and scattered the pieces without eating them. They extracted the paper fortunes and waved them around, making me glad the hot tea was still in its pot.

"Oh, look," Cabot said, a lot louder than necessary, as he bounced into me waving his paper fortune in the air. "Mine says, 'You can fool *all* of the people *some* of the time.'"

"Hey, cool," Cal interrupted, "mine says, 'You can fool *some* of the people *some* of the time.'"

He took a breath and Lissa added smoothly, "Mine says, 'You can fool *some* of the people *all* of the time.'"

And now Risa, so eager and excited at being included she nearly fell out of her seat, shouted, "But you can't fool *all* of the people *all* of the time."

As I sat open-mouthed, wondering what was going on, a well dressed, older gentleman left his table and came to ours. "Do your cookie fortunes really say that?" he asked.

My kids went into orbit, howling like hyenas at a full moon. Embarrassed, I leaned forward to answer him and saw our waitress laughing harder than the kids and realized she was in on their set-up.

I raised my eyebrows and looked at the man, unsure how to answer him. Should I (A) apologize? (B) deny any involvement and hope he'd believe me? (C) slither under the table until he went away? But life is good and I got to choose (D) none of the above.

A huge grin crossed his face as the light dawned. "It's true, you *can* fool some of the people. . ." he said, returning to his table laughing so hard he was shaking. A moment later there was a chorus of laughter from his companions.

The rest of our meal was more or less calm, once the kids finished negotiations with the waitress over changes in the menu and requests for extra soft drinks. We finished eating and while my off-spring were shoving each other out of the booth and struggling into their coats, I walked to the counter by the door to pay the bill. As I added an appropriate gratuity—a gift of gratitude that I considered generous—until I looked back to signal the kids to join me at the door, and saw four coins lying on the table—one at each child's place.

Chapter Thirty Five

"So, you can fool some of the people. . ." Remembering made me smile as I looked for Ethel in the lounge the next morning, anticipating her reaction at my kids' not-so-impromptu performance. I set my bowl of fortune cookies on the table, taking a couple to dunk in my coffee.

"What makes you so happy?" John asked scooping up half a dozen cookies. "Gotta take more than one—might not like the fortune in the first one."

"I understand perfectly, John. Getting just the right fortune is so important. However, one can always improvise."

"Improvise? Like how?"

"I'll have my kids come in and show you some day. I wish Ethel would hurry up and get here, I have to tell her what they did last night. And try to leave a couple for her," I said looking pointedly at the rapidly emptying plate. I broke my cookie apart and began dunking it before reading my fortune. "Oh, yuck. It says, *Listen with an open mind.* Borrrring. Besides, I listen with my ears."

John groaned. "First you want to tell a teacher a story about kids, like we're not neck-deep in kid stuff already. Then make it worse by making a stinky pun like that." He staggered theatrically away from me, holding his nose and sank onto the sofa. "Oh, all right, BJ, go ahead. I'll listen, but I'm not sure whether with my ears or my open mind."

"No," I said with a dismissive sniff, "you have to wait until Ethel gets here."

"Why? You got something against Ethel?"

"Who's got something against me?" Ethel asked, coming in quietly behind us and studying the cookies for just the right one before seating herself gracefully alongside John. She arranged her apple green skirt modestly over her knees and scowled at John who was mimicking her by pulling his red, white and blue plaid shirt over his stomach. "You nut," she said, laughing.

"Ethel," I said, ignoring John who was pretending to be insulted, "you will not believe what my kids did last night at the Chinese resta. . ."

"There isn't much I wouldn't believe about your kids," she interrupted. "Remember, I've met them."

 "Right," I said, handing her my cup for safety reasons as I sat down beside her. "Well, anyway," I said, ignoring the interruption, "I took them to a Chinese restaurant last night. . ."

"I have to tell my wife that one," John said when I finished. He opened his last cookie, and with another theatrical gasp said, "I don't believe it! My fortune says *You can fool some of the people...*"

"But," Ethel broke in, "you can't fool *me* any of the time. John, I said it before and I'll say it again—you really are a nut." John's attempt to look pathetic was an utter failure.

"But before that, Ethel, while we were in the car going to the restaurant, I told the kids that yesterday one of my students tossed a new word at me—oviperous, so of course they had to one-up me with their new words. I leave it to your imaginations how my sons incorporated masticate, uvula and thespian into classroom conversations. Well, actually, Cal thought about uvula, but changed his mind."

A sudden explosion of laughter told me we'd been overheard and now it seemed everyone wanted to one-up my kids.

"I have only fulsome praise for people who use oxymorons," Vic snorted, holding his nose. The tee shirt he wore today was even brighter than his red sweatshirt. "Most people don't know it means stinky."

"Which one means stinky, Vic, oxymoron or fulsome?" John asked.

Before he could answer, Marla said, "Well I've got a really nice word. Definitely not a stinky one. Once when we were shopping, my husband, who thinks he's smarter than me and likes to use words he thinks I won't know, said a bright yellow skirt I liked in a store window looked effulgent. I told him I thought it was pretty. So then he got all smug and said effulgent means bright and shiny. So I went in and bought it and told him to *effulgent this* and handed him the charge slip." The women laughed, but the men groaned.

"Good for you, Marla," Ethel said when she stopped laughing. "Hey, BJ, you've always liked yellow. Let's go shopping and I'll buy you something yellow, like some effulgent #2 pencils."

I hugged her. "Oh, thank you, Ethel, you are so perceptive. I can always use more #2 pencils."

A few moments later, after people had drifted into small groups, Patricia said, "I rather like the word sophophobia. . ." I blinked in surprise. Patricia seldom engaged in casual conversation. In her no nonsense white cotton blouse, brown denim slacks and sturdy brown brogans, to me she looked the antithesis of Marla's word, effulgent. Fortunately, Patricia couldn't read minds, and finished her sentence, "since it means fear of learning, and probably explains why most of my students forget to take their books home."

"What does?" I *almost* asked when it took me a moment to remember what she'd said.

Now, as if reading my mind, she said, "They suffer from sophophobia." She sounded so much like a judge in a spelling bee that I almost began spelling it.

Throughout, Nick Archer remained silent—he was too busy writing on the back of an envelope he'd pulled from his jacket pocket.

"Good morning, Staff," Roark said from the door. After some perfunctory return greetings, the room was silent. Roark strode to the table, saying, "I'm glad most of you are here. I have the students' standardized test results for you." He shoved the nearly empty cookie bowl aside to make room for the stack of papers he carried.

"How come, if he's so glad we're all here, he isn't smiling?" I whispered to Ethel. She didn't answer, just imitated John and elbowed me in the ribs.

"I have the packets in order of grade level, kindergarten first, sixth grade last," Roark said. "Please come get your packet when your name is called." The lucky few who weren't classroom teachers made hasty retreats. "On the top printout of each packet," Roark said, lifting the top sheet and holding it up, "you will find that each class, as well as the school as a whole, scored above district level. This would indicate that we have some outstanding students as well as some competent teachers. Congratulations."

"I think that's what is called *damning with faint praise*," I whispered, and slipped just out of Ethel's elbow range.

Hers was the first name called. "Your class this year scored higher than last year's," Roark told her. Ethel smiled and thanked him as she accepted her packet and waved goodbye to the rest of us. There are some perks to teaching kindergarten.

Soon only John, Patricia and I remained. Without comment, Roark held out my packet, overriding my polite thank you to call John's name. We waited just outside the door for Patricia, but before the three of us could leave, Roark, carrying any undistributed packets, walked past us without speaking. ·

Engaged in our own thoughts, we walked toward our classrooms in an almost eerie silence. Patricia's sudden hiss startled me.

"Huh?" I asked, stopping to stare at her.

Patricia stood, rigid and still, her teeth clenched, her eyes angry slits and her hands balled into fists. "I said *Ass*. *What an ass!*" she repeated with snaky sibilance. "And that's my other contribution to the word of the day: A-S-S, ass!"

I gaped in fascination at the woman I had never before seen display anger. She'd always seemed to be in tight control.

"He called me competent! Competent! That pedantic ass!" She stormed off toward her classroom, the sibilant ssss sounds fading only when the door slammed shut.

John shook his head in awe. "Do you know that's the first time I've seen her lose her cool and I've worked with her for over five years? Remind me never to refer to her as competent." Still shaking his head, he walked past me and into his classroom.

I stood for a moment, looking from John's to Patricia's closed doors, decided the excitement was over at least for now, and went through my door. I dropped the packet of tests on my desk and hurried to open the draperies as well as the outside door, eager for the sun's warmth and light. A breeze, fresh and clean swept in and I smiled. Still smiling, I sat, as any competent teacher should, in my competent chair at my competent desk and began, competently of course, to read the above district level test results of my more than competent students.

Chapter Thirty Six

"Competent, schlompetent," I thought with growing elation at every test result. Now, only Derek's and Roger's remained. I deliberately saved them for last, the way I used to save the one best bite for last—the juiciest bite of steak, the fudge on the sundae, the icing on the cake. And there, in black and white, was the proof of what they knew and I knew—both boys were off the charts in every subject. Laughter bubbled up inside me until it burst out loud and unrestrained. I snatched their papers up, needing to share my delight with Ethel. But of course, right then the bell rang. I placed the stack of test results to the side of my lesson plans and nearly skipped to the door to welcome my class.

My effusive greeting made some of them give me a puzzled glance before they returned my smile. As they settled in their seats, I took the packets of chocolate cookies from the drawer. "Everybody have a cookie," I said. Now there was a little wariness permeating their puzzlement, but they accepted the cookies. I didn't keep them in suspense. "Your test results came back today," I said, "and you all did great! I am so pleased with you and I know your parents. . ."

"Are you going to pass them out?" Billy interrupted, too eager to waste time waiting for me to finish my sentence or to raise his hand.

"Can't," I answered without reprimanding him. "District policy says I have to give them to your parents, but you can tell

them they're coming, either in the mail or with your report cards."
Roark hadn't specified which.

"If I get my mom to come in tonight can she get mine and can I come with her?" Skye asked, following Billy's lead of not raising her hand.

I laughed, knowing how she and the others felt. "I wish I could, but there are things the district says I have to do first." I ignored their groans. "But," I said, "I guess parents can pick them up before report card time."

"How soon will that be? Can I come too? Can we bring my little sister? We have a hard time finding sitters," Skye paused only because she ran out of breath and now waited for me to answer.

"I'll have to let you know, and yes and yes," I replied.

Skye frowned in concentration as she tried to connect each of my responses to her questions.

The classroom atmosphere remained charged all morning. Both the kids and I found it hard to concentrate on mundane things like spelling and math, and it was with a sigh of relief that I heard the lunch bell. They washed up, ate, and ran for the playground in record time. The door was still swinging shut behind them when I scooped up Derek's test results, my grade book, and the pages from his notebook I'd copied, and hurried down the hall to share Derek's success with Ethel. On a sudden impulse I made an abrupt change of plans and went instead to Roark's office, believing that for the first time he'd be glad to see me.

Marla did a double take at my cheerful, "Is Rick in?"

"Why?" she stammered, "Did he send for you?"

"Nope, I have something I think he'll be happy to see," I said, silently adding, "There has to be first time for everything."

"Let me check if he's in," she replied, although both of us could hear him moving about in his office. She rose and crossed the short distance to his open door. Still smiling, I remained standing by her desk.

Looking in, Marla said, "BJ's here to see you," and flashed me a puzzled look as she returned to her desk.

Coming only to his door, Roark said, "You want to see me?"

His voice, flat and uninviting kept me from approaching him. "Yes," I said, speaking as one professional to another, "I want to show you something outstanding." With the test results on top, I held the materials I'd brought toward him.

"I've seen them."

"But not the log Derek kept, and the consistent rise in his grades as well." I fanned out the pages from his log, my grade book and the test sheet.

"Is there some reason you think I need to see all that?" he asked, waving his hands as if brushing away a bug.

I took a deep breath. "Well, you know he was retained in third grade while his twin sister wasn't and I thought maybe we could find a way to let him skip sixth grade and catch up with her now." My voice faltered as Roark stared at me with stony indifference.

"I'm much too busy to do the necessary paperwork this late in the year. You should have brought it up earlier." With slow deliberation he turned his back and reached for the door knob.

"But the test results only came back this morning," I said, still believing that concern for Derek would override his dislike of me.

He shut the door.

Chapter Thirty Seven

"I do not understand it, Ethel. I just don't! It's outrageous! It's... it's... unprofessional!" I waved my arms around like I often did when I was angry and my voice grew louder than was prudent in the lounge. Even when I started gasping for breath, I was unable to stop. "Ethel, he absolutely refused to consider letting Derek skip a grade. He wouldn't even look at the notebook! He shut the door! What kind of principal is he, anyway?"

Light-headed, I swayed into Ethel who caught hold of me. Seeing John and Vic beginning to thread their way toward us, I laughed. "Do you suppose they're coming to your rescue thinking I was attacking you?"

She took a step back, kept a wary eye on my coffee until she was out of spill range, and fixed her long-suffering look on me, the one with half closed eyes and one raised eyebrow that she knew irritated me. I spun away from her and smacked into Vic.

"Hey! Be careful where you splash that stuff!" Vic yipped, staring in dismay at his soggy shirt front. "Only women look sexy in wet tee shirts. Besides, I liked it the color it was."

"Just look at it this way. Your shirt probably saved the custodian a mop-up job. You got a problem with that?"

"From where we were standing, I'd say it sounded like you were the one with a problem." Vic's tone was mild but his grip wasn't as he caught hold of my wrist, the one attached to the offending coffee cup.

"Me? A problem? Gee, how could you tell?" I snapped. Then quickly added, "I'm sorry, Vic. You're right. I do have a problem, but it definitely isn't with you. I'll get some paper towels and wipe off your shirt."

"Forget it!" Vic released my wrist and hurried out reach. "My wife has a thing about women messing with my body—even my chest."

With flying-liquid no longer a threat, John moved closer to ask, "Care to tell us what brought on this attack on my friend Vic? It's obvious there's a problem—other than messing with Vic's chest, I mean."

I took a sip of what remained of my coffee and grimaced at the tepid cookie dregs lying at the bottom of the cup. Lowering it as well as my voice, I told them of Roark's latest assault and asked, "Just exactly what is wrong with him? Wouldn't you think he'd be eager to have Derek's success on his record?"

John gave me a wry smile, Vic shrugged and Ethel asked, "Are you sure you want an answer to that?"

"Of course I want an answer. Why not? Why do you even ask?"

A couple of staff members looked toward me as my voice rose.

Ethel remained silent until they lost interest before she said, "Think about it. From his first day here you've challenged Roark. You discovered, I might say the hard way, on day-one that he has no sense of humor. While you, on the other hand, have the world's weirdest sense of humor. Sometimes even I can't figure out what you're laughing at. So of course he assumed you were laughing at him. Maybe he saw this as his chance to even the score."

"But he didn't come after me—he went after a student. So how is that getting even with me?"

"Through your Achilles heel, BJ. Everyone knows the one sure fire way to get to you is through your kids, your students as well as your own." Ethel spoke with the quiet patience one uses with people who are not quite bright.

"Yeah, kids are easy targets," John affirmed, his tone as disgusted as his expression.

"But he's Derek's principal," I argued, looking from one to another. "He's paid to look out for his students! It's...it's...it's his job!" My naïve comment was met with the silence it deserved and I was relieved when the morning bell sounded. After a hug from Ethel and quick pats on the arm from Vic and John, we joined the others leaving the lounge. Waiting at the door, Patricia Soames gave me two thumbs up.

.

Chapter Thirty Eight

The next morning before class, the outside door to my classroom crashed open and Roger, followed by Petey, bounded in, swerving around desks and chairs to reach my desk. "Guess what, Ms. McCall," they shouted, stumbling over each other physically and verbally. "Guess what Ms. Soames told me," Roger shouted in a voice filled with excitement. "She asked me to come to her classroom last night after school and she said she wanted to start a chess club next semester and she wants me to be the captain and when I told her how good Petey is she said he could be my co-captain if we want."

He gasped for breath and Petey broke in, "And we can invite anyone who wants to play and I get to help choose because I'll be the co-captain." He leaned across my desk, his face, glowing with pride. "Isn't that rad?"

"That certainly is rad," I agreed, sharing their happiness as I contrasted Roger today, so flushed with joy and purpose, to the sullen, withdrawn boy I'd encountered at the start of the year. Beside him Petey stood tall, confident and happy.

Their message delivered, they forgot me and turned, friends on a mission, to race for the door, eager, no doubt, to spread the word and begin taking applications. "I wonder if Skye plays chess," Roger asked Petey. The door shut and they were gone.

For a few moments I sat basking in their afterglow. Soon the sounds of children shouting and laughing drew me to the window.

273

Watching them and absorbing the rays of the June sun, my body warmed and my spirit was restored. From the distant baseball diamond, a swirl of dust spiraled up, caused perhaps, by a runner sliding home. I lifted my cup in a silent salute to all the children whose light overcomes the shadows cast by the Roarks of the world.

"Is it safe to come in?" John asked.

Startled from my silent reverie, I said, "That depends on your definition of safe, John."

He joined me by the window. "I've been thinking about what you said about Derek and I may have a solution. Not as good as his being promoted to junior high, but not too bad. Or, as they say in Chinese, it's *hogomo*—better than nothing."

"Hogomo?" I asked, and turned to make a flippant reply. When I saw the same look he'd had when he told me about his plan to surprise his wife with a trip to Italy, I changed my mind. He was serious.

"As you know, BJ, Patricia and Vic and I have been discussing our next year's students and we each know about Derek and Roger. Also, Vic's tried for a couple of years to interest Derek in playing basketball, thinking he'd be a natural with his height, but he always refused. Not just basketball, Derek wouldn't take part in sports of any kind. And Roger, until now, was too unpredictable to be part of a team. Now Vic's going to try again with both of them."

The possibilities left me speechless, a unique situation allowing John to complete what he came to say. "Patricia said Roger and his sidekick Petey leaped at the chance to start a chess club. It's something she's been considering for awhile and this seems like a good time to begin. But I believe you've already been informed of this," he said with a grin indicating he'd overheard the boys. People in the next county probably heard them. "And now," he said as his grin grew so wide I hoped it wouldn't interfere with his hearing, "for the *coup de grace*."

I blinked—John speaking French as well as Chinese? Oh, I knew this was going to be better than good.

"I guess, BJ, if you trusted Derek to go at his own pace in math, I'll continue the same way. But I think I'll add a caveat. At least once a week he has to tutor another student of my choosing. No point in letting him hoard all that brilliance and I could use the help. Patricia is going to see if it's successful and if it is, she's going to try it with some of her students." He paused, waiting for my reaction.

It took me a moment to process what he'd told me—John and Patricia working as a team, using my idea. "Oh, John, what a genius you are. You hit the ball, you are a star, made a hole in one, that's better than par." I grabbed his arm and began dancing around as excitement bubbled up inside me, not caring that my spur of the moment quatrain wouldn't win any prizes.

John extricated his arm and fled across the room, flinging my door open before calling out, "Hey, hey, hey, good buddy BJ, cut out the touchy feely stuff. My wife's as possessive as Vic's. And if that's your idea of poetry—it doesn't scan!"

"Right," I yelled after him, "but it's competent." The deserted hallway echoed John's laughter and the slam of his classroom door.

Chapter Thirty Nine

"It's the last day. The last day! Tomorrow we all sleep in," I called out through the open car window to my kids who waved and cheered from the steps as I backed out of the carport. Once on the road, I waved and blew kisses until I rounded a curve in the road that took them from my sight.

That June day was lovely. The sun scattered flashes of gold off car windows and in the distance the elegant Mt. Rainier stood caped in sparkling snow. Taking advantage of the extra hours of daylight, I'd washed and waxed my car after work yesterday, and now it shone in all its scarlet glory. Such a day called for music, and I spun the car radio dial until I heard the sensuous voice of Don Ho crooning *Tiny Bubbles*. I joined him, loud and off-key. The driver passing on my left smiled through his open window and waved. His car was red and shiny, so I knew we were soul mates.

The myriad fragrances of June enveloped me when I slid from my parked car. Then, just as I'd done for nine months, I slung my purse strap on my shoulder, grabbed my brown bag lunch, wedged my thermos under my arm, hip bumped the car door shut and strode up the walk, but the exhilarating sense of the approaching summer's freedom made this day different. The sun shone brighter, the earth and grass and flowers smelled richer and the sky glowed bluer.

An abrupt ear-splitting roar set every nerve vibrating. Spewing a gray contrail of exhaust fumes, the power mower flew from around the building with Mark hunched over the wheel like a race car driver. Speeding past me, he snapped a quick salute, pushed his blue and white Brakeman Bill hat to a cockier angle and called, "Enjoy. . ." His words were swallowed up by distance and mower roar, so I waved to his receding back, wondering what he wanted me to enjoy.

The springy lightness of my new white sneakers energized my walk, and I knew they'd make hauling supplies less tiring and climbing ladders less hazardous. And, coupled with my blue jeans and red cotton shirt, gave me a positively patriotic look.

For a moment I stood watching the sun light flickering through the leaves of the far trees; when I heard the returning mower's roar I hurried inside. After placing my can of cashews on the table in the empty lounge, I walked the quiet hallway to my classroom. Except for the text books stacked below the white board and a few items near the bottom of one wall, it was stripped and bare, ready for its annual summer cleaning. Beige walls, brown floor and dark drapes may not a prison make, but they sure don't pack a lot of personality, either. Robbed of its usual clutter, my desk was drab and lifeless— the in-and-out boxes, like the book ends, were empty, the photos of my kids were gone.

The hollow sounding thunk of my purse when it landed in the bottom drawer testified that, like all the other drawers, it, too, was empty. Even at the sight of the residue coating the bottom of my cup, I poured in some coffee. I lifted the stack of report cards from the center drawer along with the year-end certificates of award, set them all on the front corner of my desk and leaning back with a sigh with pleasure, propped my feet next to them.

My coffee finished, I swung my feet in their pristine white sneakers to the floor and walked to the front of the room to begin loading the text books onto the rolling cart, the one labeled "Multi-media room only" that I'd appropriated yesterday after the librarian left, knowing I'd have it back in its usual parking place before it was missed. Teachers were expected to haul every text book, encyclopedia, dictionary and manual to the storage area, located at the farthest end of the building from my classroom. A job I wasn't about to do armload by tedious armload, not even in brand new sneakers.

The care with which my students had stacked their books meant my job was finished within half an hour and humming, I returned the cart to the still uninhabited multi-media area. Done, I perched on a corner of my desk, not the corner with the report cards, to survey my demolition handiwork and saw no books, no glittering alphabet, no assignment on the white board. But, because I'd saved it for one last activity, the student art work covering the lower half of one wall relieved the barren drabness. After the students retrieved their art, I'd allow them to rip down the exposed construction paper background and laugh with them as they raced each other to stuff it in the hallway trash barrels. I expected noise, laughter and mass confusion—exactly what I wanted for their final memory of their year with me.

I reached for the stack of report cards to review them one last time. Below the grades were my comments. Each began with a memorable achievement of that student during the year and I wanted to relive those moments. Soon they would be gone, assigned to another teacher, but for now they were still mine. Skimming through what I'd written, I smiled and sometimes laughed out loud. "What a great class!" I said to the empty room. "Nothing, absolutely nothing is needed to make this school year more perfect."

"Wrong," I thought as Roark's voice from the intercom broke the stillness, "one thing would make the year more perfect—Roark getting laryngitis."

I scowled as he intoned each item on the flier-du-jour we'd found in our boxes yesterday: "The awards assembly will begin at 0930."

Reading my flier, I lip-synched along with him, "Make sure all report cards are ready before the students arrive, but do not hand them out until after the assembly."

"Blah, blah, blah," I added, wondering if he just enjoyed giving orders or if he thought some of us were illiterate. His voice on the intercom was sharp and had a metallic edge that hurt my ears. "Following dismissal, all members of the faculty are to meet in the lounge at 1:30 this afternoon for final instructions."

"What? Don't you mean 1330 hours?" I said to the intercom. I waited for him to remind us to wash our hands before we ate, but there was a click followed by silence, so I figured he was through. At least for now.

My hallway door flew open. There, arms akimbo, stood Ethel, flanked by Vic and John all of whom stared at me expectantly. I stared back, noting that Ethel's idea of casual dress, even today, was not a skirt and blouse, much less a pants suit. No surprise, it was a teal dress with a flared skirt that skimmed just below her knees, and ivory leather mid-heel pumps. She tilted her perfectly coifed head and uttered, "Well?" and waited as if I should know the correct response.

"Well what?" I asked.

"Well, hey, hey, hey, good buddy, BJ," John interrupted, pushing in front of Ethel, "it's the last day of school. We need our fourth musketeer to go foraging with us in the lounge."

"Of course you do, John," I answered, "how can only THREE of you FORage?"

"Oh, BJ, that was awful. Even for you," he groaned.

"I know. I'm sorry." I could tell he didn't believe me. "But I'm worried, John. I haven't seen you in white sneakers since opening day. I know you only own two shirts, both red, so in your blue jeans aren't you afraid everyone will think we're twins?"

"Oh, dear, you're right. Even I can't tell you two apart now," Ethel moaned theatrically, rolling her eyes.

"Just one small correction," Vic said. "Hasn't anybody noticed me? You two aren't twins," he paused for dramatic effect as he elbowed his way in front of them, "we three are triplets!" He struck a Charles Atlas pose displaying his red t-shirt, blue jeans and white sneakers. "But you'll just have to risk people not being able to tell us apart, BJ, because today's lounge is made to order for you—wall to wall goodies."

"Then it's a lot different from when I went in earlier with my poor lonely little can of cashews."

"How odd," Ethel gave me her slit-eyed, raised eyebrow look. "Imagine no food waiting for you when you got here in the middle of the night as usual."

"Enough talk," John interrupted, "There are a gazillion people in there already, so let's try to get there before everything is gone. Besides, I want each of you to try some of the stuff my wife made." He was already backing out the door. "It's an old Italian recipe and I can't remember what it's called, but it's sweet and tastes great and be forewarned, I promised her I'd repeat every comment made about it."

"Wait just one second," I said. I half-filled my coffee cup, hitched my purse onto my shoulder and after closing the door, linked arms with my companions and the four of us swept down the hall. "We're not strutting enough to be musketeers," I said and nearly pulled them and myself off balance as I attempted a drum majorette knee lift. As a strut it failed miserably and I was grateful my coffee cup was only half full.

"Your strut," Vic observed, "looks more like the Scarecrow staggering toward the Emerald City of Oz than d'Artagnan heading into battle," making Ethel and John whoop with laughter.

"Not funny," I muttered. But they ignored me.

We found the lounge crowded around a table exceeding Vic's description. John's wife's sweet chewy concoction covered in chopped pecans was fabulous and I enjoyed the second piece as much as the first. We circulated separately among the volunteers, playground aides, office personnel and faculty, all engaged in lighthearted conversation, high calorie treats, and frequent bursts of laughter. When it was time to leave, I figured everything would be gone before the midmorning break, so taking a few with me might be a good idea.

Back in my classroom, stuffed with junk food, sloshing in coffee and basking in the afterglow of friendly camaraderie, I couldn't resist the noses pressed against the window as kids peered in at the clock or milled about near the door. Stuffing my sticky stash in an empty drawer, I opened the door, saying, "OK, since it's the last day, you can come in early." In they tumbled like water over rocks in a river and eddied around me, exuberant and bubbling. All the rules of proper entry were forgotten and I didn't care and I realized I'd been right the first time. Nothing, not even silencing Roark, could make this a more perfect year.

It took a few moments longer than usual before some of the students noticed me standing silently at the front of the room in my *Will the class please come to order* stance. One by one they took their seats and looked at me in quiet expectation. I scanned the room, saw there were no absentees and handed the attendance slip to Allison, who returned in record time, afraid she might miss something good. When she was back in her seat, I said, "As you know, there will be an awards assembly this morning. When it's over, we'll come back here and I'll give you your report cards."

"All I want to know," Billie interrupted, "is did anybody flunk?"

"Flunk?" I repeated. "Are you asking if one of my students dared to flunk?" I raised my voice in mock horror. "Absolutely not! I don't allow it!" I waited while they gave exaggerated sighs of relief, before adding, "In fact, you kids are so smart and worked so hard, I didn't even give anyone an F or even a D. Not even one. How about that?" My rhetorical question elicited laughter, high fives and excited voices before I finished my sentence.

"Not even me?" Billie asked skeptically.

"Not even you, Billie," I answered dead-pan, making the class laugh again.

The intercom announced it was time to go to the gym for the awards assembly and while the order in which we were to proceed was read from the flier for those faculty members considered too dim to read it for themselves, we filed quietly out of the classroom and down the hall.

The massive double doors into the gym were propped open. Beyond them, shadowy sunlight filtered through the high caged windows. It flickered on the beige walls and spilled in ripples through the hazy air in which dust motes danced like bubbles in water. Below, anchored like sunken logs on the mud colored hardwood floor, were rows of brown folding chairs. My students took their assigned seats facing a portable stage with three wood steps on the left. In its center, flanked by three folding chairs, was a lectern under the basketball hoop.

Students sat in ascending grade levels with the kindergarten in front. I leaned against a wall watching my students and keeping the stage in my peripheral vision. At a movement from the stage, I turned to see Stanley Jacobs, who'd been in my class a year ago, take his place as student body president in the nearest chair. Mindy Yarborough, PTA president, took the one on the right.

I looked toward Stan's classmates seated behind my class, pleased to see several of my previous year's students watching him with pride and I remembered what a great class they had been. So different, but just as wonderful as this year's. Next year they'd be in junior high and my current students would be in the last row of seats.

The hum of voices stilled. From the back of the gym, Roark strode down the center aisle to the base of the stage, executed a sharp left turn, climbed the three stairs, and crossed to the lectern. Only the creak of the steps and the staccato tap of his leather heels broke the silence. His light gray suit, ice blue tie, starched white shirt and gleaming black shoes were a sharp contrast to the casually dressed faculty and students. I'd never seen him in casual attire, and had to choke back a giggle, wondering if his idea of casual would be a dress shirt, tie, cut-off shorts and garters holding up black dress socks tucked into white sneakers. Remembering the results of a previous unsuppressed giggle, I kept this one in check.

Sports awards, music awards and student helper awards preceded grade level academic awards and my attention wandered until the fourth grade awards began and my interest perked up as I wondered which of them would be in my class in the fall.

When my name was called, I climbed the creaking stairs, and took my place, like each of the other teachers, half way between the stairs and the lectern. I nodded in polite recognition to those on the stage. When I looked at the students in the audience, I was swept by a sense of sadness and resentment that so many would not receive awards; like Jody who discovered there was more pleasure in cooperation than in trouble making, Billy who always included less popular kids in playground activities, Allison who drew beautiful pictures and Roger who was organizing a chess club. Every year it was like this and I wondered why we recognized only a select few. I took a deep breath, smiled and one by one, called the names of my authorized five.

"But," I said quickly as the fifth recipient left the bottom step to return to her seat, "I have a sixth award." Pretending not to notice Roark's disapproving look, I spoke faster and faster making it difficult to interrupt me. "It's a special one. In addition to exceptionally high academic achievement in all areas, this student worked independently to exceed grade level expectations and often took time to help others who needed help." Unable to continue without taking a breath, I made it a quick one and made eye contact, which was easy since nearly every student was staring at me. "Derek Hall, will you please come receive your award?" Still in his seat, Derek sat motionless staring at me. "Me?" he mouthed, his face registering confusion and disbelief.

"Yes, Derek, you," I answered. He rose, never taking his eyes from me and slowly walked to the stage.

I held out the slip of paper, the inexpensive paper certificate.

"Thank you," he whispered as he took it. He left the stage, like one in a trance. His classmates patted his arm and whispered congratulations as he stepped past them to his seat, but I wondered if he heard them. For the remainder of the assembly he sat with his head bowed, his eyes focused only on the piece of paper he held with both hands in his lap.

When the assembly ended, I led my students from the gym. I glanced back and saw Derek, following his classmates, still looking down at the award he held. I waited at the classroom door, returning the smiles of my students as they passed me. I felt a gentle touch on my arm and I turned. For a moment he said nothing, just looked at me, then, his voice filled with wonder, Derek whispered, "I never got an award for anything in my life before."

I remained motionless as he walked away.

.

Chapter Forty

Nine months—September to June, another year—over, finished, done, except for the final staff luncheon and a few goodbyes. Ahead, three months without Roark. What came in September, well, like Scarlett O'Hara, I'd think about that tomorrow.

It wasn't long before I tossed my purse across the front seat and drove out of the parking lot, enjoying the tantalizing daydream slipping seductively through my mind as I covered the miles home. I could almost smell the fresh hot coffee I'd sip as I lay on my deck lounge gazing peacefully at sunlight dappled maples clustered below me in the ravine while a gentle breeze whispered across my face.

My dashboard clock read 2:30 when I coasted into the carport and my four burst off the porch, waving and cheering as the boys bumped and shoved each other impatiently. Once the engine died, they mobbed me as I flung the car door open.

"Can we go to the beach? It's summer and it's really hot today. Please. Oh, please?" the boys pleaded, striving to mimic the famous sad-faced clown whose name I can never remember.

"Hot? It's barely 70°", I protested. "The lake hasn't had time to warm up yet."

"That's OK. We like it cold."

Through all this, Lissa and Risa remained silently on the sidelines. At my questioning look, Lissa shrugged, "It's fine with me. I'm just going to lie on the blanket and read."

"Me, too," Risa said.

"Woof!" Laddie added, racing around and batting everyone with his tail.

I laughed. "Oh, all right, but you boys had better not complain if you freeze to death." I handed my empty thermos to Lissa and reached for my tote bag to drop off in the den on my way to my bedroom for a sweat shirt and my old beat-up sneakers. No way was I wearing my gorgeous new white ones to the beach.

"Don't forget your beach towels and a jacket to come home in," I yelled from my closet. There was no answer and I yelled again. Three yells and it's time to investigate. I looked in the kitchen and kids' bedrooms, but all were empty. Hearing voices from the carport, I closed my eyes, crossed my fingers and took a deep breath before taking slow steps toward the door. I turned the knob, hoping I'd see nothing tied to the roof of the car or hear a dog barking in the trunk.

(Illustration by Cabot Fuqua)

B J moved to an island in Western Washington when she retired
after teaching for 25 years. Her four adult children and their
families live nearby with her grandchildren, her just rewards for
raising Lissa, Cal, Cabot and Risa.

(Photo by Don Schmidt)

Made in the USA
San Bernardino, CA
15 November 2015